Penguin Handbooks

## The Cotswold Way

Mark Richards was born in 1949 in Chipping Norton, Oxfordshire. He was educated at Burford Grammar School before training for a farming career. He discovered the pleasures of hill walking through a local mountaineering club. He became friends with Alfred Wainwright, the creator of a unique series of pictorial guides to the fells of northern England, who encouraged him to produce a guide to the Cotswold Way, which was followed by guides to the North Cornish Coast Path and Offa's Dyke Path. Subsequently he has mapped, illustrated and written for numerous walking guides and magazines. Most recently he has completed a set of three walking guides to the Peak District National Park. Mark plays an active role on the National Register of Long-distance Paths committee. The Register, launched in 1986, acts as an advisory service for all those involved in the development of long-distance paths in Britain.

Mark Richards is happily married with two lively children, Alison and Daniel.

## The Penguin Footpath Guides

*Already published:*

The Brecon Beacons National Park
Dartmoor for Walkers and Riders
The Devon South Coast Path
The Dorset Coast Path
The North Downs Way
The Ridgeway Path
The Somerset and North Devon Coast Path
The South Downs Way

# The Cotswold Way

Mark Richards

Wayfaring Tree berries

Penguin Books

*Dedicated to my mother and father*

Penguin Books Ltd, Harmondsworth, Middlesex, England
Viking Penguin Inc., 40 West 23rd Street, New York, New York 10010, U.S.A.
Penguin Books Australia Ltd, Ringwood, Victoria, Australia
Penguin Books Canada Ltd, 2801 John Street, Markham, Ontario, Canada L3R 1B4
Penguin Books (N.Z.) Ltd, 182–190 Wairau Road, Auckland 10, New Zealand

First published 1984
Reprinted 1987

Made and printed in Great Britain by
Richard Clay Ltd, Bungay, Suffolk
Filmset in Monophoto Univers

# Contents

# Acknowledgements

I would like to record my thanks to Arthur Cundall, of the Worcestershire Nature Conservation Trust, who not only accompanied me on an eight-day traverse of the Cotswold Way during the autumn of 1982, but also assembled the fascinating natural history notes at the end of each route description. His task was made vastly easier by the valuable contribution of Miss Sue Everett (at that time Field Officer for the Gloucestershire Trust for Nature Conservation), with additional suggestions supplied by the Avon Wildlife Trust. I am greatly indebted to Ted Fryer, Head Warden of the Cotswolds A O N B, who proved a valuable source of advice as well as scrutinizing the manuscript and maps. My typists, Dorothy Parry Billings and Lilian Planer, deserve mention, having deciphered my scrawl without complaint. However, most surely this guide would not have been possible without the active support of my wife, Helen, who checked the text while I entertained Alison and Daniel – a family effort indeed!

While neither the author nor publisher can accept responsibility for errors and omissions, great care has been taken to ensure that the guide is factually correct. The author would welcome constructive comment from readers. (Letters should be addressed to the author, c/o Penguin Books Ltd, 536 King's Road, London S W10 0U H.)

# Introduction

The Cotswold Way advances for 100 miles, the length of the Cotswold escarpment, from the City of Bath to Chipping Campden. It is the model long-distance walking route. Despite its merits of accessibility and good-quality walking, the Countryside Commission have not yet seen fit to designate it as an official long-distance path. Instead it comes into the category of 'Recreational Path', which qualifies it for only a 50 per cent grant towards maintenance and improvement; hence several unfortunate road sections remain where, with full status, the 100 per cent grant aid available would have made possible the creation of attractive footpath alternatives, thereby up-grading the route.

None the less, the Cotswold Way is a very fine route. It was originally inspired by Tony Drake, who for over thirty years has been an influential campaigner for the footpath network of Gloucestershire.

The National Parks and Access to the Countryside Act of 1949 made provision for the designation and creation of long-distance paths. Hence, in 1953, the Gloucestershire Committee of the Ramblers' Association submitted plans for a Cotswold Way to the National Parks Commission. Though acknowledged and mentioned in the Commission's annual report of that year, the Cotswold Way was nevertheless pigeon-holed, the emphasis being placed on the development of other seemingly more prestigious routes like the Pennine Way.

When, in 1968, the Gloucestershire County Council prepared its recreational plan for the countryside, it proposed the designation of a Cotswold Way route, using existing rights of way. The Way was launched with some haste, and minimal pomp, during National Footpath Week in 1970, receiving the qualified support of the Ramblers' Association, who felt, rightly as it has transpired, that this would jeopardize its ultimate recognition as an official long-distance path – despite the Countryside Commission's home-base shift from London to Cheltenham (the holiday centre for the Cotswolds!).

One of the proud boasts of the Cotswold Way is that it is the best waymarked route in Britain. While other routes may challenge this claim, there is little doubt that every care has been taken to give the public confidence to use this route. In 1975 a programme of complete waymarking was begun called 'Operation Cotswaymark'. A coordinated effort between the Ramblers' Association and the Cotswolds Warden Service obtained permission from over a hundred landowners to waymark the whole Way in both directions. The Countryside Commission's code of painted YELLOW ARROWS for footpaths and BLUE ARROWS for bridleways were supplemented by ORANGE ARROWS where the route had to follow motor roads. In every case a WHITE SPOT the size of a ten penny piece was set inside the arrow to distinguish the Cotswold Way, as often several rights of way diverge from a given place.

conventional waymark
on the Cotswold Way

Also at difficult path junctions the 'headless arrow' technique has been employed: straight stems show each individual path, but only the Cotswold Way has an arrowhead. Where it is imperative that walkers should follow a precise line, for instance, across a cultivated field, a white target disc has been erected. In towns, waymarking is often put on the upright part of kerbstones. On occasion other specific waymarked routes may be seen directing at variance with the Cotswold Way. For instance, an arrow with a coloured tail is a Cotswolds Warden Service circular route (described in one of their special guides); a yellow spot indicates prescribed circular routes in the Stroud locality; horseshoes blaze bridle-trails through Witcombe Woods and a golden crown denotes the Wychavon Way. The evolutionary process of change and improvement of the Cotswold Way ensures that this guidebook is always liable to be out of date in some particular, so walkers are advised to comply with waymarking where this differs from the route shown in the guide.

A team of thirty volunteers maintain the chain of footpaths and bridleways that constitute the Cotswold Way, though any walker is encouraged to report damaged stiles or other obstacles seen en route directly to the Head Warden of the Cotswolds A O N B, c/o Shire Hall, Gloucester – for whom the Cotswold Way represents an important brief.

The Cotswolds Voluntary Warden Service, coordinated and administered by the Head Warden, serves the broader Cotswold region too – acting as practical watchdogs through patrolling, maintenance and conservation work and caring for the wellbeing of the countryside. New recruits with energy and a will to cherish the very special characteristics of the Cotswolds are welcome to join an active local group.

# The Cotswold layer-cake

The topography of the Cotswolds falls into two distinct zones:

(a) the rolling gently corrugated uplands alternating high wold with sylvan valley. This great band dips eastward to blend into the clay Thames basin;

(b) the escarpment, facing W and N, receding like sea-cliffs and permitting numerous inlets, some shallow bays, some deep fiords, penetrating far into the dip slope. (Compare the wide bowl-shaped Witcombe with the long trench-like Ozleworth Bottom valley.)

Why should this escarpment be such an impressive feature?

The great Cotswold layer-cake, consisting of Jurassic limestones and Lias sands and clays, was forced to tilt. Consequently the clays and sands are continually slithering down. This instability has a direct effect on the overlying oolitic rock, which crumbles, for want of support. The resultant hummocky pastures are common scarp-face features.

The rhythmic succession of these clays, sands and limestones represents an ascending geological time scale, whereby the older rock lies generally beneath and W. The Lias clays were formed in a rather deep muddy sea. The sand indicates a shallower sea, with incoming rivers bringing sand from high ground, whereas the limestones tell of a clear warm shallow sea. The S Cotswold in the immediate vicinity of Bath and Cold Ashton are capped with Great Oolite. This recedes, to be replaced by the older Inferior Oolite throughout the remainder of the Cotswold Edge country.

The retreating escarpment has left several isolated hills, known as outliers – for instance Dundry Hill S of Bristol, Cam Long Down, Robinswood Hill and Bredon Hill – indicating the former extent of the limestone uplands. Much modification has taken place along lines of weakness through to glacial times, with the N/S strike of the series influencing the course of the River Severn.

The waving, irregular band of limestone belonging to the Jurassic series that sweeps diagonally across the breast of England, from the Dorset Coast to the North Yorks Moors, has provided man with a beautiful building material. Nowhere, throughout its course, is it more abundant than in the Cotswold region. It is this most amenable stone which has enabled the creation of buildings that are the archetype for the whole limestone belt. These oolitic limestones have a knack of blending whole villages subtly into their landscape, varying in hue from the silvery white of Painswick to the golden ochre of Chipping Campden. The study of Cotswold building stone and architectural idiosyncrasies is one of the most rewarding elements of any exploration of this homogeneous region.

As a general rule steep-pitched roofs indicate the earliest houses, necessary to cope with the great weight of stone tiles (largely obtained by mining the lower Great Oolite and wafered by frost action). In turn this gave scope for roof-space to be included in the upper floor, hence the development of the characteristic window gables with mullioned windows and drip-moulding to encourage water to run off the walls away from the windows; on occasion string-courses serve the same purpose: notice them particularly on church towers.

Oolitic freestone is extracted relatively easily, and when freshly quarried can be sculpted to form beautifully decorative motifs. In time it hardens to endure several centuries before frost action makes its surface friable. One further virtue emanating from its ease of extraction is that it can be sawn into regular plane blocks to give neat ashlared walls, clearly evident in the solid elegant town houses of Painswick and Chipping Campden.

That there are so many fine houses dotted throughout the region is the direct result of one economic phenomenon. During the 13th, 14th and 15th centuries the wealth of England was not expressed in gold or oil, but in wool.

As a means of making warm clothing, sheep must always have played an important part in this temperate climate. Good breeding practice had evidently created in the Cotswold breed such a long-stapled heavy fleece with a shaggy mane appearance that the sheep became nicknamed 'the Cotswold Lion'.

From the Norman Conquest, trade with the Low Countries increased and the demand became voracious for good-quality wool. Buyers came from as far afield as northern Italy to take advantage of the free trade and low export dues. At that time the Cotswolds were vast unenclosed sheepwalks and the region was a prime source of this staple commodity. The Enclosure Acts did not really envelop the wolds until after 1760, the first Acts in the Cotswold region relating to Horton in 1664 and Farmington, near Northleach, in 1713.

From all this activity there arose a new wealthy elite, wool tycoons who amassed large fortunes on the back of the sheep. These merchants, however, increasingly relied on middlemen, the wool broggers, who collected the fleeces and were then able to store, assess and supply the required quantities of wool to the merchants and clothiers. The raw wool trade declined during the 15th century through monarchical intervention demanding ever higher taxation on exports – quite literally a wealth tax on the merchants. It is also ironic that, subsequent to Edward IV's gift of Cotswold rams to the Spanish court, their native coarse-fleeced Merino stock was so improved that its heavy fleece and staple quality excelled those of the Cotswold Lion.

The cloth trade of the 17th and 18th centuries created a broader-based wealth. From the entrepreneurs of this time emerged the first middle classes, sufficiently well-off to afford stone-built houses of the kind that proudly adorn Wotton, Painswick and Campden today.

## A geological feast

Along the Cotswold Edge, progressing N from Bath, the spectator is witness to a series of revealing views. In the early stages these are to S and E, while constantly the abrupt escarpment permits generous prospects to the W and later N. There is more than just scenic sustenance to be digested from this theatre, for it further stages a quite remarkable range of geological time.

The earliest rocks on view, represented by the Malvern Hills, are composed of Pre-Cambrian formations which belong to the most ancient geological category. It has been established that the period of their crystallization from sedimentaries into rocks occurred between 580 and 600 million years ago, prior to which they may have been shales and sandstone laid down 1,000 million years ago. The ridgewalk from Chase End Hill to North Hill (the Pre-Cambrian Way!) is not only the finest high-level walk in the Midlands but provides geologists with a rare exposure of the major structures which form the framework of Britain.

Rising conspicuously to their S is May Hill, dome-shaped and sporting a clump of trees planted in celebration of Queen Victoria's Golden Jubilee. This isolated hill is composed of Silurian sandstone laid down between 425 million and 405 million years ago in a shallow shelf sea. Next come the Old Red Sandstones of the Forest of Dean, which accumulated during Devonian times in an arid sub-equatorial desert lowland of 405 million to 350 million years ago. Fourth in line come the equatorial Carboniferous limestones, sandstones and coal measures found in the complex country about Chepstow, Bristol and the Mendips, and cover the period 350 million to 270 million years ago. Fifth in sequence are the Triassic rocks in the undulating country beneath the Cotswold scarp. These Keuper Marls and Rhaetic Beds were laid down some 225 million years ago. The Jurassic rocks of the Cotswolds themselves belong to the period 180 to 135 million years ago while to the E, beyond the Upper Jurassic Oxford Clay beds, the next escarpment step, that of the Wiltshire Downs, is composed of brilliant white chalk laid down over the period 135 million to 60 million years ago, during Cretaceous times. In the Severn and tributary valleys there are areas of drift like the windborne Cheltenham Sands or the glacial deposits of gravel, together with alluvium of floodwater deposition. Clearly the area exhibits quite superb juxtapositions and is an immensely rewarding location for the study of the earth's history.

## Natural history

To walk the pathways of England is fundamentally an elemental experience. The pleasure of a day in the countryside is influenced by the state of the path and the prevailing weather, but more importantly the onus is on each walker to gather in all the subtle variations and textures of the natural world and thereby feel a part of the whole.

Nature Conservation Trusts operate in every county. Besides the establishment and management of reserves they work to maintain a future for wildlife generally by providing free advice to members, private landowners and statutory bodies concerned with land management. They depend on members' subscriptions, grants, legacies and donations to finance their work. Without the

Trusts many of the attractions of the Cotswold Way (and elsewhere) might have been destroyed. Never before has man's ability to modify his environment been so powerful. Change is to some extent inevitable and in fact demanded by the needs of our population and society. However, equally urgent is the need to strike a balance between all the pressures upon the landscape and the conservation of sufficient near-natural areas for the future. Those who care for the countryside and its wildlife should join their County Trust:

Avon Wildlife Trust, 209 Redland Road, Bristol, B S6 6YU.

Gloucestershire Trust for Nature Conservation, Church House, Standish, Stonehouse, Gloucestershire.

Worcestershire Nature Conservation Trust, The Lodge, Beacon Lane, Rednal, Birmingham, B47 9X N.

## Link paths

Two comparable routes linking to the Cotswold Way have recently been developed to expand opportunities for the public to explore the varied country-side leading from the Cotswold Edge.

The Wychavon Way, pioneered and established by the Wychavon District Council, leads through the deep rural heartland of Worcestershire. It has been sensitively developed and comprehensively waymarked, cleared, and equipped with the necessary stiles and footbridges. It branches from the Cotswold Way at Winchcombe, heading N for Bredon Hill before taking a wide sweep W to conclude beyond Droitwich on the River Severn at Holt Fleet Bridge. An excellent guide is available price £1.50 through local bookshops or direct from the Wychavon District Council, 37 High Street, Pershore, Worcestershire, and from the Worcestershire Nature Conservation Trust (see above).

The Limestone Link was pioneered by the Avon Area of the Ramblers' Association. At the time of writing (January 1983) the route has been cleared but only partially waymarked, but during the course of this season a programme of complete two-way waymarking and stile erection will be effected, bringing it up to Wychavon Way standards. This route offers a diverse countryside, branching from the Cotswold Way at Cold Ashton and wending S with a link from Bath. It sweeps W through an attractive tangle of hills to join the West Mendip Way at Shipham. For further information contact Mr Cyril Trenfield, Bristol Avon Area R. A., 38 Oakdale Court, Downend, Bristol B S16 6D U. Both of these routes are 40 miles long and represent two good week-end walks each.

An unwaymarked 'Heart of England Way' joins the Cotswold Way at Chipping Campden. Consult the detailed guide published by Thornhill Press, 24 Moorend Road, Cheltenham, Glos.

The Oxfordshire Way, developed by the Oxfordshire branch of the C P R E, on the other hand, is extremely well waymarked and equipped. As it commences from Bourton-on-the-Water in the Gloucestershire Cotswolds, numerous very appealing links to the Cotswold Way are apparent, and that missing dimension, the waters and villages of the dip-slope wolds, can be added to the scarpland traverse of the Cotswold Way – a real bonus!

## Planning the walk

It is often stated, and rightly so, that long-distance paths were not created for record-breaking or human endurance tests (nor for mass invasions treading down the crops!). You may wish to complete the entire route in one fell swoop. That choice is yours alone. In truth the Cotswold Way offers up its mystique sparingly, most often to a gentler stratum of walking ambition. If you allow yourself the time really to admire the countryside, the satisfaction will persist into an after-glow – much to be preferred to blisters!

Take for instance Bath, whose full splendour cannot be comprehended within the impatient urgency of a tight walking schedule. Plan on your first day to stroll and absorb the scale of the place, casting the Cotswold Way briefly to the back of your mind. Let this city offer up its architectural wizardry until your itching feet can no longer be denied. You can then set forth in buoyant mood cheered by sublime images of a truly amazing city.

The way rises high upon Lansdown's breezy wold, then stretches forward weaving and undulating through an intricate tapestry of country revealing a rare richness in history and rural charm, to reach a climax at Chipping Campden. In the words of John Masefield:

> On Campden Wold the skylark sings,
> In Campden town the traveller finds,
> The inward peace that beauty brings
> To bless and heal tormented minds.

In the opinion of the author the Cotswold Way is best executed northbound. Walking in this direction, the more distinctive of Cotswold features lie ahead, acting like a lure, drawing the walker irresistibly on. The prevailing SW wind is to one's back, and the escarpment grows in stature with commensurately expanding views and the walker bounds forward in anticipation and is duly rewarded.

To enjoy the Cotswold Way as a walking holiday it would be wise to set aside ten to twelve days for the complete end-to-end march, though it is no less a pleasure to attack it piecemeal, one or two days at a time. A folding bicycle is a tremendous boon, as only one car is then necessary, using a cycle-back plan. But do lock the bike and if possible ask to leave it in some safe place out of sight.

## Clothing

If you are not deterred by the winter season and are prepared to meet any adversity – driving rain, a bitter, cutting wind – then the essential shell protection will be carried as basic kit. For the majority, however, seeking the kindest seasons for their expeditions, bad weather is not welcomed with the same masochistic fervour. Nevertheless it is prudent to consider carrying some form of waterproof, a light mac or cagoule, possibly nylon over-trousers too. A word of warning: never wear jeans on long walking trips – when wet they cling bitterly cold against the skin. Shorts are most refreshing, but do not overlook the effects of sunburn and cold winds (chapped knees!). Light, loose-fitting clothes permitting ventilation are generally preferable, with resort to a wind-proof jacket and/or a light sweater sensible precautions. Be smart, but let comfort take precedence. Tramping through fields, woods and lanes can be muddy and brambles can tear!

The preparation of your feet is of paramount importance. The ability to walk freely is so taken for granted by many that they approach a walking holiday with careless abandon. The shock of pounding the feet incessantly day after day can give rise to tender spots and more general foot discomfort. So think ahead and wear only well-broken-in, preferably light-weight, flexible boots or stout shoes. Let them be neither too tight nor too loose for otherwise assuredly you will suffer! Loopstitch woollen stockings are the most comfortable accompaniment, though most wool-based socks are successful. Avoid reliance on acrylic or nylon socks for any distance, as they do not absorb foot perspiration adequately, becoming harsh against the skin. You may find a little vaseline useful in reducing friction, but apply it at the outset, not at the onset of pain! If you sense localized hot spots, stop immediately and give that area of the foot the protection of a plaster, otherwise you will all too soon have reason to rue your inaction!

Carry some food and a refreshing drink, but consume neither in such a prodigious manner that you feel bloated (beer at a welcome mid-point hostelry should be drunk with caution – half a pint will suffice to carry those aching limbs resolutely on). Wear an easy-fitting rucksack or daysack and if backpacking avoid loads of over 30 lb. Do not shackle yourself as a beast of burden. Walk with your head up, a light heart and a spring in your step!

## Accommodation and transport

It is to the good fortune of Cotswold wayfarers that the Gloucestershire Area of the Ramblers' Association have devoted considerable effort to the compilation of a most comprehensive guide. The *Cotswold Way Handbook* covers the full range of accommodation options on or near the route, together with places for refreshment. Bus, rail and taxi services are detailed, together with sound advice on walking schedules and the main opening times of places of interest en route.

This essential booklet is revised every two years and can be obtained from The Ramblers' Association, 1/5 Wandsworth Road, London SW8 2LJ, price 45p, plus postage.

A further bountiful source of transport advice is the *Cotswold Bus and Rail Guide*, published annually by the Gloucestershire County Council.

A scheme under serious consideration is the establishment of 'stone tents' at 8-mile intervals along the Cotswold Way. These camping barns would provide simple yet comfortable accommodation for walkers who would like to undertake the walk on a low budget. They would be suitable for either families, small groups or the lone traveller, who otherwise find the Way poorly equipped for camping or backpacking. A possible 'pack-carrying' scheme, to relieve walking parties of their burden between night stops, is also being considered. Both projects would be developed through the Cotswolds Warden Service.

## How to use the guide

This book has been designed not merely as a practical handbook to the many intricacies of the footpath Way but more importantly to cheer and entertain the walker by developing a healthy regard and curiosity for this precious country-side.

The guide is divided in two. The first part provides basic navigation orientated specifically for northbound walkers (Bath to Chipping Campden), who thus follow the facing map up the page. Natural history notes have gained preference over southbound direction notes, on the grounds that waymarking is sufficiently reliable when coupled with the detail on the map to keep walkers on the straight and narrow without encumbering the text further. Outline profiles accompany each map, forewarning of strenuous climbs or easy passages, and the nature of the surface underfoot, whether path, track or metalled road. Throughout the text the directions north, south, east and west, together with right and left, have been abbreviated to: N, S, E, W and R, L; while the Anglo-Saxon Old English language (up to c. 1150) and the medieval Middle English language (up to c. 1500) have been shortened to O E and M E.

The second part is the general commentary referring to each map, with line illustrations to relieve the print and direct attention to special features. The text has not been exclusively shackled to the Cotswold Way – indeed frequent diversionary comments are made on items of interest well off the route map. To get a fuller enjoyment walkers should carry the appropriate O S Landranger map to enable them to locate places referred to and learn more about the broader Cotswold region. The guide will then become a stepping stone into the Cotswolds rather than a blinkered chase! The Ordnance Survey 1 : 50,000 Landranger maps covering the Cotswold Way are: No. 172 Bristol and Bath, No. 162 Gloucester and Forest of Dean, No. 163 Cheltenham and Cirencester, No. 150 Worcester and the Malverns, and No. 151 Stratford-upon-Avon.

# Book List

## General Landscape

Barraclough, Marian, *Exploring the Cotswold Edge*, Thornhill Press, 1979.
Brill, Edith, *Life and Tradition on the Cotswolds*, Dent, 1973.
Crosher, G. R., *Along the Cotswold Ways*, Cassell, 1976.
Finberg, H. P. R., *The Gloucestershire Landscape*, Hodder & Stoughton, 1975.
Morris, John, *The Domesday Book: Gloucestershire*, Phillimore, 1982.
Smith, A. H., *The Place-names of Gloucestershire*, 4 vols., Cambridge University Press, 1964.
Smith, Brian, *The Cotswolds*, Batsford, 1976.
Smith, Brian and Ralph, Elizabeth, *A History of Bristol and Gloucestershire*, Darwen Finlayson, 1972.
Tann, Jennifer, *Gloucestershire Woollen Mills*, David & Charles, 1967.
Wright, Louise, and Priddey, James, *Cotswold Heritage*, Hale 1979.

## Architecture

Pevsner, Nikolaus, *The Buildings of England: North Somerset and Bristol*, Penguin Books, 1958.
Pevsner, Nikolaus, *The Buildings of England: Worcestershire*, Penguin Books, 1968.
Verey, David, *The Buildings of England: Gloucestershire: The Cotswolds*, Penguin Books, 1979.
Verey, David, *The Buildings of England: Gloucestershire: The Vale and the Forest of Dean*, Penguin Books, 1980.
Verey, David, *Cotswold Churches*, Batsford, 1976.

## Local History

Cunliffe, Barry, *The Roman Baths*, Bath Archaeological Trust, 1978.
Donaldson, D. N., *A Portrait of Winchcombe*, Published by the author, 1978.
Houghton, C. C., *A Walk about Broadway*, Ian Allan, 1980.
Hyett, F. A., *Glimpses of the History of Painswick*, British Publishing Co., Gloucester, 1957.
Kersley, George, *Bath Water*, Bath City Council, 1979.
Lindley, E. S., *Wotton-under-Edge*, Museum Press, 1962.
Powell, Geoffrey, *The Book of Campden*, Barracuda Books, 1982.
Robertson, Charles, *Bath: An Architectural Guide*, Faber, 1975.

Town Trail leaflets are also available at Bath, Wotton-under-Edge and Painswick.

## Geology

Dreghorn, William, *Geology Explained in the Severn Vale and Cotswolds*, David & Charles, 1967.

Geologists' Association Guide No. 36, *The Cotswold Hills.*

Institute of Geological Sciences, Solid and Drift one-inch Map series:
Sheets: 265 Bath; 251 Malmesbury; 234 Gloucester; 235 Northleach; 217 Moreton-in-Marsh.

## Walks

Cotswolds Warden Service series (from Gloucestershire County Council, Shire Hall, Gloucester): *Walks from Coaley Peak Picnic Site; Walking around Painswick; Cooper's Hill Nature Trail; Hill Walks around Cheltenham; Walking around Winchcombe; Country Walks around Broadway; Country Walks around Chipping Campden; A Walk to West Littleton and Dyrham; A Walk from Wotton-under-Edge; Woodland Trails from the Fiddler's Elbow Picnic Area (Cooper's Hill).*

Ramblers' Maps of the Cotswolds (special 3-colour composite 2½-inch maps showing all rights of way, commons and line of Cotswold Way – superb productions): Currently available: No. 2 Cleeve Hill; No. 3 Birdlip; No. 4 Stroud and Sapperton; No. 5 Dursley. In preparation: No. 1 Chipping Campden. Proposed: No. 6 Cotswold Way – South; No. 7 Bourton-on-the-Water. Available from the Ramblers' Association, 1/5 Wandsworth Road, London SW8 2LJ.

Sale, Richard, *The Cotswold Way*, Constable, 1980.

Sale, Richard, *A Visitor's Guide to the Cotswolds*, Moorland Publishing, 1982.

Lewis, June, *Walking the Cotswold Way*, David & Charles, 1986.

A.A./Ordnance Survey Leisure Guide, *Cotswolds*, 1986.

# Route Guide
## and Sectional Maps

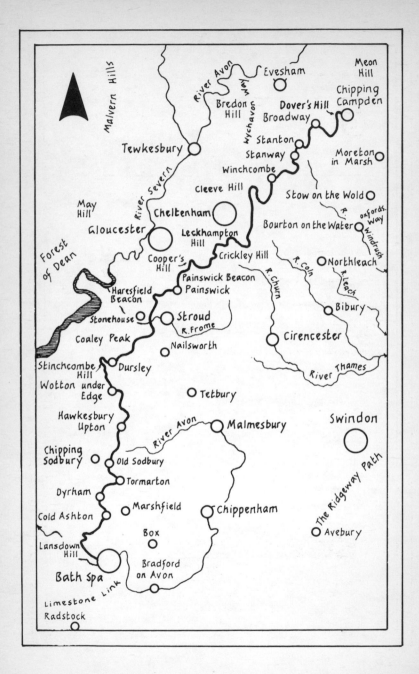

# KEY

• • • • • • • • • • • • • The Cotswold Way

——————————— Route on metalled surface

(11) Mileage from Bath   MAP SCALE: 2½ = 1 mile
   — all distances are given in miles

· · · · · · · · · · · · · Other visible paths or tracks

·····················  hedge or fence  ∞∞∞∞∞∞ wall

⸙ quarry or  ოო trees or      triangulation
   earthwork  ოოwoodland  △ column

▚ buildings  + church  ▲ Youth Hostel ⁂ tumulus

════════ metalled         Direction of
            lane              North
═══▦▦▦═══ minor road

▦▦▦▦▦▦▦▦▦▦ major road       PH. : Public House
                              P.O. : Post Office
▨▨▨▨▨▨▨▨ motorway                    footbridge
                              FB
■▬■▬■▬■▬■ railway

W : strategic waymark        River or
G : gate or gateway          Stream
g : hunting or wicket gate   with an arrow
K : kissing gate             to show direction
S : stile or substitute fence   of flow

The numbers in the margin locate the Northings
and Eastings (grid lines) on Ordnance Survey maps

53

19

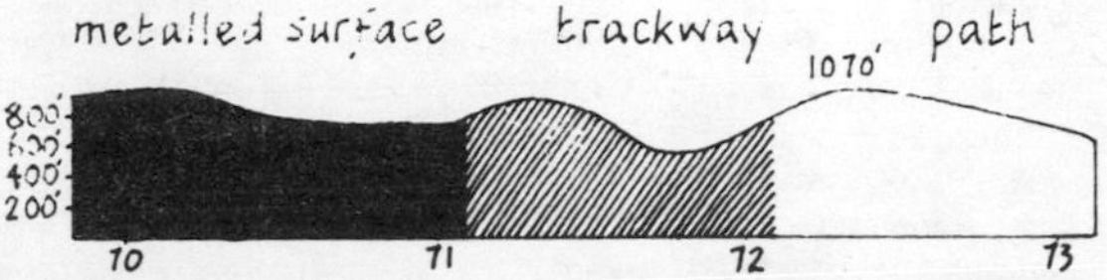

   metalled surface    trackway      path
                                  1070'
 800
 700
 400
 200
     10        71        72        73

The gradient profile is graduated in 200 feet
intervals and shows high points and mile points
plus three types of route surface.

# 1. Bath and Weston

See commentary, pp. 81, 84

The Cotswold Way starts at the Abbey Churchyard, before the Abbey West front and the entrance to the Pump Room. Leave the precinct northwards through the passage, crossing Cheap Street into Union Passage. Cross Upper Borough Walls (street) into New Bond Street, going L then R in Old Bond Street and turning first L into Quiet Street, which becomes Wood Street, thereby entering Queen Square. Go R round the Square to turn R into Queen's Parade and join the Royal Avenue. Advance across Marlborough Lane by the Victoria Monument into the Royal Victoria Park, turning first R up to Weston Road. Cross directly up the path between the High Common and the 'pitch and putt' golf course. Go L with the Sion Hill road, past the Gothic Cottage, to reach Summerhill Road, and turn L to enter the alley leading steeply down past The Retreat by Primrose Hill to a (fixed) kissing gate. Go forward to a stile and proceed ahead (do not be lured R with the obvious track) to a squeeze stile – note the loop at its base for big boots to slip through! The confined passage leads down into Purlewent Drive (housing estate). Bearing R, follow the pavement, seeking the somewhat obscure passage L shortly after Lucklands Road. This soon broadens and becomes Church Road. The Way next enters the churchyard R, passing in front of the church to descend Church Street. Cross the side street, passing the fish and chip shop, then, opposite Mills and Mills, cross to the traffic island and proceed directly up Anchor Road, entering Pennhill Road. Branch R at the kissing gate to cross the recreation ground (football pitch) to a stile and ascend the pasture to an awkward pipe rail fence-cum-stile, going R onto Penn Hill.

Royal Victoria Park, Bath, provides a fitting introduction to the trees which dominate the Cotswold Way. Beech, ash and lime stand alongside the less frequent sweet chestnut and cedar, splendid specimens which have matured during the past century. Beyond, the path beside High Common golf course is lined with horse chestnut and plane trees, while in Sion Hill, as well as limes and beeches, the list can be extended by rowan and holly. The N side of Summerhill Road is lined with limes.

Ivy-leaved toadflax, whose lilac flowers are profuse throughout summer and autumn, grows readily on the wall surrounding All Saints church, Weston, and in many similar places along the Way. Like the dainty wall rue, on the same wall, it thrives with its roots in the porous mortar. Churchyards are usually intensively managed, regularly mown and tidy. Where wild corners can be kept, however, they provide welcome sanctuary for wildlife.

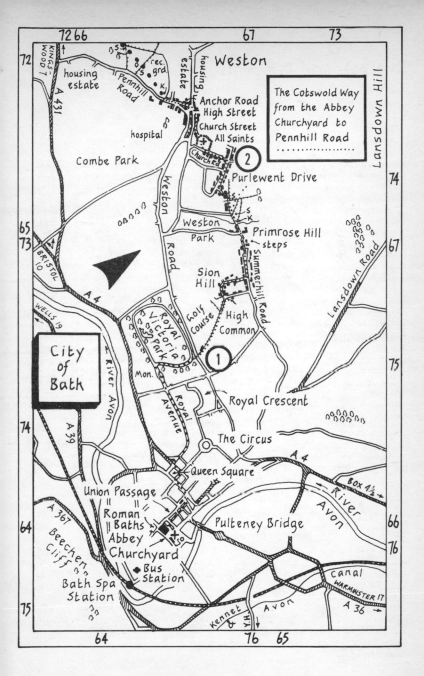

The Cotswold Way
from the Abbey
Churchyard to
Pennhill Road
.................

City
of
Bath

200'
375'
380'
1
2

# 2. Penn Hill and Lansdown Hill

See commentary, p. 87

Passing the trig point, proceed with the hedge to a further pipe rail obstacle, and contour the pasture crossing a stile to join the minor road at Pendean Farm. Advance up the lane onto Dean Hill and continue round under Kelston Round Hill. The bridleway, prone to churning up in wet weather, has been divided off to give walkers dry footing and stiles to reach the cross-ridge track. Follow the track R beside the cultivated field leading up towards the Lansdown Hill plateau edge. Branch at the waymark post L to Prospect Stile (the stile is in fact a poor railing substitute). Go L along the scarp top to a stile adjacent to the race course starting rails, advancing to the entrenchment of Little Down Hill Fort, turn R at the midpoint breach, then turn L through the hill fort enclosure to a stile. Descend the hollow way to the waymark post, turn R, and continue, keeping to the same contour, to a gate. Soon after join a track which rises to a gate above Pipley Wood. The track runs beside the golf course and passes a barn to a junction. Turn L, stay on the track until it descends to a gate and branch up R through a wall corner gap. From the golf enclosure stile, proceed beside the wall on course for Hanging Hill trig point.

Leaving Bath behind, the ascent of Dean Hill permits a wide expanse of landscape to be studied. Weathering and erosion over the millennia have created the broad undulations of foundered Lower and Middle Jurassic strata, particularly along the north side of the Avon valley above Bath. The harder Great Oolite, resting like a layer of hard icing on the silts and sands which form the 'stale cake mixture' beneath, is reached at the race course boundary. The track up Dean Hill is lined with a wealth of flowering herbs all characteristic of the calcium-rich rubbly soil: vetches, white campion, hardheads, ladies' bedstraw, scabious, basil and agrimony, with occasionally purple milk vetch, and sunspurge emerging from the mixture of grasses. The king of all thistles, woolly thistle, may also be found. This stretch is a delightful excursion in itself.

Wayfaring tree, most often encountered as a shrub, is first met where the hedge begins in Dean Lane. The wrinkled leaves are distinctive, its flowers showy and the berries a delight to nose and eyes. Commonest on the lime-rich soils of southern England, it is typical of the Avon section.

Lichens are a noticeable adornment of the stone walls on the Way to Prospect Stile. They are a sure indicator of air free from impurities. Like the mosses that also flourish there, they are often unnoticed and unappreciated. Close examination reveals their beauty.

Toadflax grows in large patches on the otherwise uniform grassland near the starting rail of the race course. This even sward should be compared with the old pasture, full of large anthills, immediately after the golf course is passed. Pipley Wood contains ash and larch, with hazel and elder in the shrub zone mingling with traveller's joy and ivy. A good place for birds and small mammals.

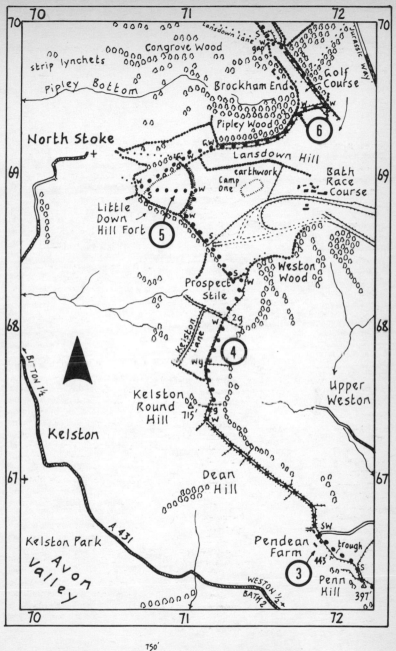

70 71 72

Lansdown Lane

Congrove Wood

strip lynchets

Pipley Bottom

Brockham End

Golf Course

Jurassic Way

gap

Pipley Wood

W

W

**North Stoke**

fw

69

+

W

W

s

W

Lansdown Hill

earthwork

Camp One

Bath Race Course

69

Little Down Hill Fort

5

W

s

Weston Wood

Prospect Stile

s

W

68

2g

Kelston Lane

W

68

4

wg

Kelston Round Hill

715'

g

W

Upper Weston

67

+

Kelston

Dean Hill

67

Kelston Park

A 431

Avon Valley

Br-TON 1½

SW

trough

Pendean Farm

445'

s

3

Penn Hill

80

397'

WESTON ½
BATH 2

70 71 72

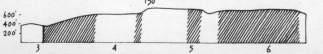

750'

600'
400'
200'

3      4      5      6

# 3. Hanging Hill, Hamswell and Greenway Lane

*See commentary, p. 90*

Following the scarp-top wall the Way reaches the trig point on Hanging Hill. Cross the stile and turn R to follow the fence and the old wall to a gate. Scrub hugs the wall, confining walkers, until this gives way to an access road which brings the Way to the Lansdown Road. Go R, seeking the stile in the fence L, onto a track leading to the Granville Monument. Pass down to the wall stile, following the wall and fence round to another wall step stile. Take the track down the bank leading to a gate into a lane. Leave the lane where a gate and gateway confront the Way, take the L gate and follow the hedge round L down to a stile. The Way descends diagonally across the pasture to a stile. Proceed down the bank to the Goudie's Farm access track. Take the gate to the R of the cattle grid, branching from the track to a gate onto the Hall Lane track, and go L past the cottage. Taking the first gate R, go past the dutch barn. The Way crosses three pasture fields by two gates to a hunting gate by a wet coppice. Joining the concreted track, go L uphill, passing Hill Farm. This is Greenway Lane.

Elm disease swept England in the 1970s, leaving behind innumerable skeletal relics of this once-dominant hedgerow tree. Regenerating growth from the old boles of both common and wych elm may be found, the latter especially in the south of the Cotswold Way. Of particular significance however are the few mature common elm trees in the lane beyond the Granville Monument: examples of a very small minority of disease-resistant specimens which survived.

Winter sunshine, illuminating ash, beech and hawthorn near the monument, brings out form and colour which are concealed in summer. The subtle green of moss on silver bark and misty purple drifts where the shrub zone is densest contrast with the yellow-orange of willow along the damp hedgerows and streamside.

Lords and ladies are common along many of the shady hedge banks and woodland paths. The arum lily, to give it its botanic name, flowers early and can easily be overlooked, but in autumn the fleshy scarlet fruits clustered on the leafless stem are eye-catching. It can be found in Greenway Lane, the banks of which are rich with many hedgerow plants: meadow cranesbill, toadflax, bedstraws, basil and scabious abound in summer, replacing the violets and other early flowers. The hedge itself is worthy of remark for its diversity of species, many of which, like ash and elm, are true woodland constituents.

The aromatic mint, fleabane and other semi-aquatic plants which grow in the damp stream bed near Hill Farm are an irresistible attraction for bees, hover flies and similar valuable pollinating insects. Marshy areas are fast being drained and with them go many forms of wildlife. The continued existence of this patch is to be hoped for.

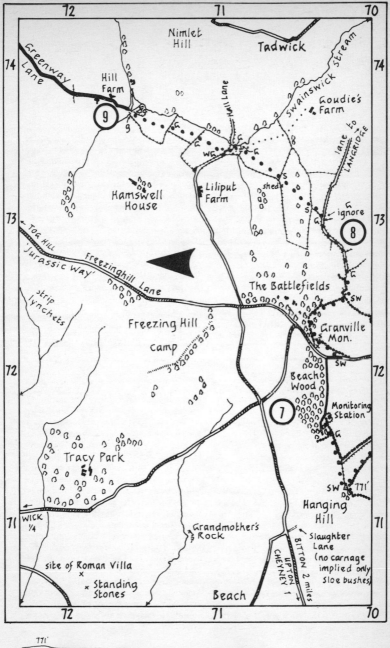

Greenway Lane

Nimlet Hill

Tadwick

Swainswick Stream

Hill Farm

⑨

Hall Lane

Goudie's Farm

lane to LANGRIDGE

WC

Hamswell House

Liliput Farm

shed

S

S

ignore

⑧

74

74

73

73

72

72

71

71

Tog Hill

'Jurassic Way'

Freezinghill Lane

strip lynchets

Freezing Hill

Camp

The Battlefields

SW

Granville Mon.

SW

Beach Wood

⑦

Monitoring Station

Tracy Park

SW

771'

Hanging Hill

WICK ¼

Grandmother's Rock

BITTON 2 miles
UPTON CHEYNEY 1

Slaughter Lane
(no carnage implied only sloe bushes)

site of Roman Villa   ×
        × Standing
           Stones

Beach

72

71

70

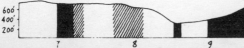

771'

600'
400'
200'

7          8          9

27

# 4. Cold Ashton and Dyrham

See commentary, p. 94

Advancing up Greenway Lane, the Way crosses the busy A46 to enter Cold Ashton up the steep rise. Pass the Manor and Old Rectory, taking the lane L to the church. From the kissing gate proceed past the church to a further kissing gate, follow the wall to yet another kissing gate, then cross the busy A420 directly to the White Hart public house. Go L on the pavement till a gate R gives access to a cultivated field. Cross this diagonally to a stone stile. The ensuing cultivated field is also crossed diagonally to a stile onto the A46 at Pennsylvania. Advance up the lane opposite to a gate, keeping company with the hedge, to another gate onto the narrow road, going L to the first gate R (do take care, as the corners are blind for traffic and ill-suited to pedestrians). Proceed down the pasture to a stile (built onto a hunting gate) into Dyrham Wood. Obvious paths lead to L and R. However, the Way advances directly down the (sometime) stream bed ahead, only breaking out as water materializes! Reaching a stile (of similar construction to the last), leave the wood and descend the pasture to a hunting gate and plank footbridge. The Way veers L on a green track across the pasture to a stile, then follows the cultivated field headland to a gap and crosses the next cultivated field down to a pond. From the stile follow the hedge, crossing three stiles, to join the minor road at its entry into Dyrham village. Go L and R at the junction, passing the gates (no access) to Dyrham House, and continue till a lane R leads the Way out of the village by the park wall through three gates on course for Tormarton.

Cold Ashton village is built mainly on the Great Oolite, but walking north, across A46, the soils are fuller's earth clay and sands. Guelder rose, wayfaring tree and blackthorn grow in close proximity here, along the short stretch of track at mile 11, and produce a succession of white blossoms in spring. Beyond, Dyrham Wood is on the unstable sands, the lower slopes indeed being an old landslip area. The neglected hazel coppice, with occasional oak standards, tells of an old wood once managed for the crop of hazel: raw material for hurdles, implements and early forms of building. In their prime such woods were ideal for bluebells and nightingales. At the N boundary, where dense elder, ash and oak predominate, there is ideal cover for leaf warblers in spring, and a rewarding hunting ground for marauding sparrowhawks. Below the wood the tiny stream is lined with large old oak and ash, field maple and hawthorn. It is a head-water of the River Boyd, which joins the Avon near Keynsham.

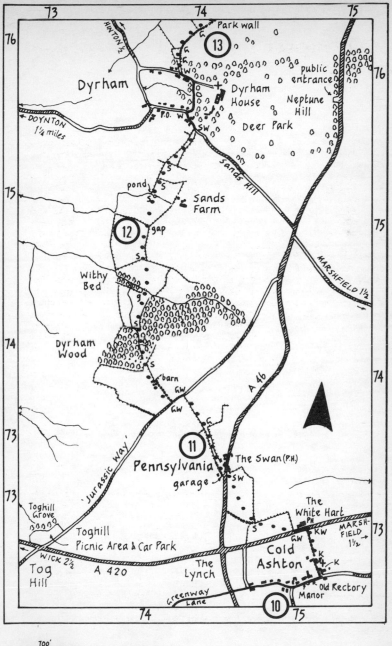

Map labels:

- 73, 74, 75 (top)
- 76
- Park wall
- 13
- HINTON ½
- public entrance
- Dyrham
- W
- Dyrham House
- Neptune Hill
- ← DOYNTON 1¼ miles
- P.O. W
- Deer Park
- SW
- Sands Hill
- 75
- pond
- S
- S
- S
- Sands Farm
- 12
- gap
- S
- MARSHFIELD 1½
- Withy Bed
- 75
- 74
- Dyrham Wood
- 'Jurassic Way'
- S
- barn
- GW
- GW
- A 46
- G
- 73
- 11
- Pennsylvania
- garage
- The Swan (P.H.)
- SW
- 73
- Toghill Grove
- Toghill Picnic Area & Car Park
- The White Hart
- PH
- KW
- MARSH-FIELD 1½
- GW
- S
- K
- K
- Cold Ashton
- Wick 2½
- A 420
- The Lynch
- Tog Hill
- Greenway Lane
- Old Rectory
- Manor
- 10
- 74
- 75

700'
600'
400'
200'

10    11    12    13

29

# 5. Dyrham, Tormarton and Dodington Park

*See commentary, p. 97*

The Way ascends beside Dyrham Park wall to emerge into Field Lane. Go L to the road junction, cross to the hunting gate, follow the hedge to a further hunting gate, at which go R, adhering to the field margin and seeking a passage through the wood onto Beacon Lane (a severed portion of the A46). Proceed through the picnic area (toilets), cross the A46 to the lay-by and go L, crossing the motorway on the E side. Take the first road R and again R, and proceed to the footpath sign L. Cross the stone stile, cross the pasture to a further stone stile, go down the ensu-ing pasture to a gate and pass the new house into Tormarton village. Turning R past the post office, then L, cross the stile (L) opposite the church and follow the top of the bank to a gate beside a barn. Go L, then cross the stile R beside the Old School House. Advance to cross two minor roads via opposing stiles, entering a cultivated field, and retain course to a stone stile. Cross, with care, the A46 to a narrow gate, descending to a hunting gate, and descend the cultivated field to a footbridge and stile, advancing across the next cultivated field N W.

Where the B4465 is crossed, way-faring tree is close by the stile in association with other shrubs. This may well be an 'old' hedge, for those planted as a result of the 19th-century enclosures were invariably quick-growing hawthorn. Ecologically these are of less importance than the old-established mixed-species hedges that often still follow parish boundaries.

The M4 Motorway may well contain interest for naturalists! The banks are almost free from human interference and unless scrub takes a firm hold they may develop a varied flora and fauna. It takes several years for an orchid to reach the flowering stage and in wildlife terms the embankments are still young. Viewed from the A46 overbridge the larger herbs – hard-heads, vetches, etc. – are visibly established already. Both rook and kestrel have readily adopted this man-made habitat as a feeding zone, indicating by the latter species that small mammals abound in the grass. The verges of A46 and those of the lane approaching Tormarton are also not without interest. Meadow cranesbill and scabious bloom in summer, blue against the shaly limestone wall bordering the latter.

Tormarton still has a number of simple botanical delights in odd corners, police-man's helmet, silverweed and watercress to name only a few. Making a list during the walk through the village would be an interesting diversion.

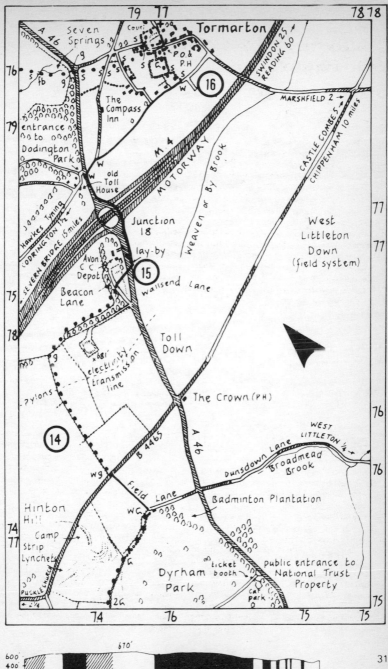

# 6. Dodington, Old Sodbury and Little Sodbury

*See commentary, p. 99*

The Way reaches a fence beside a copse. Follow it to a gate, then down the steep pasture, crossing two stiles and a low bridge, to a stile where the route crosses the park exit drive. Continue to a gate onto the road at Coomb's End. Go R up the hill, taking the gate L after the cottages. Follow the hedge, pass through the ungated gap and descend to a stile partially hidden by brambles. Now aim diagonally L above the pond to a gate in the paddock fence, proceeding to a gate into Chapel Lane and turning R into Old Sodbury. At the crossroads go forward into the farmyard between the garage and Cotswold Lane, passing through to a gate, veering R to a stile in the field corner and turning R up the pasture bank to enter the churchyard. Pass in front of the church to the lychgate, seeking the signpost pointing L up beside the primary school to a hunting gate. Advance with the hedge beneath the scarp bank to a gate, here joining the ascending path R. At the top go through the gate L and pass through the earthworks of Little Sodbury Hill Fort. Short of the farm buildings (note the dew pond) veer L to a hunting gate. Go R then L with the descending lane to a gate and so onto the minor road running below Little Sodbury Manor.

Dodington Park is typically English. Fine specimen trees and shelter belts abound, many of great age and near the end of their life-span. Notable are horse chestnut, ash, lime, oak, beech, sycamore, plane and regenerating elm where the dead trees have been cleared. There is little planting of trees in this spacious manner nowadays and future generations will not be able to experience the pleasure of this scene when these have fallen. Yet a few newly establishing oaks are to be welcomed along the drive to the house at Coomb's End.

Old Sodbury church is approached by climbing the scarp over Lias clays to reach the harder marlstone on which it is built. An ancient larch is near the church gate and a fine old sycamore nearby. The short stiff clamber to reach the hill fort is along a damp path, lined with hart's tongue fern, arum lily and dog's mercury. Elder is present, as it so often is in the neighbourhood of badgers, whose footmarks may be detected in the moist ground.

The short sward within the hill fort contrasts with the adjacent woodland grasses. It supports harebell, cowslip and other delicate herbs. In autumn, the ubiquitous autumnal hawkbit brightens the turf. Grassland butterflies – common blue, marbled white, small heath, etc. – fly on warm summer mornings, but though wild thyme is here, the large blue, whose larvae fed on that plant, is no more. Extinct in Britain, it was recorded last century from a few Cotswold stations. Chalk hill blues are a handsome substitute in a few localities.

Giant hogweed, growing 10 ft tall, can hardly be overlooked in the roadside vegetation at mile 20. It towers over the surrounding elder, dogwood and bindweed. The whole of this verge is a good wild place.

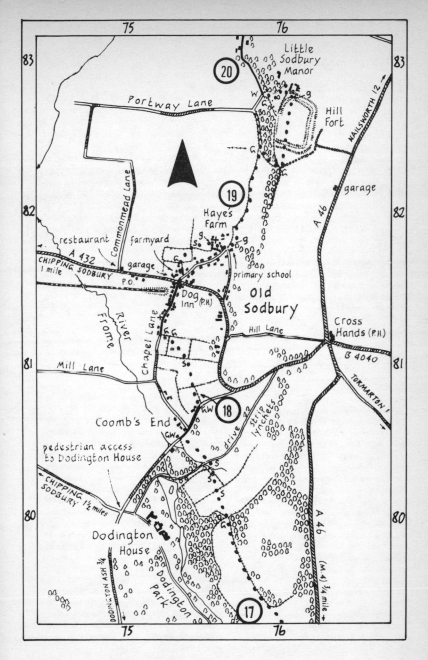

75 76

83 83

○20

Little
Sodbury
Manor

Portway Lane

Hill
Fort

NAILSWORTH 12

Commonmead Lane

○19

garage

A 46

82 82

Hayes
Farm

restaurant

farmyard

g
S

g

CHIPPING SODBURY
1 mile

A 432

garage

G

primary school

Dog
Inn (P.H.)

Old
Sodbury

River Frome

Chapel Lane

Hill Lane

Cross
Hands (P.H.)

B 4040

TORMARTON 1

81 81

Mill Lane

S

○18
GW

Coomb's End

drive

strip
lynchels

GW

pedestrian access
to Dodington House

S

CHIPPING
SODBURY 1½ miles

O

S

Dodington
House

G

A 46

80 80

DODINGTON ASH ¾

Dodington
Park

○17

A 46
(M 4) ¾ mile

75 76

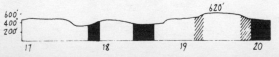

600'
400'
200'

620'

17    18    19    20

# 7. Little Sodbury, Horton and Bath Lane

*See commentary, p. 102*

The Way passes Little Sodbury church, turning R at the road junction. Turn L beside the cottage, climbing the fence by the back door. Follow the hedge to a hunting gate, continuing to a field gate, descend below the dam and then rise steeply to a further hunting gate. Now cross the large cultivated field to a gate into a short lane into Horton. Follow the road R then L, towards Horton Court, leaving the road R at the foot of a hill short of the house. Ascend the pasture to a gate into the woodland. A clear track proceeds ahead. However, watch for the divergence L up and along a path leading to a stile out of the beech woodland. The Way climbs the rough pasture to the fence, continuing to a gateway. Hold to the hedgeline, passing through the gate, and advance below the barn across the pasture (sometimes a motor scramble course) to a stile. The Way runs parallel to Highfield Lane along the cultivated field headland, swinging L round the shed to a stile. Continue to a gate where Bath Lane is joined (at its junction with Highfield Lane) and go L along this ancient trackway.

A variety of trees may be studied between Little Sodbury and Horton. In Little Sodbury churchyard grow yew, holly, beech (including the copper-foliaged variety), but above all giant sequoia. Pollard ash follow, on the route N, while at the lake new planting has been undertaken. The pool itself is relatively new, yet already attracts some wildfowl in winter. Emergent reed mace indicates shallows and a likely breeding place for some species of dragonfly. Waters are few on the Way and in the local context this one is potentially valuable.

Holm oak, dark and evergreen, lines the approach road to Horton Court. English oak, ash, horse chestnut and beech also occur in the same stretch. Many of these woodland species support parasitic bracket fungi which are evident throughout the year. Autumn, however, will bring forth the bulk of the years crop of fruiting bodies: toadstools. Beechwoods and conifer plantations are among the more productive areas for fungi, but caution should be exercised when their edibility is in question. Identification can be tricky and mistakes lead to discomfort or even death.

Bath Lane sees the wayfaring tree again a principal constituent of the hedge alongside the route. Hawthorn, blackthorn, elder and maple, with the stature of small trees, are also present. This should be an attractive place for migrant thrushes in winter, though wayfaring berries are a delicacy eaten by resident blackbirds almost before they ripen.

Rarities will occasionally be mentioned throughout this guide, but those who require detailed directions to localities will have to look elsewhere. The purpose of these notes is to stimulate the interest and point the way. The commonplace is often beautiful.

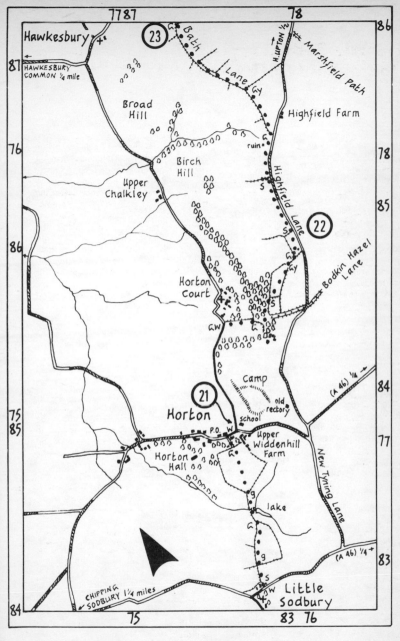

# 8. Hawkesbury Upton and the Kilcott Valley

*See commentary, p. 105*

Bath Lane emerges onto the minor road. Go straight on to the duck pond. At the junction go L along the pavement to the Somerset Monument. Then follow the road, regretfully bereft of pavement, until a lane takes the Way R. Do not continue with the lane but go through the gate facing the road and across the pasture to a gate into Frith Wood. Go into the wood and follow the track to the R to join the track that starts at the hunting gate at the corner of the pasture. Emerging from Claypit Wood at a gate, follow the hedgeline down to a gate into a sunken lane leading down to Lower Kilcott. Turn L, following the valley road beyond Kilcott Mill to the lane leading into the Tresham valley R. Watery Lane (well named, as wet-season walkers will know) is followed for 200 yards, then turn L up a lane (also liable to be muddy), partially obscured on the map by mile 26, to a hunting gate.

Claypit Wood is the first of the many large woodlands traversed on the walk north. It is a mixed primary wood showing evidence of recent sympathetic management and a return to the oak standards which must once have been associated with a hazel coppice. Where the route departs from the fields a mature elm survives with scrub wych elm, hazel and common elm nearby. Wayfaring tree and maple are also present, and in the thicker places old man's beard tumbles from the canopy. The steep-sided and wooded terrain in this area is particularly attractive to buzzards, which are frequently seen along the scarp between Kilcott and Wotton-under-Edge.

The Kilcott Brook is fed by springs which rise from the scarp. Where the banks are ungrazed they are fringed with meadowsweet, willowherb, hard rush, water mint, forget-me-nots and occasional clumps of marsh marigold. This once commonplace plant is now increasingly difficult to find owing to the drainage of its favourite marshy habitat and the damaging maintenance of river banks.

The Gloucestershire Trust for Nature Conservation manages Midger Wood as one of its reserves, which number more than fifty. Its exploration makes a worthwhile detour for the serious naturalist. Again it is ancient woodland of oak, ash and field maple, which also contains some steep species-rich grassland. The diverse woodland flora includes herb paris, lily of the valley and meadow saffron, while along the shady banks of the Kilcott Brook, which rises above the wood, there are many ferns, liverworts and mosses. Throughout the year there is varied bird life, with owls, woodpeckers, nuthatch and sparrowhawk resident. A leaflet about the Reserve is available for 60p. from the Trust.

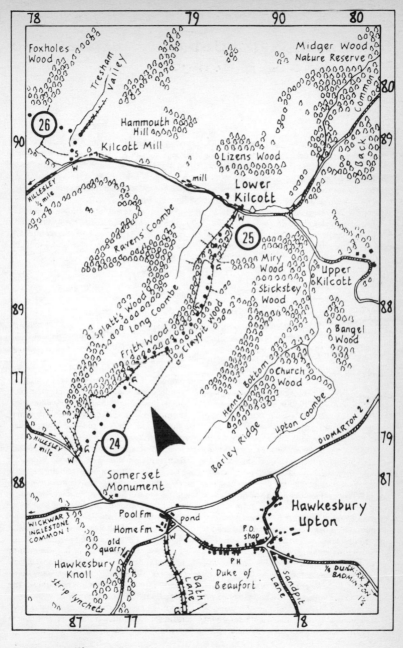

# 9. Alderley, Wortley and Blackquarries Hill

*See commentary, p. 108*

Follow the bridleway beside the hedge via four gates onto a track, directly into Alderley. Turn R following the road signposted to Tresham, then at the road junction cross into Kennerwell Lane. At the bottom cross the bridge. Advance through a gate to the stile, then walk more or less diagonally across the cultivated field to an imposing ladder stile. Go directly across the minor road through the gate and along the lane, diverging at a stile R. Ascend the hollow way onto Wortley Hill. Keep to the main track until a waymark post directs you cryptically L down into the scrub to a stile. Follow the fence above the amphitheatre (strip lynchet) to a gate on Tor Hill, go R to a gate where the Way rejoins the plateau top lane. At the minor road go L down Blackquarries Hill, bound for Wotton-under-Edge.

The spindle tree is not uncommon on lime-rich soils, though easily overlooked except in autumn, when the curious pink berries ripen. Hardly ever more than a tall shrub, note the example growing in the hedge after the left turn at mile 27 (near waymark on corner).

Wortley hollow way rises between exceedingly steep banks which are composed of soft unstable sands and clays, sparsely vegetated with ivy and hart's tongue fern. Here, as in many densely wooded habitats, the flowers are at their best before the dense canopy of leaves has formed, primroses making a magnificent display in April, while on the slopes are scattered plants of pale wood violet and celandine. At the top of the climb the track is fringed by a mixture of shrubs and trees, including sycamore, coppiced ash, sallow, wayfaring tree, honeysuckle and old man's beard.

Wortley Hill woods are much poorer in terms of wildlife than the woods of the Kilcott valley because they are recent in origin and consist entirely of conifers. Where the track emerges into an area of younger planting there are still a diversity of plants, including agrimony, scabious, salad burnet and, in the dry sandy soil, odd remnants of viper's bugloss. As the larches develop these flowers will be shaded out.

Nitrogen-rich fertilizers, applied to the pastures beyond the woods, will have improved the yield of grass. Note, however, that most of the flowering herbs have been eliminated, except in the fringe under the boundary fence, where harebells, scabious, goat's-beard and hoary plantain still survive.

Overlooking Coombe, the route passes briefly through a narrow, steep-sided woodland. Coppiced ash and hazel is present, together with a number of wild cherry trees. Dog's mercury is evident through the year, but the moschatel or 'town hall clock' clothes the ground only in April.

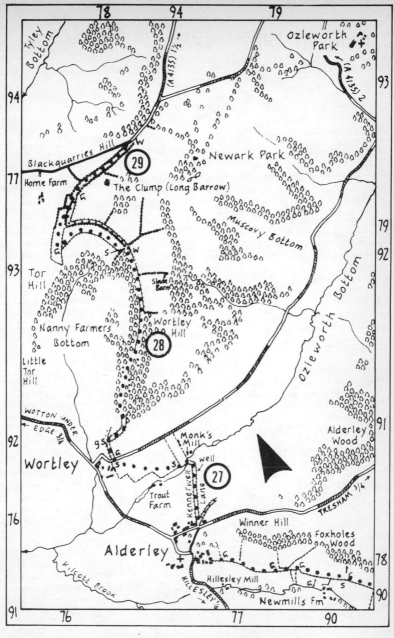

Tyley Bottom

Ozleworth Park

(A 4135) 1½

(A 4135) 2

94

93

Blackquarries Hill ·W· ㉙

Newark Park

Home Farm

The Clump (Long Barrow)

77

G

Muscovy Bottom

79

S W

92

Tor Hill

93

Slade Barn

Wortley Hill

Ozleworth Bottom

Nanny Farmers Bottom

㉘

Little Tor Hill

WOTTON UNDER EDGE 3¼

Alderley Wood

91

92

G S
G

Monk's Mill

S

well

㉗

Wortley

S

TRESHAM 3/4

Trout Farm

Kennerwell Lane

76

Winner Hill

Foxholes Wood

Alderley

G

78

Kilcott Brook

HILLESLEY

Hillesley Mill

G S

91

76

94

79

Newmills Fm

90

77

90

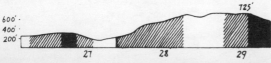

600'
400'
200'

725'

27    28    29

# 10. Wotton-under-Edge and North Nibley

*See commentary, p. 113*

The road descends steeply. Take the path diverging R leading down to a minor road. Walk down into Coombe and at the stream go L along its bank, crossing a minor road at Holywell, and advance into Valley Road to emerge onto Coombe Road, turning L into Wotton. Turn L into the churchyard, pass in front of the porch and go down Church Walk. Veer steeply R (short of the Potters Pond road) up the narrow passage in The Cloud and cross the road into Church Street. Turn R up Long Street (which becomes High Street) and at the junction continue into Bradley Street, bearing up to Gloucester Street, and turn L. Beyond the Old London Road junction cross to ascend (with the hand rails) the steep path up onto Wotton Hill. Cross the road to the stile, angling up L to the Jubilee Clump, and continue up round to a stile. Now follow the field headland to join the track through Westridge Wood, keeping R at two waymarked forks and passing the earthworks of Brackenbury Ditches hill fort. Reaching a gate, advance with the L-hand fence to the topograph and Tyndale Monument on Nibley Knoll. Do not descend on the footpath directly below but go R to a stile in the old quarry scrub to descend Wood Lane L. Emerging on the road at North Nibley, go R and L along The Street, branching down Lower House Lane R.

A Cotswold stream is briefly followed from Coombe towards Wotton-under-Edge. Thick hedges on the S side provide good cover for birds, while the wide variety of waterside plants includes brooklime, golden saxifrage, hemlock, water dropwort, great hairy willowherb, meadowsweet, water forget-me-not, monkey flower, yellow flag and water mint. The low-lying pasture N of the path near Wotton contains a few marsh marigolds.

Westridge Wood has been planted with conifers (mainly larch) following clearance of the deciduous trees, which now remain only on the steepest and mostly W-facing slopes. For half a mile the path runs above such a strip of beech and ash, where the ground beneath is carpeted with wild garlic and dog's mercury, with some nettle-leaved bellflower and golden rod flower in summer. Further along, where there are wild cherries in the woodland, the spring flora is very fine, with abundant wood anemones and the occasional primrose.

Brackenbury Ditches is approached along a ride, through thinned mature beech, plantations of larch and areas of open ground where masses of primroses grow. Parts of the ride are fringed by coppiced hazel, sallow and the occasional wild cherry. Many typical woodland flowers grow here, including pale wood violet, common violet, wood anemone, bluebell and dog's mercury. Wild roses grace the path in June and wild raspberry is also present.

Nibley Knoll is a species-rich limestone pasture, the best places for wild flowers and butterflies, especially blues, being the steep slopes around the Knoll and in the old limestone quarry to the NE. The quarry is geologically important and shows a complete cross-section through the Inferior Oolite from Cotteswold Sands to the Trigonia Grit. Below, beech and ash, growing on the unstable sands, are a forerunner of the glories yet to come.

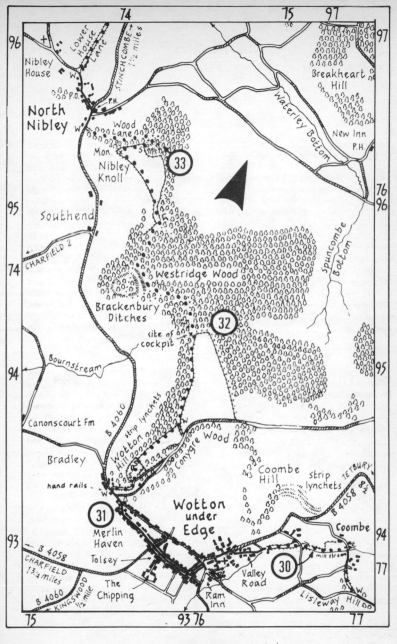

74 · 75 · 97

96

+

Lower House Lane

STINCHCOMBE 1½ miles

Nibley House W.

P.O.

North Nibley W.

P.H.

Wood Lane

Mon. Nibley Knoll

S. Mill

Breakheart Hill

New Inn P.H.

Waterley Bottom

33

95

Southend

96

CHARFIELD 2

74

Westridge Wood

Spuncombe Bottom

Brackenbury Ditches

site of cockpit

32

76

94

Bournstream

B 4060

Canonscourt Fm

Bradley

strip lynchets

Wotton Hill

Conygre Wood

Coombe Hill

strip lynchets

TETBURY

B 4058 8¼

95

hand rails

W.

Wotton under Edge

Coombe

31

Merlin Haven

Tolsey

30

Valley Road

mill stream

B 4058

CHARFIELD 13.4 miles

B 4060

KINGSWOOD ½ mile

The Chipping

Ram Inn

Lisleway Hill

94

93 · 76

77

75 · 93 76 · 77

650'

30 · 31 · 32 · 33

# 11. Stinchcombe Hill, Dursley and Cam Peak

*See commentary, p. 118*

The Way descends with Lower House Lane to cross the B4060 (use extreme caution). Go forward to cross Doverle Brook, taking the stile off the minor road L. Climb the pasture to a stile, proceed with the hedge to a stile onto a minor road and go L. Leave the road R at a stile, ascend to the fence (do not cross the first fence stile) and follow to the waymarked stile. Continue to a stile, descend through the hollow way decorated with gas pipes (hence the smell!), then ascend the scarp woodland track onto Stinchcombe Hill plateau. Go L on a grand tour of the promontory. The path keeps to the edge of the golf course playing area round Hollow Combe (note the attractive path from the first spur contouring out to Drakestone Point) to the Tubbs Seat. Follow the edge path past the ordnance column, down to the viewpoint shelter. The perimeter path proceeds beside a wall, diverging at an old quarry R, and crossing a short section of fairway to an old stone marker, here joining the Whiteway track. The waymarked route continues diagonally across the golf course with a bridleway onto the tarmac road, thereby reaching the club house. However, the author's preferred route keeps L, with the plateau edge for superior views, into the upper fringe of Sheep Path Wood, passing a seat viewpoint over the Dursley neighbourhood. This optional route goes in front of the golf course maintenance sheds onto a clear green track to the club house. Branch L down the steep waymarked path through the scarp woodland onto Hill Road, turning L and entering Dursley via May Lane and going R along Parsonage Street to the Market House. Advance down Long Street, branching R past the entrance to Chestal House onto a confined path which rises (assisted by newly cut steps) into a paddock over a stile, quickly followed by a further fence stile leading to a field gate and stile. Follow the headland to a stile and enter Drake Lane over another stile. Proceed R to the road junction, climbing the stile on the corner, and cross the pasture to a field gate onto the minor road opposite Downhouse Farm. Go R, then R again, over the stile to climb the steep path over Cam Peak.

Park Wood is the first of the five escarpment beechwoods, containing a number of enormous ancient trees. Ash is also present with some scattered hazel coppice, while on the woodland floor grow hart's tongue fern, polypody, wood spurge, primrose, melick and spurge laurel. Other specialities include white helleborine and stinking hellebore, which are locally distributed in similar woods in this area. Emerging from the wood and traversing above it, it is seen to be fringed with shrubs that include whitebeam, birch and wayfaring tree.

On Stinchcombe Hill the S-facing slopes are prime limestone grassland, carpeted with many typical herbs, including early purple orchids and yellow flowers of rock-rose. The woodlands below the hilltop are a mixture of beech and larch. Overall the hill is a fine place for all sorts of wildlife – there is beech woodland, scrub and species-rich grassland – a scene which is fortunately not too uncommon along the escarpment, northwards to Cleeve Hill.

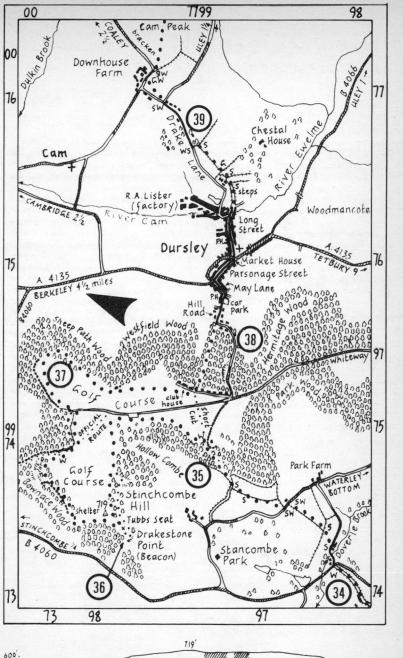

00

Dulkin Brook

Cam Peak
bracken
COALEY 2½
ULEY 1½

Downhouse
Farm

76

Cam

GW
GW
SW

39

Drake Lane
WS
S

Chestal
House

River Ewelme

River Cam

B 4066
ULEY 1

77

← CAMBRIDGE 2½

R.A.Lister
(factory)

G
S
S
S steps

Woodmancote

Long
Street

Dursley

PH.

Market House
Parsonage Street

May Lane

A 4135
TETBURY 9 →

76

75

A 4135
BERKELEY 4½ miles

B4060

Sheep Path Wood

Westfield Wood

Hill
Road

PH.
car
Park

38

Hermitage Wood

Whiteway

97

37

Golf
Course

club
house

short
cut

Park Wood

75

99
74

OFFICIAL
ROUTE

Hollow Combe

35

Park Farm

WATERLEY
BOTTOM

S

Golf
Course

S
SW
SW

Downace Wood

Stinchcombe
Hill

shelter
719

Tubbs Seat

x
Drakestone
Point
(Beacon)

Stancombe
Park

S

Doverle Brook

← STINCHCOMBE ½
B 4060

36

34

W

74

719'

600'
400'
200'

34   35   36   37   38   39

# 12. Cam Long Down and Coaley Peak

*See commentary, p. 122*

The Way descends to the R of the main depression to join the path on its slanting ascent of Cam Long Down. Parade along the undulating summit ridge before descending to a well-obscured stile below the trees. Descend the pasture to a stile in the hedge corner, continuing with the L-hand fence line to a gate onto the minor road. Go forward to the bend and branch L along the farm access track. Proceed up past Hodgecombe Farm almost to the B4066 at the top of Crawley Hill. A most enjoyable departure from the Way is the grand tour round Uleybury, which is best started from this point. The Way, however, promptly slips L onto a descending woodland path which soon contours beneath the old quarry wall, reaching the scarp foot at Tickshill road end. Re-mount the scarp up the old hollow way, gaining the main road. Go L then immediately L again a short way down Frocester Hill, branching R onto the old quarry path which leads through to the Frocester Hill spur and topograph. Go through the adjacent kissing gate within the Coaley Peak picnic site and follow the scarp-top fence.

Dog violets – a rather uncommon species in Gloucestershire – distinguishable by the yellowish spur to the flower, occur sparsely on the slopes of Cam Peak and Long Down. Short grass on the slopes is confined to trampled tracks, while elsewhere the invasion of bracken is almost complete. The bracken betrays the presence of the underlying acidic Cotteswold Sands.

Coaley Wood is very varied in character and quite different from the beechwoods further north. In the S, tall mature beech are dominant, giving way to massive coppiced specimens beyond Crawley Barns, while in the centre and N of the wood dense pole ash and hazel coppice with sycamore and a few oaks are to be seen. There are fewer flowers as the tree canopy becomes denser, but wood anemones, dog's mercury and primroses occur throughout, while on the damp shaded banks in the upper parts of the wood hart's tongue, shield and polypody ferns find ideal conditions, together with mosses and liverworts. Masses of golden saxifrage flower here in spring.

The Gloucestershire Trust for Nature Conservation manages a strip of steep grassland and a disused quarry, S of the Coaley Peak picnic area, as a nature reserve. The land is owned by the National Trust. The quarry shows an exposure of the Inferior Oolite and although its floor is threatened by ash scrub, clothed in ivy and old man's beard, parts are periodically cleared to encourage primroses, early purple orchids, valerian and other colourful plants. The upper part of the grassland possesses a typical limestone flora, with salad burnet, rockrose and cowslip as prominent species. It is a good place for butterflies. Lower down, on the sands and clays, where the soil is deeper, bracken and tall herbs such as rosebay and hemp agrimony flourish. Grasshopper warblers formerly bred regularly on these slopes, but have not done so for some years, possibly because of increasing recreational pressures. The Gloucestershire Trust maintain the grassland condition by carefully controlled burning.

44

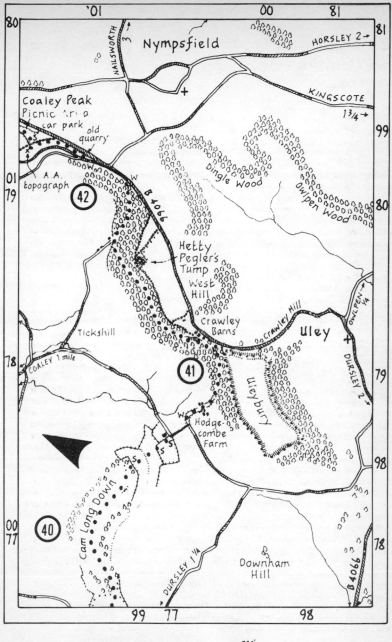

'01     00     81

80    81

**Nympsfield**

NAILSWORTH 3

HORSLEY 2 →

+

KINGSCOTE

13/4 →

99

**Coaley Peak**
Picnic Area
car park   old quarry

A.A.
topograph

01
79    80

Dingle Wood

Owlpen Wood

W

B 4066

42

Hetty
Pegler's
Tump
West
Hill

Crawley Hill

OWLPEN 1/2

Tickshill

Crawley
Barns

**Uley**

+

78

COALEY 1 mile

41

Uleybury

DURSLEY 2

79

W

Hodge-
combe
Farm

S S

98

S

S

Cam Long Down

00
77

40

DURSLEY 1 1/4

Downham
Hill

B 4060

78

99   77     98

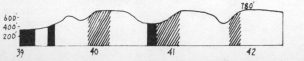

600'-
400'-
200'-

780'

39     40     41     42

# 13. Stanley Wood, Pen Hill and Peckstreet Farm

*See commentary, p. 125*

The Way passes through the kissing gate, crossing the enclosure to a stile beyond the information building. A clear path skirts the necessarily well-fenced quarry rim down onto a track. Go R, following the fence line nearly to the road, where an obvious path leads L through the upper woodland. Watch for the track crossways. Do not take the broader descending track, instead fork R to cross a rising track before emerging from the wood at an awkwardly angled fence (soon to be replaced by a stable stile). Hug the foot of Stanley Wood, only moving away on approaching Woodside Farm, cross a stile and enter a rapidly overgrowing enclosure (path subjected to brambly tendrils). The rising path enters mature woodland, advancing unhindered beneath Pen Hill. The Way is directed by barbed fencing to the point where Pen Lane, near a metal gate, enters the woodland. Go down this lane to the metal stile and descend the pasture to a stile into a narrow lane, soon emerging with an access lane into Coombe Lane and proceeding into Middle Yard. Go L then at the corner R by the old chapel to a stile and advance to the fence, crossing the field diagonally L to a stile. Follow the L-hand hedgeline to a stile, then cross the ensuing cultivated field to another stile and join the farm lane going R through the farmyard to a gate into pastureland. Retain the obvious track down, via a stile, onto the road by the giant Stanley Mill, going R to cross the River Frome.

The picnic area at Coaley Peak is managed by Gloucestershire County Council, who, with advice from the Gloucester Trust and the Nature Conservancy Council, maintain a species-rich grassland around the car parking area. In particular, the once widely cultivated sainfoin grows there. It is an excellent place for butterflies, with nine species to be found in a typical year. Opposite the information building deciduous trees have been planted – a welcome sight – notably hazel, field maple and beech.

Buckholt Wood is entered near a quarry with a sheer face, where redstart and jackdaw may breed. The top is flanked by wayfaring tree. Stanley Wood was probably similar in character to Coaley Wood before parts were cleared and re-planted with a mixture of conifers. Cypress at the S end date from the early 1980s, while larch plantations are present further NE. Elsewhere there is still dense pole beech, with a mixed coppice of ash and hazel. On the open banks below the wood many primroses grow and just before re-entering the trees there is a small area of limestone grassland. Quaking grass, large specimens of common spotted orchid, yellow wort and centaury may all be found, but the slope is becoming invaded by sallow scrub and will not remain open for very long.

Pen Hill Woods are contiguous with Stanley Wood. Tall beech trees are dominant, although small blocks of larch and pine are also present. Sanicle, ivy and sweet woodruff cover the woodland floor. Violets, wood spurge and golden rod are sparsely distributed, while spurge laurel and wood anemones are abundant on the steep W-facing slope.

Red admirals delight in the nectar of ivy flowers! A luxuriant growth swarming up a long dead tree near mile 44 rewards the insects and observers in September.

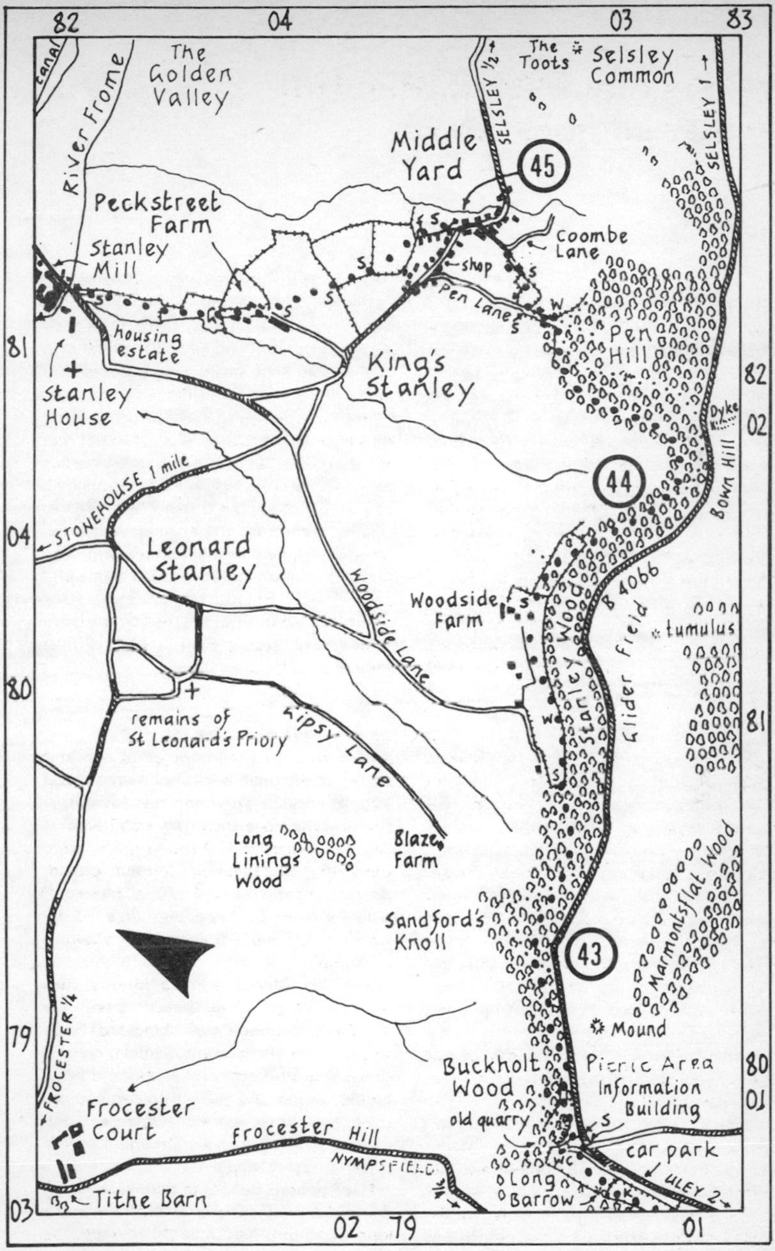
82
04
03
83
canal
River Frome
The Golden Valley
The Toots
Selsley Common
SELSLEY ½
SELSLEY 1
Middle Yard
45
Peckstreet Farm
Stanley Mill
Coombe Lane
shop
Pen Lane
Pen Hill
housing estate
King's Stanley
Stanley House
81
82
02
Dyke
Bown Hill
44
STONEHOUSE 1 mile
04
Leonard Stanley
Woodside Lane
Woodside Farm
Stanley Wood
B 4066
Glider Field
tumulus
80
remains of St Leonard's Priory
Gipsy Lane
81
Long Linings Wood
Blaze Farm
Marmontsflat Wood
Sandford's Knoll
43
FROCESTER ¼
79
Mound
Buckholt Wood
Picnic Area Information Building
80
01
old quarry
Frocester Court
Frocester Hill
car park
NYMPSFIELD 1¼
Long Barrow
ULEY 2
Tithe Barn
03
02
79
01

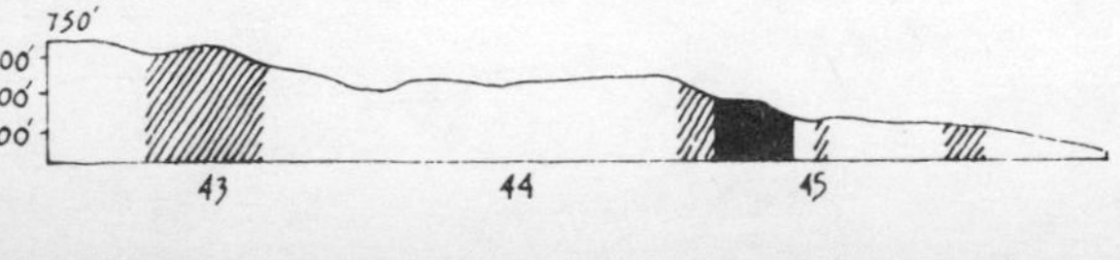
750′
600′
400′
200′
43
44
45

# 14. Ryeford, Westrip and Standish Wood

*See commentary, p. 130*

The Way proceeds upon the pavement, crossing the Stroudwater Canal, then turns R at the road junction, passing under the school footbridge. Subsequently the route turns L up a path between hedges, passes a football pitch and climbs over a railway footbridge. The Way bears R, crossing three stiles above an old brickworks (now a car depository). Crossing a pasture to a stile, follow the hedge down to a muddy gate, then climb the pasture to another stile, continuing up a further pasture to a stone stile onto the road at Westrip and go R.

Watch for the waymarking pointing L up between the houses to a stile. Advance up the bank to another stile, then across a field to the stile, onto a minor road. Go L then R into Three Bears' Wood, passing through to a stone stile. Go R to the track leading up Maiden Hill and pass through two gates to reach a crossways. Taking the main lane ahead, watch for the branch path L, short of the minor road, shortly cross the stile and retain the ridge path through Standish Wood.

The River Frome, now quite small, was a powerful torrent in the ice age, and was responsible for cutting the deep valley in which it now runs. The descent from Pen Hill and the re-ascent beyond Ryeford therefore cross a wide range of geological strata. The lighter soil of the Dyrham Silts, near King's Stanley, gives way to the alluvium in the valley and the successive terraces of former river levels before the permanent pastures of Doverow Hill, sited on the foundered strata of Upper and Middle Lias clays and sands, are reached. The land here, and in the Painswick valley further N, is quite steep and mostly used for beef rearing, sheep or dairy farming.

Broad-leaf cockspur thorn, tough and spiny, decorative at all seasons, lines the road by the sports field of Wycliffe College.

The Stroudwater Canal is fringed with colourful waterside plants, including purple loosestrife, forget-me-not and policeman's helmet. Reed canary grass and pond weeds dominate the scene in late summer. If the canal is filled in, another freshwater habitat, valuable for dragonflies and other aquatic creatures as well as sedge warblers, mute swan and moorhen, will have been lost.

Beech woodland is the most important wildlife habitat on the rubbly limestone soils between Stroud and Birdlip, a large number of woods being of national importance in terms of their plant and animal life. Most are managed for timber production, which discourages trees other than beech and the occasional ash. Typically, there is a thin understorey of holly, yew and whitebeam. A number of plants which are nationally rare or of restricted distribution grow in this important habitat, including angular solomon's seal, bird's nest orchid, stinking hellebore and lily of the valley. Standish Wood is the first of these escarpment beech woods, which also contain much larch.

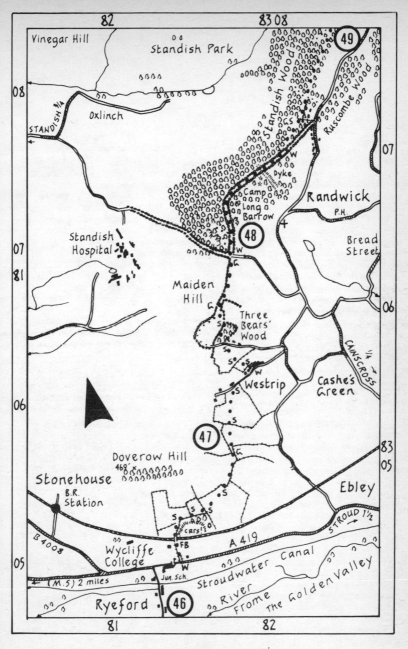

# 15. Haresfield Beacon, Scottsquare Hill and Washbrook Farm

*See commentary, p. 132*

The Way advances upon the main path, swinging L via a stile to join a track rising up from Standish Wood. Short of the road, pass L through the National Trust car park, going forward to the topograph, before veering N back from the spur to pass through the trees L, following a clear path below the wall and crossing a choice of two stiles at the down wall. Proceed to rise up towards the road again, veer L on the waymarked path through the earthworks, following the fence to a stile, and continue to the ordnance column and beacon site viewpoint. Backtrack along the W edge of the Ring Hill promontory, crossing a stile, then descend to the farmyard gate, there joining the minor road and going L. Take the track R above Ringhill Cottage, which leads unerringly past the Siege Stone round to Cliffwell House and the well. Turn R up the minor road and branch off L onto the waymarked track leading through Halliday Wood. The track runs on under Stockend Wood. Watch carefully for the path leading R up through Stockend Wood onto the minor road on Rudge Hill. Cross the road, keeping L of the old Scottsquar Quarry, descend the old pasture to a track in the birch, go R then down L at the wall corner. Proceed across the B4072 and down the lane towards Jenkins Farm. Take the stone stile L short of the farm, crossing to a fence stile, then descend the pasture, seeking a footbridge and stile. Continue past the new barn and round Washbrook to a gate. Swing R up to a stile, following the L hedgeline to cross the next pasture.

Buzzards, perhaps as many as three at a time, may occasionally be seen soaring over Haresfield Beacon, although they no longer nest in the area. Below the topograph, where thick scrub has encroached on to the steep rough slopes, the berry-bearing hawthorns are likely to be an important source of food for fieldfares, redwings and thrushes during winter months. In summer it is a marvellous place for warblers, tits and finches. In the grassland around the quarries there are particularly fine stands of blue fleabane and a number of orchids.

Scottsquar Hill (Edge Common) is a very distinctive outcrop of the Lower Inferior Oolite and is of both geological and physiographical importance. Its rough slopes possess a herb-rich grassland where six species of orchid may be found. There is also a good range of butterflies, including small blue, marbled white and a number of fritillaries. The sward is dominated by the coarse upright brome grass which, despite not having been grazed for many years, has remained reasonably short owing to trampling and the recreational use of the common – a saving grace for many of the plants and insects.

Roadside verges have become increasingly important in recent years as refuges for the survival of wildlife, as to a large extent they are free from the pressures exerted by intensive land usage. The verge from Edgemoor Inn to Jenkins Farm, fringed with hedges and woodland plants is an example. Herb robert, yellow archangel, sweet violets, bush vetch and wild strawberry are particularly abundant on the S side of the lane.

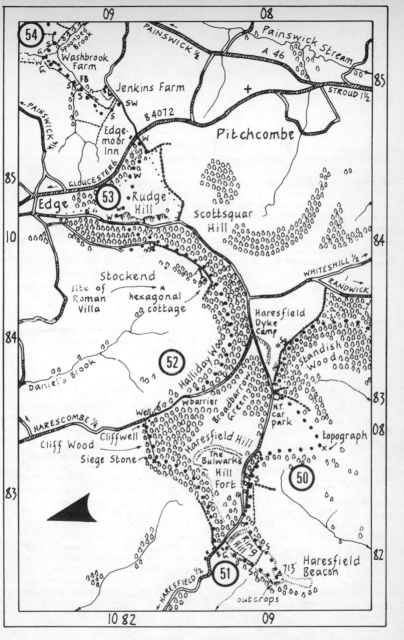

54

PAINSWICK ½

Painswick Stream

A 46

Spoonbed Brook

85

Washbrook Farm

FB

S

STROUD 1½

Jenkins Farm

SW

B4012

S

W

Edge-moor Inn

PAINSWICK ¼

+

Pitchcombe

W

85

GLOUCESTER 6

53  • Rudge Hill

Edge

W

Scottsquar Hill

10

84

WHITESHILL ½

RANDWICK

Stockend

site of Roman Villa

× hexagonal cottage

Haresfield Dyke Camp

84

52

Halliday Wood

Standish Wood

83

Daniel's Brook

W barrier

Broadbarrow Green

N.T. car park

HARESCOMBE ¼

Well

Cliff Wood  Cliffwell

Siege Stone

Haresfield Hill

topograph
×

The Bulwarks Hill Fort

S

50

83

Ring Hill

713

Haresfield Beacon

82

HARESFIELD ½

51

S

outcrops

10 82

09

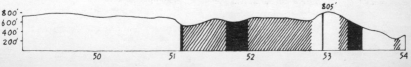

800'
600'
400'
200'

805'

50          51          52          53          54

# 16. Painswick and Painswick Beacon

See commentary, p. 135

Cross the pasture to a stile in the fence, then climb the next pasture with an old hedge-line to a rail stile. Pass through a passage between gardens, proceeding to the Edge Road via two stiles. The waymarked route through Painswick leads L along New Street. However, the prettiest route advances in front of the church, then by St Mary's, Friday and Bisley Streets to rejoin the formal route up Gloucester Street. A pavement assists progress along the Gloucester Road. Pass through The Plantation R. On emerging, veer R across the lower golf course fairway and an unenclosed minor road. Keep above the cemetery, and soon join a well-marked path, passing Catsbrain Quarry to join briefly the upper road across Painswick Hill. Branch R, either keeping to the fairway margin up the ridge onto Kimsbury (this may soon become the waymarked route) or advancing with the clear track N E. By The Castles join the metalled lane proceeding down towards the Royal William. Take the track branching L through woodland on course for the Portway (Upton St Leonards road).

The environs of Painswick Beacon are a Cotswold Common where grazing rights are no longer exercised. As a result, many of its slopes have been invaded by scrub and self-sown Scots pine, thus reducing the extent, if not the interest, of ground long famous with botanists. The richest areas are the scattered dips and hummocks left by quarrying; such open W facing slopes that remain are around the Beacon, where both frog and musk orchids grow. Among the shallow limestone workings one of the earliest plants to flower is the hairy violet and soon afterwards the thriving colonies of limestone butterflies successively take to the wing. Large blues, now extinct in Britain, were last found here in 1932.

Pope's Wood is now part of the Cotswolds Commons and Beechwoods National Nature Reserve. Like many of these woods it is managed for a commercially viable timber crop and there is frequently evidence of forestry activity. Management techniques vary, from replanting after felling to leaving the wood to its own devices, later selecting and thinning out the best saplings which have naturally regenerated. The latter approach, if natural regeneration is good, may be the most sympathetic to conservation in these important primary woodlands. In Pope's Wood, rowan, wild cherry and birch grow as well as whitebeam and yew with wood anemone, sweet woodruff, dog's mercury and sanicle on the woodland floor. Where open glades and rides occur a lusher flora develops and associated with it a richer insect life. In particular, silver-washed fritillary butterflies may be seen in July, in the vicinity of violets, which are the sole food plant of its caterpillar.

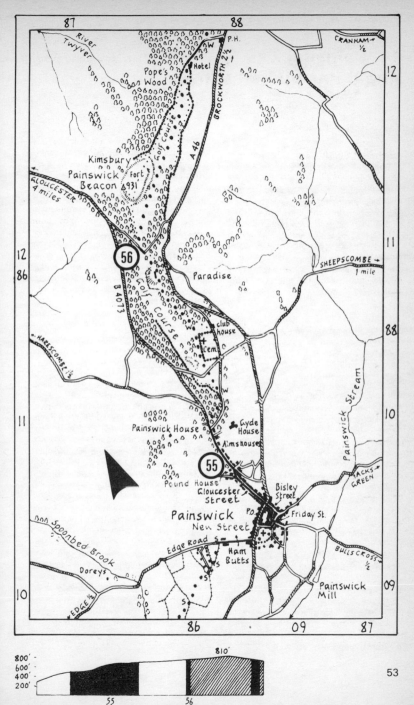

# 17. Prinknash Corner, Cooper's Hill and Witcombe Woods

See commentary, p. 139

Cross the Upton (Portway) road and go R with the park wall to the Prinknash Corner junction. Cross onto the Birdlip road, branching L just opposite the Cranham turn to ascend with the wall. Cresting High Brotheridge, descend steeply (a future modification may avoid this section by zig-zagging N of the settlement site – watch the waymarks here). A nature trail leads round Brockworth Wood from the Fiddler's Elbow car park – the Cotswold Way coincides with part of it. Follow the colour-coded trail posts thus: blue from above the quarry, brown R through the hedged connecting lane, orange along the track N, branching R with the black posts to reach the open common leading N to the maypole (the trail continues round by yellow, red and green posts to the lane at brown). Descend L (direct descents via the cheese-rolling slope are ill-advised!), swinging R below an outcrop to a new kissing gate, beyond which pass through the car park and turn R along the minor road. Passing through the gate, retain the main track, keeping to the base of Witcombe Woods.

Rough Park Wood and Buckholt Wood are also part of the National Nature Reserve. The S end of Rough Park is mainly tall, thinned beech with a sparse understorey of holly. Woodruff, herb robert, sanicle and dog's mercury are the principal components of the flora in summer. White helleborine could also be encountered. Under the current wildlife legislation it is now illegal to uproot *any* wild plant without permission from the landowner, and in addition there are many plants which are legally protected from picking. White helleborine is one. Preserve the beauty of the flowers in a photograph, but please, in your endeavours to select the best camera position, have a care for what else may be trampled underfoot!

Cooper's Hill local nature reserve encompasses Upton Wood and the western flank of Brockworth Wood. The former consists of old hazel and beech coppice, with some invasion by sycamore. Dense drifts of bluebell and wild garlic bloom beneath. Where the canopy is more open, as in the areas where thinning of the beech has recently commenced, taller herbs flourish. There are clearly marked nature trails around the reserve, for which an explanatory leaflet is available from The Haven at the foot of the hill.

Tall beech trees continue to dominate the walk through Brockworth Wood, Cooper's Hill Wood and indeed on to Witcombe Wood – a superb and ancient scene. Primroses, wood anemones and sweet violets are scattered on the steep slopes, while thick ivy clothes some of the trees. Fallow deer roam the quieter parts and, after dusk, badgers, those controversially persecuted and seldom-seen mammals which find the sandy soils of the escarpment favourable for excavation of the set. On the N side of Cooper's Hill sycamores are vigorously invasive of the beechwood as they are in some other woods in the area. This common tree was introduced to Britain 400 years ago.

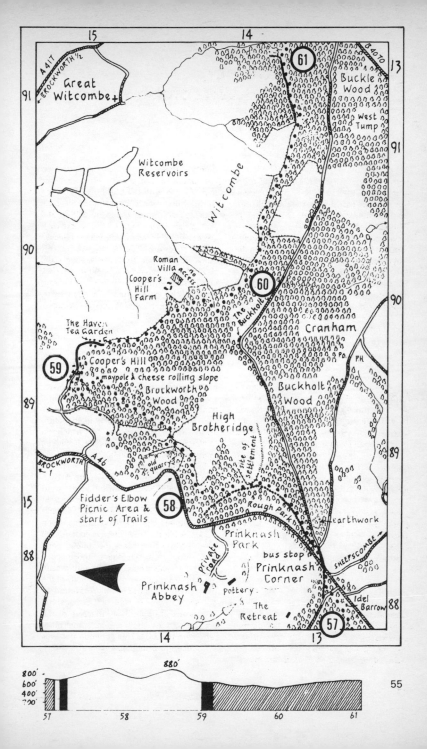

55

# 18. The Peak and Crickley Hill

*See commentary, p. 141*

The Way is well waymarked, though walkers should study the map if in doubt. The route begins to ascend more acutely, following the old quarry (which has been enveloped by Cotteswold sand landslipping). At the top of this rise, branch L off the main track (there are three paths diverging at this point) and follow the terrace-way down to the wall, branching sharp R up the narrow trod to cross the Birdlip Hill road directly, following the clear track out to The Peak. Backtrack along the edge, entering a strongly fenced pasture through a gate (it is planned to erect a stile here), and keep to the edge, crossing a stile to come up onto the Barrow Wake viewpoint. Follow the pavement down to the Air Balloon public house, crossing at the traffic island to the gate. Veer L to follow the fence out to the hill fort promontory, crossing a stile. Retain the edge, pass through the camp portals by the viewing platform (erected to reduce erosion) and Country Park car park to a stile. Follow the outer margin of Short Wood towards Shurdington Hill.

In Witcombe Wood, N of the Cotswold Way, cypress plantations have recently been added to the original woodland. On the steep oolitic limestone, S of the track, beech is still dominant and here, as elsewhere, different stages of the management cycle may be seen. Most of the conifers are on foundered clays and sands (the presence of wood sorrel is indicative of sand). Elsewhere in the wood, lily of the valley, white helleborine, bird's nest orchid and angular solomon's seal are among the 'special' plants.

Peak Plantation is mainly larch, pine and beech, with some yew, holly, hazel, hawthorn and wild raspberry and gooseberry in the sparse shrub layer. Much of this woodland is comparatively recent in origin, and although a locally valuable habitat for wildlife it is not in the same category of importance as the large beechwoods.

Chalk hill blue butterflies, glow-worms, common lizards, adders and grasshoppers all revel in the sunny warm conditions on the stony slopes of Barrow Wake. Redstarts nest in the old stone walls and musk orchids may be found in the short limestone turf.

The kiss of death awaits those who flirt with the lovely lady – Belladonna! Deadly nightshade grows round Crickley. Its large black berries are very poisonous!

The Devil's Table is a natural pedestal formed by erosion of the Pea Grit, a crumbly limestone which is exposed along the flanks of Crickley Hill. The cliffs here are a feature of considerable geological importance that contrast starkly with the green pastures and arable fields on the Lias below. The formation of the valley is partly due to a fault. Its occurrence can be determined by examination of the rocks exposed by quarrying.

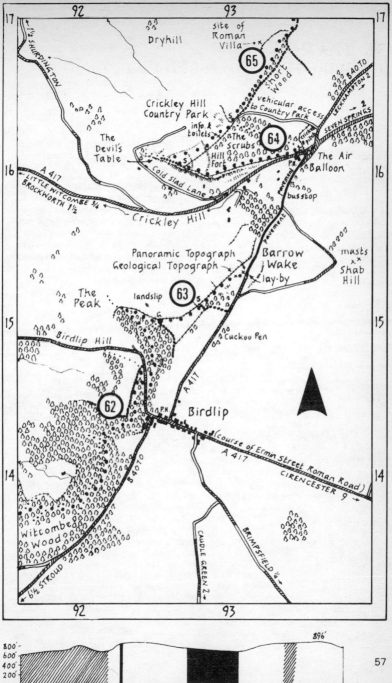

Dryhill

site of Roman Villa

⑥⑤

Short Wood

Crickley Hill Country Park

vehicular access to Country Park

The Devil's Table

info. & toilets

The Scrubs

⑥④

LECHAMPTON 2

B4070

SEVEN SPRINGS 2

Hill Fort

The Air Balloon

A 417

LITTLE WITCOMBE ¾

BROCKWORTH 1½

Cold slad Lane

pavement

Crickley Hill

bus stop

Panoramic Topograph
Geological Topograph

Barrow Wake

masts
×× Shab Hill

The Peak

landslip

⑥③

lay-by

Birdlip Hill

Cuckoo Pen

⑥②

A 417

Birdlip

(course of Ermin Street Roman Road)

P.H.

B4070

A 417

CIRENCESTER 9

Witcombe Wood

CAUDLE GREEN 2

BRIMPSFIELD ¾

6½ STROUD

896'

800'
600'
400'
200'

62    63    64    65

57

# 19. Shurdington Hill, Leckhampton Hill and Seven Springs

*See commentary, p. 144*

Keeping to the W of the fence cross two stiles to join Greenway Lane. Proceed R, passing an old army camp, and, crossing the B4070 carefully, enter Ullenwood. Where the road swings R take the lane L, beside the first fairway of the golf course, rising above Salterley Grange Hospital to join Hartley Lane. Go L downhill, watch for the less than obvious path R running above the quarry and out to the hill fort, with a spur route L down to see the Devil's Chimney and Dead Man's Quarry. The waymarked path keeps to the edge, weaving a joyous course along Charlton Kings Common. Proceed into the pasture field, following the hedge down to the lane. Where this joins Hartley Lane a puddle invariably hampers progress! Advance to the busy crossroads, go directly across to follow the lane for Upper Coberley. At the time of writing this is not the waymarked route, which points up the A436 to Chatcombe Pitch (totally unsuitable for walkers). Plans are afoot to adopt the route shown in this guide.

Barrow Piece Plantation is a narrow strip of planted beech, pine and larch on Shurdington Hill which shelters land on its E side from the prevailing SW winds which buffet the scarp. Rough scrubby slopes fall to the W, with springs emerging at the junction of Lias clays and sands at the foot of the hill. Such springs are a feature of the escarpment. They result from surface water, percolating through the porous oolite and sands, reaching the impervious clay. Their occurrence dictated the siting of the older, isolated habitations.

Barn owls are resident in the Ullenwood area and a number of landowners have consented to the use of specially made nest boxes for them. They are provided by the Gloucestershire Trust for Nature Conservation to encourage this now uncommon species to increase in numbers.

Robin's Wood Hill and Churchdown Hill, visible across the valley from near the Devil's Chimney, were once part of the Cotswold mass. Aeons of preferential erosion have left them as outliers, their underlying sands protected by the marlstone and oolite caps.

Leckhampton Hill, owned by Cheltenham District Council, is a Site of Special Scientific Interest. Together with Charlton Kings Common it contains a variety of habitats: species-rich grassland; thick gorse; quarry faces and stone walls; and a small area of beechwood. The steep slopes of Leckhampton Hill are good for butterflies and reptiles. The diverse flora there includes rockrose, small scabious, thyme and ploughman's spikenard, which also feature near the path with centaury and felwort. Both Leckhampton and Salterley Grange quarries contain classic geological exposures of the freestones. Ragstones at the top have been used for the boundary walls.

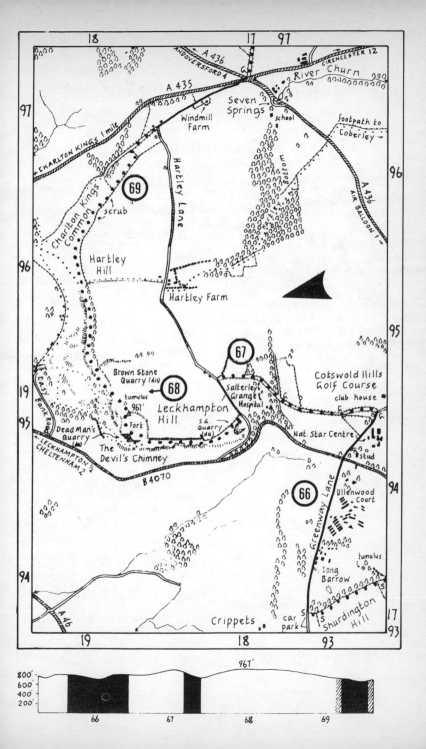

# 20. Seven Springs, Wistley Hill and Lineover Wood

*See commentary, p. 148*

The lane joins the Upper Coberley road, rising onto the wolds. Branch L onto the track which advances towards Needlehole (signposted to Wistley Hill), diverging L at the angle to cross the cultivated field by the dewpond (very muddy at times) to a hunting gate in the corner. Follow the field boundary to the gate into Chatcombe Wood, thereafter retaining the track along the edge of the wood to the A436. Cross directly by facing gates and follow the track descending through the conifer strips and a gateway and a gate. Slant R down the very steep scarp bank on a thin trod to a hunting gate. Descend towards Old Dole, veering R at a waymark post to reach a further hunting gate into Lineover Wood. The route is clear, passing the head of a pasture, then, before the end of the pasture, forking R to a gate (the three cleared strips were made in 1982). Veer L to a stile, then descend to the old railway and the A40. An awkward stretch beside the young plantation is liable to be muddy and therefore slippery, so be careful!

Chatcombe Wood is a marvellous bluebell wood. Approached from the 'pylon field', it is seen as still dense beech, with ash, where in summer the ground is carpeted with dog's mercury. But further N, towards the A436, the original woodland has been altered by conifer planting and recent felling. Primary woodland indicators, such as angular solomon's seal and small-leaved lime, were recorded in the past, while meadow saffron may still be found by the conifer plantation. Unfortunately, a large section of the primary woodland was cleared in 1979 and ploughed.

Moles as well as badgers find the sandy soils to their liking in Chatcombe Wood and, with the abundance of berried shrubs that are in the hedges to the S and alongside the route in the N of the wood, wood mice and squirrels should also thrive (sadly, only grey squirrel nowadays – the red have gone).

Lineover Wood 'hangs' off the escarpment and faces N over the Chelt Valley. In the S it is on the Inferior Oolite but the wood slopes steeply down over the Cotteswold Sands to the undulating Lias. The deeper soils allow fine oaks to grow and these, with ash and hazel coppice, are the principal elements of the wood. Larch has been sporadically planted, amid two blocks of conifers. Old documents show a wood on this site in the 9th century, suggesting that it has been forest for at least 600 years. The inter-related complex of wildlife which has evolved in that period – mosses, ferns, fungi, insects, flowers, birds, shrubs and trees – cannot be re-established once it is destroyed. Much, perhaps, is rarely seen, or appreciated, though that could scarcely be true of the bluebells, lilies of the valley and wayfaring trees in May. The remaining deciduous element of Lineover Wood is well worth conserving.

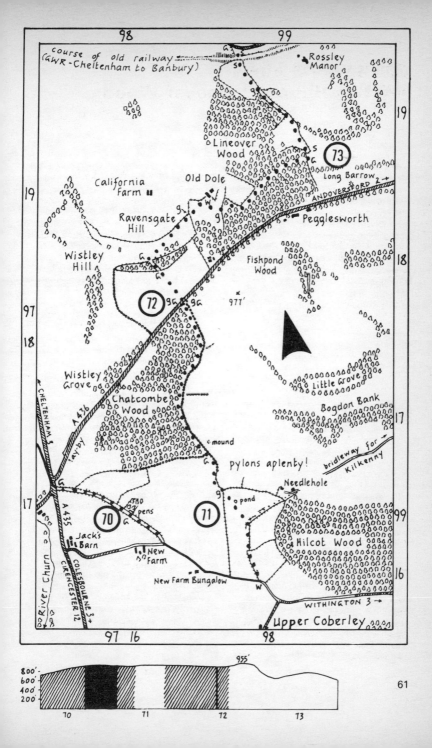

course of old railway
(GWR-Cheltenham to Banbury)

Rossley Manor

Lineover Wood

73

California Farm

Old Dole

Long Barrow

ANDOVERSFORD 2

Ravensgate Hill

Pegglesworth

Wistley Hill

Fishpond Wood

72

977'

Wistley Grove

Little Grove

Chatcombe Wood

Bogdon Bank

mound

pylons aplenty!

bridleway for Kilkenny

Needlehole

70

71

pond

Jack's Barn

Hilcot Wood

New Farm

New Farm Bungalow

WITHINGTON 3

Upper Coberley

CHELTENHAM 3

A 436

LAY-BY

A 435

COLESBOURNE 3

CIRENCESTER 12

River Churn

800'
600'
400'
200'

955'

70

71

72

73

# 21. Dowdeswell Reservoir and Piccadilly

*See commentary, p. 150*

Crossing the railway follow the track down to a gate onto the A40, go L on the pavement, passing the Reservoir Inn, diverging R down the lane leading under the dam. A path proceeds up beside the woodland fence and can be uncomfortably slippery. Cross a stile higher up and soon leave the perimeter fence on a path leading R in a triangular enclosure to a stile. Aim across the cultivated field to a target waymark NW. Cross the Ham Hill by-road, following the field boundary by two gates onto the minor road from Whittington. Proceed N, turning L at the skew junction, descending the old road, veering R beneath the woodland fringe, then going R through a gate and up a stony track to a gate. Pass on through this quarry (watching for the wild antics of motor-cyclists) to the track junction, descend a few yards, then cross the fence R, proceeding through the dense gorse on a clear path.

Dowdeswell Reservoir is not visible from the Cotswold Way but, for the birdwatcher, may be worth the short detour in winter months. Public access is not permitted, but good views can be obtained from the road of any migratory wildfowl. A booklet is available from the Gloucestershire Trust for Nature Conservation, which gives a comprehensive list of all the birds which have visited or bred on the reservoir. The Trust has a Nature Reserve agreement with the owners, Severn Trent Water Authority.

Herb Paris and lily of the valley were part of the ground flora in Dowdeswell Wood before it was clear-felled during the 1970s and replanted with conifers. It was formerly a fine oak/ash/wych elm wood on Upper Lias clay. A small remnant of old ash and hazel coppice remains to the west of the Cotswold Way, where masses of bluebells and wood anemones, flowering in spring, provide a stark contrast to the barren floor below the dense conifers to the east. Pale wood violet and moschatel should be sought under the coppiced beech at the top of the climb.

Old hedges are often ancient woodland remnants. Age can roughly be found by counting the different shrub and tree species in a 100-ft length and multiplying by 100. The hedge line from Dowdeswell Wood to Arle Grove is an example to try, for it includes wayfaring tree, wild rose, ash, holly and hawthorn as well as other species. Across the lane all except old ash pollards have been removed, leaving a few violets, cowslips and dog's mercury isolated between intensively farmed grasslands.

An avenue of old pollarded beech trees frames the rolling oolitic-based landscape east of the lane at mile 76, complemented by the ragstone wall beneath. They are a joy at all seasons.

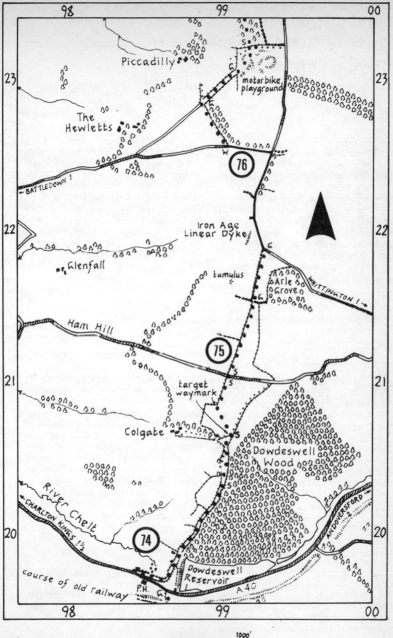

Piccadilly

The Hewletts

motorbike playground

76

← BATTLEDOWN 1

Iron Age Linear Dyke

Glenfall

tumulus

Arle Grove

WHITTINGTON 1 →

Ham Hill

75

target waymark

Colgate

Dowdeswell Wood

River Chelt

ANDOVERSFORD 2 →

74

CHARLTON KINGS 1½

Dowdeswell Reservoir

course of old railway

P.H.

A 40

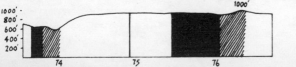

63

# 22. Happy Valley and Cleeve Common

*See commentary, p. 152*

The path rises to the stile. Now descend the lateral valley, join a track that sweeps N, and pass through a gateway beside a beechwood to a gate. Go L downhill, veering R up the track to, and beyond, the hunting gate, eventually rising to the gate onto Cleeve Common. Advance along the edge to Castle Rock, diverging R up to the trig point, descending NW with waymark posts in abundance. Veer R above The Ring and go obliquely L on a track leading towards the club house. However, branch R above the old quarry, keeping close under the gorse and off the fairways. At the wall-end cross the ridge-track and descend abruptly due S, joining a clear grass track leading to the Washpool. Continue beyond the pond, retaining the valley floor path, until a waymark post directs you steeply L (ESE). Where the path levels, take the L fork (avoiding the parallel gallop), then where these reunite veer L with the vehicle tracks. Shortly a post directs off obliquely L, again with a new trod, through a shallow valley depression and on to join a gallop. Turn L to the gate off the Common.

Happy Valley is part of Prestbury Grasslands which, together with Cleeve Common, form an area of more than 3 square miles (about 1,250 acres) of prime limestone grassland and associated habitats. The escarpment in particular is a pure delight for botanists and butterfly lovers alike. Cleeve Common is scheduled as a Grade 1 Site of Special Scientific Interest by the Nature Conservancy Council in recognition of its importance as part of Britain's natural heritage. It is a popular recreational area, well used by casual visitors, walkers and golfers. At the same time it is common grazing land and a nationally important wildlife habitat. The common thus has to satisfy a multitude of sometimes conflicting requirements and is an example of how a balance must be obtained between the different demands on the countryside.

Musk, frog and bee orchids may be found on the very steep slopes and round the shallow limestone workings on the common. In general, the vegetation ranges from short sedge-rich turf to tussocky upright brome and tor grass. Of considerable interest is the localized presence of both calcifuge (acid-loving) and calcicole (lime-loving) plants which, in places, grow close together owing to the localized outcrops of sand through the limestone cap. Glow-worms and the stripe-winged grasshopper are two of the commoner insects to be found on Cleeve Common.

The Washpool is fed by a stream which issues from the ground higher up the valley, at the junction of the lowland clay and the overlying sands. Five species of orchid grow on this side of the common, which is another particularly promising area. Any notable observations of wildlife, here or elsewhere on the route, would be welcomed by the appropriate County Nature Conservation Trust.

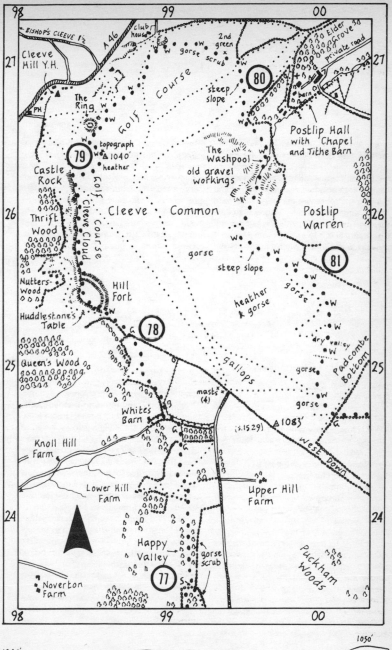

Cleeve Hill Y.H.

PH

BISHOP'S CLEEVE 1½   A46   club house

gorse   scrub   2nd green   ×

80

steep slope

Elder Grove   Private road

The Ring   W   W   Golf   Course

barn

Postlip Hall with Chapel and Tithe Barn

79   W   topograph   W   △ 1040'   heather

The Washpool   old gravel workings

Castle Rock

Thrift Wood

Golf Course   Cleeve Cloud

Cleeve   Common

Postlip Warren

Nutters Wood

Hill Fort

gorse   steep slope   W   W   81

Huddlestone's Table   W

78   G

heather & gorse   W   W   dry valley   W   Padcombe Bottom   gorse

Queen's Wood

G   G

masts (4)   ×   Gallops   W   gorse

White's Barn

(S.1529)   △ 1083'   West Down   G

Knoll Hill Farm

Lower Hill Farm   Upper Hill Farm

Happy Valley   gorse scrub   77   S   Puckham Woods

Noverton Farm

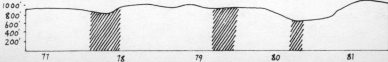

1050'

1000'
800'
600'
400'
200'

77   78   79   80   81

# 23. Wontley Farm, Belas Knap and Sudeley Castle

See commentary, p. 156

Track down to Wontley Farm, swing up L, then go R through the gateway before the Hill Barn lane. Follow the wall to Belas Knap, passing in front of the false portal. Leave this enclosure N, via a stile and a gate, then go down the cultivated field margin to a kissing gate. Descend steeply through the woodland to a stile onto the Charlton Abbots road and go R. Descend the lane L and follow the clear track down to Wadfield Farm, passing round to the R of the buildings to a gate. Descend with the hedge, crossing two stiles, veering L to a stile, cross over a plank bridge to another stile, then diagonally cross a cultivated field to a double-stiled footbridge. Continue across the ensuing cultivated field to a stile, then rise with the ridge and furrow to a kissing gate onto the minor road. Go L into Winchcombe.

Once the Cleeve grasslands are left behind, wildlife and near-natural areas are few and far between. The scenery is dominated by arable fields and occasional conifer plantations, with dry limestone valleys to the east of Wontley Farm, where the steeper slopes support some permanent pasture, most of it improved. Once away from the escarpment the change in the appearance of the landscape is most marked, although the oolite is still just below the soil surface.

Belas Knap is an island of unimproved grassland amid a sea of arable. Limestone plants, including salad burnet, glaucous sedge and hoary plantain, are particularly abundant. Beyond is a thick belt of hawthorn, providing substantial reserves of food for thrushes and excellent cover for tits and other small birds. Humblebee How below is predominantly larch and pole ash.

Mature hawthorn trees, notable in size, are a feature of the lane reached below Belas Knap. A 13-ft-tall wych elm, near the bend, is a welcome constituent of the hedge/scrub, which also includes ash, beech, apple and elder, the latter no doubt with its jew's-ear fungus. The verges hold a good flora through spring and summer, the obvious species being primrose, wood anemone, wild garlic, red campion, crosswort and vetches, with violets hidden below. Stretches of roadside such as this are the essence of the English countryside. These are possibly woodland relics, and are very well worth conserving.

Ancient oaks, isolated on the hedge lines below the Whitehills, are perhaps also forest relics. Ash is predominant in the hedges, which contain elder, bramble and blackthorn. The valley soils are the thick Lias clay.

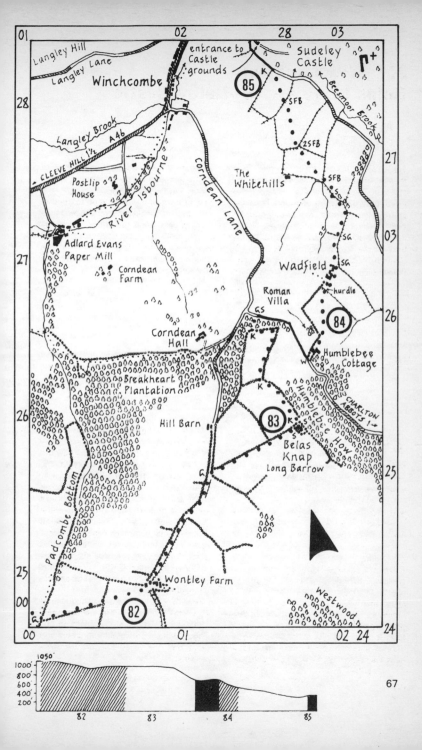

# 24. Winchcombe and Hailes Abbey

*See commentary, p. 161*

Enter Winchcombe by Vineyard Street, turning R along Abbey Terrace. Continue N by Hailes Street and Broadway Road, crossing the Isbourne at Footbridge (formerly called Fordbridge), and take the lane off the busy road R called Puck Pit Lane. The formerly muddy end to this lane has been radically improved by the Warden Service: from the fenced passage, cross the pasture to a grand footbridge, also provided by the wardens. Proceed to a metal kissing gate. Across the next pasture, the Way with its occasional original paving slabs still visible, curves gently to a kissing gate, after which a stile leads into a cultivated field. Cross diagonally to a target waymark. Joining the track, go to the gate L and pass along the blackthorn lane by two gates onto Salter's Lane. Go R then L down the short lane by Hailes Green Farm and from the gate cross diagonally to the hunting gate onto the road by the Hailes Abbey enclosure. Turn R.

Winchcombe's attractions are unlikely to pall quickly, but the dedicated naturalist may find a small diversion by identifying as many different species of wild plants as possible within the confines of the town.

The River Isbourne, fed by numerous springs that issue higher up the vale of Winchcombe, flows due N for its entire length – an almost unique event in this country. It joins the Avon at Evesham. In glacial times it may have been a much larger watercourse.

An old orchard at the bottom of Puck Pit Lane grows on still obvious ridge and furrow. Large, mature fruit trees, which often developed hollow trunks or boughs, were a sure place for lesser spotted woodpeckers, tree sparrows, goldfinches and redstarts. Modern, intensive fruit growing, with smaller trees, efficiently managed, has little room for wildlife by comparison.

Puck Pit Lane is flanked by a mixture of oak, ash, sycamore, hawthorn, hazel and blackthorn, with a rough herbaceous growth below. The whole forms a valuable line of cover. On entering the fields, pollard willows are obvious constituents of the low-lying hedgerow, a favoured Midland nesting site for little owl. These thick thorn hedges form the main wildlife habitat in this part of the Way, where it crosses the permanent pastures of Lower Lias clay. The limestone scarp runs parallel, to the east, marked by Stancombe Wood.

The sweet heady perfume which can be detected in the region of Hailes Abbey, at the time of leaf burst and fall, is emitted from the resinous leaf buds of the eastern balsam poplars which line Salter's Lane.

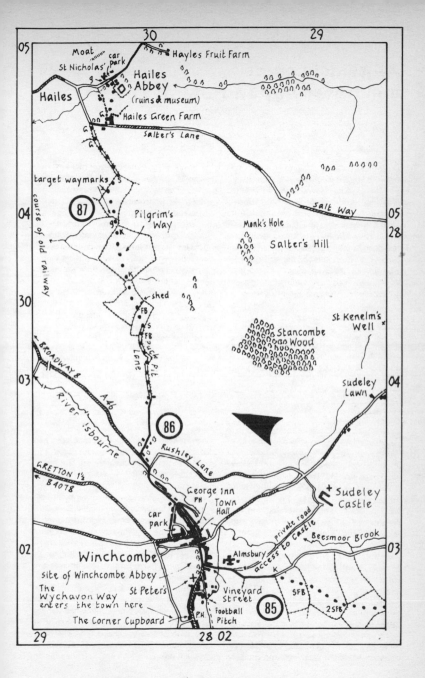

Moat
St Nicholas'
car
park
Hailes Fruit Farm
g
Hailes Abbey
(ruins & museum)
Hailes
Hailes Green Farm
G
Salter's Lane
G
target waymarks S
87
Pilgrim's Way
g
K
course of old railway
Monk's Hole
Salter's Hill
salt Way
K
shed
FB
S
St Kenelm's Well ×
FB
Stancombe Wood
Beech P.H.
BROADWAY 8
A 46
86
Sudeley Lawn
River Isbourne
Rushley Lane
GRETTON 1½
B 4078
George Inn PH
Town Hall
Sudeley Castle
car park
private road
access to Castle
Beesmoor Brook
Almsbury
K
Winchcombe
site of Winchcombe Abbey
The Wychavon Way enters the town here
St Peter's
Vineyard Street
SFB
85
2 SFB
The Corner Cupboard
P.H.
Football Pitch

400'
200'
400'

85        86        87

69

# 25. Beckbury, Wood Stanway and Stanway

*See commentary, p. 166*

The road ends at a fork. Ignore the R lane leading to the Fruit Farm and advance up the lane rising L beside Hailes Wood. When above the wood look for the 'British Standard' Stile L, and go across pasture-land via a gate and succeeding stile to climb up into Cromwell's Clump, where a hunting gate gives access to the hill fort. Follow the wall E then SE to a gate, keeping with the wall to join Campden Lane (unenclosed). Go via Sheepwash to Stumps Cross. Pass through the gate and turn L. Cross the wall next to Stumps Cross (the base of a wayside cross) following a newly created footpath (hence superabundance of waymarks!) beside the scarptop wall. Where the wall curves sharply L descend through the landslip declining to a gate, turn R descending past Lower Coscombe House via a fence stile to rejoin the original route at the gate, continuing across ridge and furrow to a stile, then down to another gate, Follow the track into Wood Stanway. Beyond Wood Stanway House take the short lane R to a gate, retain the hedgeline via three stiles onto the B4077, go L, then R by a gate on a green track down to a further gate and so onto the road leading through Stanway. Beyond the grounds, branch off R, crossing two stiles aiming diagonally across the avenue N E.

Hailes Wood is an important woodland habitat. It is one of the few remaining primary woods in the area which still contains a wide range of native trees and shrubs. Of particular importance is the presence of small-leaved lime coppice which may be seen from the track. Two other calcicoles are prominent at the W corner of the wood: field maple and wayfaring tree. The flora is varied and typical of old woodland, being especially fine in spring. Thrusting through the damp soil in April will be the fertile stems of that most primitive of plants, horsetail, in advance of the 'leafy' stems which follow in June. The wood, as a whole, is an ideal place for birds, butterflies and other insects.

Beckbury Camp is reached by a climb over the Upper Lias, finally steepening onto the Inferior Oolite cap. Large windswept beech trees are grouped by the monument.

At Stumps Cross rooks have colonized a group of beech trees, perhaps compelled to do so now that the elms they once preferred are no longer available. Another rookery near Stanway church is visible from the main street.

Marsh marigolds and primroses grow on and below the banks of a fast-flowing stream close by Stanway House. Liverworts clothe the damp stones and as the year develops the fronds of male fern and hart's tongue fern, together with herb robert, cover the ground above. Around the church are some magnificent yew trees, which are favourite places for mistle thrush. In winter, the berries are one more welcome source of food for birds. Ivy-leaved toadflax grows on the churchyard wall, while on that of Stanway House, wall rue and one or two casuals. Fine trees grace the parkland.

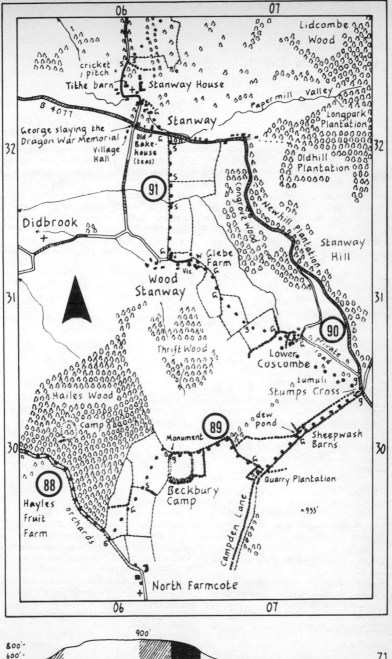

cricket pitch
Lidcombe Wood
Stanway House
Tithe barn
Papermill valley
Longpark Plantation
B 4077
Stanway
George slaying the Dragon War Memorial
Oldhill Plantation
Village Hall
Old Bakehouse (teas)
(91)
Didbrook
Stanway Hill
Glebe Farm
Vic.
Wood Stanway
(90)
Thrift Wood
Private road
Lower Coscombe
tumuli
Stumps Cross
Hailes Wood
Camp
dew pond
(89)
Monument
Sheepwash Barns
(88)
Hayles Fruit Farm
orchards
Beckbury Camp
Quarry Plantation
×955'
Campden Lane
North Farmcote

800'
600'
400'
200'

900'

88    89    90    91

71

# 26. Stanton, Shenberrow Hill and Burhill

*See commentary, p. 171*

Reaching a stile beyond a stone shed, proceed through a gateway to a double-stiled footbridge. Cross the ridge and furrow to a stile, swing round the mound, following the tall hedge to a stile and cross the ridge and furrow to a metal fence, going L with the track into Manorway. Go R up the main street of Stanton, veering R via Sheppey Corner, to a gate onto a track leading past the swimming pool by a gate. Leave the track just before a gate (watch for the waymark) and go through the hunting gate tucked in by the reservoir, sweeping low then rising to a dilapidated gate. Rise above the shed with the hydraulic ram to a stile L, then ascend the valley. Pass through the hill fort from the gate, advancing with the track to a cattle grid, pass through the No Man's Land on a track to a gate and thereafter retain this track. Fork R beyond Laverton Hill Barn down through a gate and veer L to a gate onto a lane. This leads to the sheds on the county boundary. Pass through the double gates R then the stile. Turn L.

Cowslips surviving in the pasture beyond Stanway Park indicate minimal agricultural improvement of the grassland. The ridge and furrow system, evident in several fields, further shows that the soil has remained relatively undisturbed by surface cultivation for a considerable time.

The shallow stream, crossed by a footbridge, is an example of marginal habitat, which may be retained for the benefit of many forms of wildlife – insects, birds, invertebrates – without serious loss to agriculture. The channel is thickly vegetated with docks, nettles, rushes, bramble, meadow sweet, woody nightshade, water cress, etc.

Shenberrow Hill is climbed to regain the limestone scarp, which is less well defined than at either Stinchcombe or Crickley. Its edge falls more gently over the Upper and Middle Lias, producing steep but undulating terrain of foundered sands and clays.

The boundary of the Upper Lias is marked by the emergence of springs, here pumped back to the buildings by hydraulic rams. In the hedge near the lowest ram are two notably venerable maples. As the valley abruptly narrows, the limestone pasture on each side supports such typical species as cowslip, small scabious, hairy violet and early purple orchid. Gorse, old man's beard and hawthorn form a scrub community attractive to bullfinches and yellow hammers. The whole hillside provides a complex of grassland, scrub and mixed woodland habitats supportive of a wide range of plants and animals.

Disused quarries, passed on the level summit walk, contain a few flowers, but the land use is primarily arable. Long Plantation is a mixture of larch, beech and ash, while Buckland Wood, east of Laverton Hill Barn, is primary oak woodland.

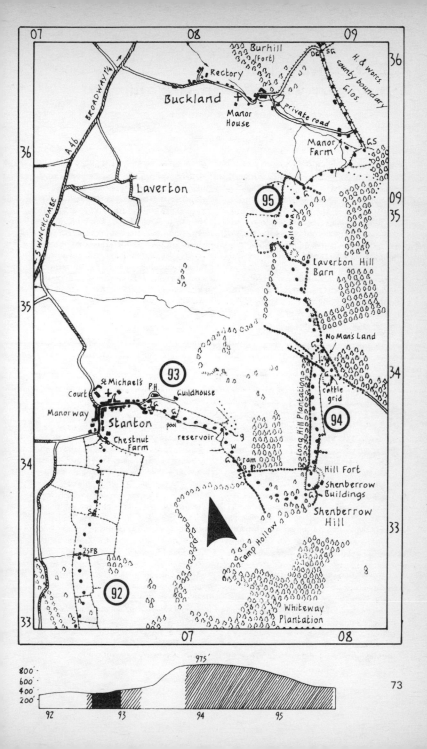

73

# 27. Broadway, Broadway Tower and the Fish Inn

See commentary, p. 176

Pass through another double gate and a stile. Keep with the hedgeline to a hunting gate into Broadway Coppice and branch R to a hunting gate. Descend the pasture, crossing a series of stiles onto the West End Lane, cross directly through the cultivated fields via two stiles onto a footbridge, ascend the pasture to a hunting gate into a lane reaching Church Street and go L. At The Green go R up Broadway High Street. Beyond the Willersey road seek the lane R, leading into a farmyard, and pass through a gate, then a stile through a paddock. Proceed straight to a gate, veering L up to a gateway, and follow the sunken track by two stiles to enter Rough Hill. Continue with the wall uphill, via four stiles, to a hunting gate into the Country Park enclosure. Pass to the L of the tower, taking the hunting gate L, and pass down the lateral valley to a hurdled gap. Continue into a further hollow to reach a gate into the Armley Bank woodland, walk straight on to the new path, crossing the road with caution near Jolly's Barn. Pass the topograph to the stile. First cross the cultivated field, then cross Buckle Street, entering The Mile Drive after crossing two cultivated fields.

Into Worcestershire where, in former time, Burhill Wood probably embraced the hedgeline which is followed at mile 96. It contains at least six shrub species, with a varied flora beneath. The county's rich woodland heritage is only minutely, albeit typically, sampled on the Cotswold Way. Oak, ash and birch with old coppiced hazel thrive on the clay at Broadway Coppice, where the canopy is open enough to allow enchanters nightshade, tufted vetch, hedge woundwort and other tall herbs to flourish after bluebells and wood anemones have died down.

Brilliant blue water forget-me-nots flower throughout the summer in the Badsey Brook, crossed near Broadway church. Like the Isbourne, this is an ancient, shrunken watercourse that cut back into the Cotswold scarp.

Broadway Street is lined with red chestnut trees. Beyond, the hill is climbed through numerous fields of crops and pasture. Spiny restharrow, whose pink flowers are shaped like those of broom, is a localized plant by the path.

Sunny June days allow the flowers, birds and butterflies to be enjoyed at leisure on the summit of Broadway Hill. Close by the Fish Inn are the commoner orchids, and tall herbs including scabious, hardheads, melilot, moon daisies, St John's wort and goats-beard, with birdsfoot-trefoil, hoary plantain, harebell and eyebright in the grasses. Butterflies, blues, whites and browns, abound. This is a sample of what the English countryside was like before the essential demands of efficient food production brought the wild corners into cultivation and improved the grass content of pastures at the expense of the 'weeds'.

The Worcestershire Nature Conservation Trust has an interest in this southern tip of the county and, like the other Trusts, will welcome observations.

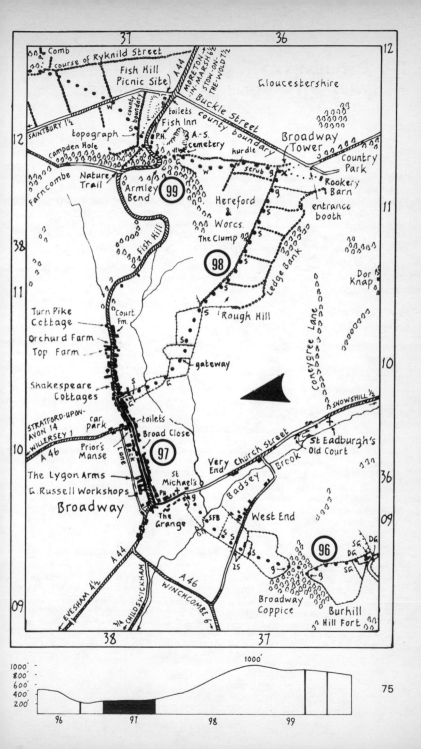

75

# 28. The Mile Drive, Dover's Hill and Chipping Campden

*See commentary, pp. 182, 186*

Follow The Mile Drive (footpath only) to a wall gap, then cross a new stile onto the road. Proceed R to the crossroads, take the Weston road L, seeking the car park R, onto Dover's Hill by a kissing gate. From the topograph promenade along the edge to the trig point and the stile in the corner. Follow the hedge down to Kingcomb Lane, turn L, then R down Hoo Lane (which becomes metalled near the end). Go R, then L by St Catherine's church, into the High Street. Beyond the Market Hall turn R into Church Street. Pass the Eight Bells Inn, swinging L up the steps by the Almshouses, to reach the steps before St James's, to end a bountiful experience.

The Mile Drive is an excellent place for seeing woodland edge birds, such as long-tailed tit, redwing, fieldfare and various finches. The thick belt of mixed thorn, hazel and ash scrub with once coppiced limes and occasional sycamores, all mingling with wild roses along the edge, provides food and cover throughout the year. Towards the N E end fine horse chestnut trees flank the path and where the road is joined an adjacent hazel coppice is lined with sweet violets.

Dover's Hill lies on the scarp edge. Its permanent rough pastures are species-poor and badly drained, being sited on Liassic clays. Some small areas of woodland, below, are mixed plantations of larch, ash and chestnut, while beyond are the clay plains of the Vale of Evesham. Providing dry conditions prevail it is worthwhile making a detour around the marked trail in the Lynches Wood. Some of the steeper parts are quite old, and typical woodland plants such as bluebell, yellow archangel and goldilocks may be seen. Woodpeckers are particularly abundant, and during autumn many species of fungi may be found on decaying wood and old tree stumps. Badgers are also active in the wood.

Readers of these notes will not fail to observe the constituents of the hedge which is followed immediately after leaving Dover's Hill. In addition to blackthorn, hawthorn and ash, a solitary wayfaring tree may be found, cut back annually with the rest of the hedge but nevertheless a fitting reminder of the walk's early stages and the relative abundance of that lime-loving shrub near Bath. Some commendable tree planting has been undertaken in the same hedge.

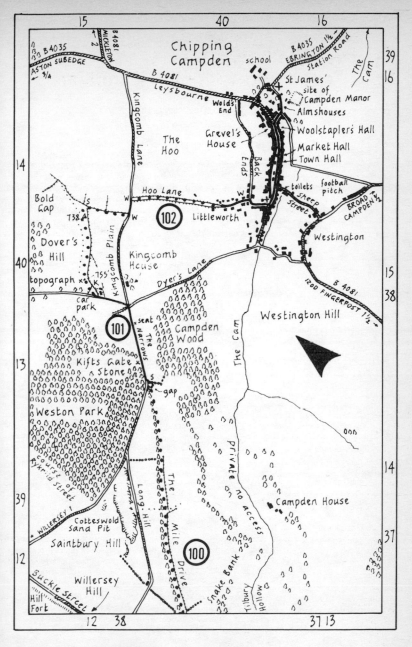

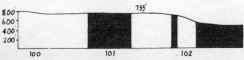

# Commentary

The west front of Bath Abbey from the Abbey Churchyard

# Bath Spa

Bath is unique in Britain, for here, owing to a fault in the volcanic structure beneath the city, hot water rises to the surface. It is these waters upon which the Romans founded their temple to Sulis Minerva and around which the 18th-century spa grew. While filtering down to a depth of some two miles beneath the Radstock and Bristol coalfield strata and percolating to the surface, the water decreases in temperature from 70°C to 45°C. This freak action, though unceasing, is not rapid – indeed tests point to a remarkable 10,000-year cycle.

The current temple precinct excavations conducted by Professor Barry Cunliffe have delved beneath the Victorian floor level to excavate areas undisturbed since Roman times. This programme, begun in 1981, is more than ever lifting the veil on the Roman occupation. The hot bubbling swamp the Roman legionaries discovered while laying their Fosse Way was already a recognized feature. Indeed Sulis was the local Celtic goddess of the hot springs, her cult being adopted by the Romans, hence the Roman name for Bath, Aquae Sulis. Further the Sulis-Minerva shrine bears all the hallmarks of a dual Romano-British cult, a spa where sacrificial acts were perpetrated upon the high altar to Sulis (represented by the famous masculine 'Gorgons Head' preserved in the Roman Bath Museum). Two centuries of careful ex-

The Gorgons
Head

Roman
Aquae Sulis

cavation have produced a major architectural monument to the Roman era, rivalling in the British context Hadrian's Wall.

Two factors contributed to the end of the first 'golden age' of Bath: a rise in the water table which flooded the temple precincts and more crucially the fall of the Roman Empire.

A period of several centuries of decay passed when the springs were ignored. Then the growing unity of the Saxon peoples, coupled with the spread of Christianity, saw the foundation in 781 of a church of secular canons, which was made monastic by Dunstan. In 973 King Edgar was crowned as the first King of all England at Bath Abbey within an evidently substantial Saxon town. Proof of the size of the town is confirmed by the seat of the Bishops of the See of Wells in 1088 being removed to Bath and, although they returned to Wells in the following century, this comparatively brief adventure is enshrined even today in the Bishopric of Bath and Wells. The Saxon church has never been revealed and the first Norman church was destroyed by a fire that enveloped the city.

The present church, begun in 1499 by Bishop King, covering only the nave area of the previous cathedral was still incomplete by the Dissolution. In the 1860s, Sir Gilbert Scott brought to fruition the beautiful fan vaulting to the nave, originally designed by Bishop King's master mason William Vertue. Under his guidance much was restored, and the lofty elegance of one of the last great churches to be built in the Perpendicular Gothic style can now be seen as it was intended.

The spectator in the Abbey Churchyard cannot fail to be impressed by the gorgeous magnificence of the W front, sensitively restored by Sir Thomas Jackson at the end of the 19th century. Flying buttresses descend from the clerestory windows, and flanking the Perpendicular W window angels ascend a fretted ladder to heaven – the product of a dream Bishop King had which directed him to the task of rebuilding. Above more angels cluster about a seated figure of Christ. Beneath, a statue of Henry VII is raised on battlements above the W door, which is splendidly carved with arms, drapery and cartouches. This was given by Sir Henry Montagu in 1617.

While the abbey obviously takes the centre stage, its Gothic grandeur has, since the end of the 18th century, been no more than an accompaniment to a rich array of Palladian buildings – the product of the second 'golden age' of the spa.

During the later years of the 17th century Bath had made substantial strides in developing as a country resort patronized by a steady flow of ailing aristocracy, who considered the hot springs efficacious in ameliorating their skin conditions, gout and fecundity, and, owing to their low mineral content, in flushing out the kidneys.

Royal patronage tipped the balance and turned a humble resort into the fashionable rendezvous. Soon after Queen Anne had paid a visit Daniel Defoe wrote, 'We may say now it is the resort of the sound as well as the sick' and 'a place that helps the indolent and the gay to commit that worst of murders – to kill time'.

Inevitably it needed men with the self-confidence and vision to set the spa alight, to give form and order to a new esteem. Firstly, with Richard (Beau) Nash, an inveterate gambler, who was made honorary Master of Ceremonies by the Corporation in 1704, Bath became the social centre of England and with the help of a dictatorially enforced code of behaviour he taught its patrons elegance.

For fifty years he influenced the pattern of social life and in the process laid a vital foundation, making it possible for two further personalities to emerge. Of these Ralph Allen provided the initial injection of cash and enthusiasm. He bought Combe Down quarries in 1727 and promoted the use of its yellow oolite limestone. He then commissioned John Wood, a rising architect, to design his mansion, Prior Park. Wood proved to be the architectural visionary chiefly responsible for the Georgian homogeneity of the Bath we see today. With the liberty of architectural expression, the image of a procession of visual centres, drawing the spectator's curiosity along and borne upon the splendour of a classical Roman theme, guided his thought and design faculties.

His son continued these themes, thereby creating within the principal sequence of Queen Square, The Circus and Royal Crescent monuments to a Palladian ideal.

The Georgian period saw many fine buildings blossom upon the scene, including Lansdown Crescent (arguably a more picturesque model of the Royal Crescent), Pulteney Bridge, the Assembly Rooms and the Pump Room. It was a time of unparalleled growth for Bath, but fashions change and the racy flamboyance of Beau Nash's day was replaced by a respectable stuffiness. Gothic Revival (heralded by Sham Castle) replaced the more gracious classical form and the Regency rich favoured new venues like Cheltenham and Brighton.

Bath had to fall back on industry to compensate. The Kennet and Avon Canal was built as a trade route across England in 1810, but this was rapidly overrun by the advent of Brunel's Great Western Railway in 1840, upon which industry developed along the banks of the River Avon.

Spa waters remained an attraction but at a more sedate level. Even the discovery in 1878 of the underlying Roman baths, while drawing a new excitement, did not resuscitate past glories. Of recent years Bath has tried to develop new themes, with its music festival and in 1965 the establishment of a university campus on Claverton Down. Today the city is a vibrant tourist and shopping centre ideally suited to the visitor.

But for the future this is not enough. Bath deserves to become a leading health resort again. Hot water therapy is by no means out-dated. Indeed, in this stress-riddled world the calming efficacy of a totally drug-free spa treatment is a progressive medical force.

# 1. Bath and Weston

The visitor to Bath who seriously wishes to see the main features and treasures needs to set aside a full day for investigation. Most walkers prefer independence and explore alone, or with family or friends, but the City of Bath provides, in season, a body of voluntary tour leaders titled the 'Mayor's Honorary Guides'. If you are visiting in a group with prior notice you can have a personal detailed guided tour (contact the Director of Leisure and Tourist Services at the Pump Room, tel. 61111, ext. 327).

With time at a premium you can take a two-hour excursion on a city coach tour operated by Bristol Omnibus from their Manvers Street bus station (tel. 64446). There are also Roman City Tours (tel. 332121).

The Abbey Churchyard is the natural heart of the city and start of the Cotswold Way. Here is the tourist information centre, with town trail leaflets and ideas for places to visit and for accommodation. Here too is the Pump Room suite, built upon the ancient hot springs, open throughout the year for morning coffee or afternoon tea in the style of a former age, with resident musicians. There is also the Terrace Restaurant overlooking the Baths.

Pulteney Bridge

Walkers with limited time should not leave without inspecting the hot springs, baths and Roman remains approached through the Pump Room (the Mayor's Honorary Guides operate here on a regular basis). These are exciting times, with new discoveries revealing not merely the Sulis-Minerva temple but evidence of much earlier occupation.

Because Bath rests deep in the Avon valley, opportunities to view the city from above abound, but the Cotswold Way for all its merits departs the wrong way to capture the best vantages. Probably the best and certainly the handiest is Beechen Cliff, across the river to the S. It is easily reached from Bear Flat or Calton Gardens. Possibly the most enduring image visitors take with them is the abundance of flowers that seem to bloom down every passage, complementing each intimate view and making this truly a floral city.

It is a wise precaution to plan your first day on the Cotswold Way with due respect for the task and possibly walk only as far as Weston, thereby allowing time to explore and perhaps more importantly to ease yourself into the walking process.

The route shown on map 1 is by no means obligatory, but does give some idea of direction, seeking trees and green spaces at the earliest opportunity. If you wish to see more of the architectural highlights with your first steps along the Way, continue up Gay Street from Queen Square, passing through The Circus, branch left along Brock Street to the Royal Crescent, then rejoin the plotted route at the Royal Victoria Park.

The Cotswold Way leaves the Abbey Churchyard, crossing Cheap Street, the medieval market street, to enter Union Passage, on the medieval Cock Lane. The sequence of Corridor, Northumberland Place and Upper Borough Walls is quite delightful, the Walls confirming that we are crossing the northern limit of medieval Bath. To the L is the Royal Mineral Water Hospital, built by John Wood and financed by Ralph Allen and Beau Nash (close by is a restored section of the medieval city wall). The Way turns L along New Bond Street to enter a broadening streetscape, going R then L to Queen Square. Started in 1729, this was John Wood's first major work. It took seven years to complete and comprises a N, E and S side uniformly modelled, each treated as a whole palatial composition. For the W side Wood chose another equally monumental treatment: two broad corner houses and a porticoed front of a third, set a good way back (this house belonged to Dr Oliver, famous for his Bath Oliver biscuits – he was buried in Weston churchyard). Passing Queen's Parade the route advances along Royal Avenue; to the R the green space was once fields leading down from a ha-ha in front of the Royal Crescent. Built by Wood the Younger, this was the first crescent-shaped terrace of houses in England. Entering the Royal Victoria Park, laid out in 1830 (the column was erected in 1837), the route swings up through High Common to Sion Hill, which has a number of classical and Gothic 19th-century villas.

The Way to Weston is not particularly meritorious, though the environs of All Saints church are quite charming. Lower Weston is very much downtown Bath, with a useful range of shops for stocking up before the journey begins

Commentary

in earnest (including a chemist and a fish and chip shop just where the route crosses into Anchor Road). Bristol Omnibus have a fare stage at the junction of Anchor Road with Pennhill Road, useful either for reaching accommodation or for starting the walk where the Cotswold escarpment begins.

The Great Bath and Abbey

## 2. Penn Hill and Lansdown Hill

Penn Hill (from the British hill-name *'penno'*, meaning prominent nose or peak) is the only place en route for a general appraisal of the City of Bath. The Abbey, whence our journey began, can readily be located overtopping roofs and trees; but so much less praiseworthy stands in between that this viewpoint cannot be considered a rival to Beechen Cliff. None the less, there are things to admire: the consistent use of Bath Stone in the crescents that rise in tiers about the steep hillsides and the integration of trees and green spaces within the city bounded so comprehensively by hills. High upon the Lansdown skyline stands Beckford's Tower, a prospect tower built in 1825–6 for William Beckford. It is open to the public at weekends and contains a small museum of Beckfordiana. It has little architectural merit. Pevsner considered it of bleak and sinister disposition and it certainly is no graceful landmark when compared with Broadway Tower, visited near journey's end. The route is now a course rising up this first Cotswold ridge on to the high plateau of Lansdown Hill, capped with Great Oolite. The summit of Kelston Round Hill, though a potentially excellent viewpoint, is strictly out of bounds. Instead walkers should content themselves with Prospect Stile. From here is seen the Wansdyke

Kelston Round Hill from Prospect Stile

ridge above Bath, backed by the broken hill country S to the Mendip Hills. To the W rises Dundry Hill (764 ft), S of Bristol, a Jurassic misfit amid the Carboniferous strata running from the Forest of Dean through to the Mendips. In the main the drainage pattern of the Cotswolds is simpler, with the dip-slope streams forming the headwaters of the River Thames. The one exception is the Bristol Avon, which rises above Old Sodbury, in effect claiming the South Wolds for the Severn and deflecting the watershed of England eastwards towards Thamesdown. Its course to the mouth of the Severn was not easily accomplished for, while it followed the strike of the Jurassic beds to Bradford-on-Avon, thereafter it ran against the dip-slope and cut a wide, deep valley so evident from this viewpoint. From Bath to Hanham Mills the river flows placidly over Keuper and Liassic clay strata, before cutting through the Coal Measure sandstone and emerging in Bristol, where it takes what appears the most un-likely course, forcing a dramatic gorge through the Carboniferous grits and limestones of Clifton Down.

With a last glance back, bid farewell to Bath, the Abbey Churchyard now some 600 ft below, and attend to the northward advance of the Cotswold escarpment. Lansdown, first named in 1067 as 'Lantesdune ecge' and trans-lated as 'the edge of the long strip of high land', is an apt description. While the Jurassic limestones may continue southward, they never again attain the stature of this great plateau nor the unification provided by the Cotswold scarplands.

The Way passes the starting gates of Bath race course. Nine meetings occur at this small, windswept course between May and October. Little Down is an interesting, if simple, example of Iron Age hill fort construction, enclosing 15 acres on a typical spur site. The rampart and ditch, though probably half

Little Down Camp

its original height, still shows how in a troubled time the Iron Age populace found it necessary to construct great defences into which they could retreat with their livestock.

There are two other earthworks upon the plateau worthy of note; neither has been accurately dated, though it seems not unreasonable to suggest that they could be connected with the camp defences constructed by Sir William Waller, the Parliamentary Governor of Bath, just prior to the Battle of Lansdown, during the Civil War (see the Granville Monument, p. 91).

From Little Down, which incidentally is the most westerly point on the entire Cotswold Way, the route tracks above Pipley Wood; notice the regular triangular holes built into the bounding wall adjacent to the golf course (were these for trapping rabbits?). The wood on the opposite hillside is in fact called Congrove Wood, 'rabbit wood!' Pipley may derive from the ME *'Pipel'*, meaning bubbling springs.

The valley below Brockham End contains traces of flanking strip lynchet terracing, which will have been developed at a time when the pressure for food exceeding the capacity of the traditional open fields, forcing desperate measures upon the peasantry, possibly at the time of the great population explosion of the 12th and 13th centuries.

The remains of a Romano-British building, together with scattered sherds over a wide area within Brockham Combe, have suggested that there may have been either a villa complex or a larger contemporary community in this vicinity.

Kelston Round Hill

# 3. Hanging Hill, Hamswell and Greenway Lane

Little Down from Hanging Hill

Hanging Hill, marked by a trig point, derives its name from the O E *'langende'*, meaning the steep wooded slope. The name Beach, a hamlet at one time within the prebend of Bitton, obviously refers to the beech trees that must have shrouded this hillside. It is a key point, for, from this vantage, the Cotswold escarpment stretches northward like some indented cliff line before the clay and marlstone sub-scarp, wave upon wave of hawthorn hedge mimicking the sea (below is the Beach!). The distant Drakestone Point on Stinchcombe Hill (mile 36), 18 miles away as the crow flies, terminates the scarp's advance; keen eyes will distinguish both the Tyndale Monument on Nibley Knoll and the Somerset Monument on Hawkesbury Knoll. Hinton Hill (encampment), marked by a prominent conifer plantation, and Tog Hill, over topping the opposite Freezing Hill, complete the scarp. To the R the next objective of the Way, the village of Cold Ashton, may be located upon the hill beyond. Conspicuous among trees is the 17th-century Tracy Park, with an early 19th-century classical front of two storeys, flanking the Golden Valley (River Boyd). Westward spreads the vast bristling conurbation of Bristol, and, still further westward the dark ridges of the Forest of Dean overtopped by the distant three peaks of Abergavenny – Blorenge, Sugar Loaf and Skirrid Fawr.

Freezing Hill means 'Frisian's Hill', though this should not be misconstrued as a reference to a modern dairy herd – it derives from an Old English nickname 'Frisa'. The exposed situation may easily explain the corrupted drift of the name, as in the case of Cold Ashton. There is a suggestion of a linear dyke on this hill, called *'eald dic'* in Saxon Charters and 'Royal Camp' on Isaac Taylor's map of Gloucestershire (1777), presumably of Iron Age date.

The Granville (or Lansdown) Monument was erected to the cherished memory of Sir Bevil Granville by his grandson, Lord Lansdown, in 1720. It was in this vicinity, and down the slope upon which Battlefields House now stands, that the Battle of Lansdown was fought on 5 July 1643. The English Civil War, precipitated by the excesses of Royal prerogative exercised by Charles I, was a time of open hostility when bloody skirmishes engaged loyal Royalist (Cavalier) and radical Parliamentary (Roundhead) forces. Sir Bevil, leading his Cornish army, mounted the heavily defended scarp, causing a Parliamentary army to retreat, but while the action was soon to prove decisive in the capture of Bath for the Royalist cause, Sir Bevil was mortally wounded and was carried to Cold Ashton Manor to die that night. The monument, sporting Granville's coat of arms and topped by a strutting griffin, has suffered from weathering.

Granville Monument

Battlefields House, seen subsequent to the monument, stands in the shelter of the wooded scarp. Built in 1836 of ashlared Bath limestone, it is castellated with octagonal turrets and Gothic windows, and it has a Tudor-style lodge.

From the Battlefields, Langridge Lane descends below a Romano-British settlement site. It offers beautifully serene views across the Swainswick valley. Green pastures, rank hedges and bank woodland draw the eye S towards the Avon valley. To the R rises Lansdown, with Beckford's Tower, and down the valley Little Solsbury Common, isolated by a narrow ridge from Charmy Down. This 20-acre hilltop is encircled by an Iron Age rampart and contains evidence of a very early enclosure possibly connected with the hill-fort builders of about the 2nd century BC. These are overlaid with traces of medieval open field baulking strips, their ends marked with the original mere (marker) stones.

Langridge was formerly in the possession of the Blathwayt family of Dyrham, and no doubt they used the lane to travel to Bath or Dyrham. In common with Swainswick and Kelston the little church has a distinctive saddleback tower. This delightful form reappears further N in the Cotswolds (though off the Way) in the Churn and Duntisbourne valleys.

Descent into the Hamswell Valley

The descent into and through the Hamswell valley is a joyous stroll. The route briefly follows Hall Lane, linking Freezinghill Lane with Tadwick at Torneyscourt. Liliput Farm takes its name from Swift's *Gulliver's Travels*; the application is therefore 'small holding'.

Hamswell House stands in a prominent springline situation. The name, first mentioned in 1276 as Hameswell, means 'spring by an enclosure' and implies that settlement preceded the present building, which dates from the 16th century, with 17th-century and early 18th-century remodelling by a branch of Dick Whittington's family (see Coberley, p. 148) Hanging Hill, Hamswell and Greenway Lane.

Regrettably Greenway Lane is not emerald turf as suggested by the name, a concrete causeway being superseded by tarmac beyond the rustic arcadia of Hill Farm. The lane must, however, be old and have served the valley over many centuries.

Little Solsbury Common

The Swainswick Valley from Langridge Lane

# 4. Cold Ashton and Dyrham

The name Cold Ashton means 'farmstead by the ash-tree'. The chilly con-notation of the first element is an accurate description, for being set high upon the plateau edge it suffers from icy draughts emanating from the Bristol Channel. The village appears in the Domesday Book as belonging to Bath Abbey and extended to 5 hides (note the present Hydes Lane – a hide was the equivalent of 120 acres). The 13th century saw the establishment of a vineyard, possibly upon the S-facing strip lynchets below the Lynch, seen on the approach to the A46.

Cold Ashton Manor

Cold Ashton Manor, partially shielded from the passing traveller by the Renaissance gateway, commands a marvellous prospect down the St Catherines valley. This Elizabethan house has a rare symmetry: the S elevation of two gabled wings and recessed centre with oval windows and classical balustrade presents a most imposing front. Oddly there seems to be some uncertainty about for whom the present building was built, though it is attributed to John Gunning (c. 1629), then Mayor of Bristol. The manor came to the Denys family at the Dissolution, from whom it was bought by William Pepwall, Mayor of Bristol 1570–75, who in turn sold it to John Gunning.

The adjacent Rectory is attributed to Thomas Key (*c*. 1510, with later additions). The lane to the church passes the former village school. Though tastefully adapted into a private residence, there lingers a sadness at the passing of such a valuable nucleating influence within this remote community.

Between 1508 and 1540, Thomas Key, at his own expense, rebuilt the main body of this church, leaving only the 14th-century tower untouched. It remains unexplained how a parish priest of the time of Henry VIII could amass the necessary wealth to undertake such a benefaction. Holy Trinity is late-Perpendicular and notable among its fittings is the pinnacled stone canopy above the oak pulpit set into the stairs of the former rood-loft.

The Way reaches the busy A420, which was formerly the direct coaching and trading route from London to Bristol. A little under 2 miles E stands the large village of Marshfield, which grew upon this route. A market was established in 1265. Later it earned borough status, and by the 16th century the largest accessible exposures of fuller's earth found in its vicinity were a major contributing factor in the village's expansion within the cloth trade. The sticky cloddy nature of fuller's earth soil may well explain the place-name, 'marshy tract of open country'. It is a fascinating place to visit, as is the nearby Castle Farm Folk Museum (open by prior appointment only) along George Lane. The oldest building is a rare 16th-century cruck-construction long house, where livestock and the farmer with his family lived either side of a common passage, with fodder and sleeping accommodation on the upper floor.

The Way advances across arable fields to Pennsylvania, a fanciful name which could have arisen as a humorous quip. The route briefly follows Toghill Lane, which coincides with the ancient ridgeway today known as the Jurassic Way, because it can be traced following the natural limestone spine from Bath over Lansdown all the way to the Lincolnshire Wolds and the Humber shore.

The route quits the wolds and goes down through Dyrham Wood, passing by Sands Farm, where two Romano-British burials in stone coffins were found during ploughing in 1932. The delightful little village of Dyrham, set snugly in the lap of the scarp, is a memorable match of church, country house and tended landscape. The house and park, together with the historic herd of fallow deer, are in the care of the National Trust and on merit come into the itineraries of many visitors to the area. All visitors are obliged to enter off the A46, unless they are National Trust members, who may enter through the churchyard, an undoubted frustration for unaffiliated Cotswold wayfarers.

The 264 acres of Deer Park are open all year, while the house and gardens are closed during the winter months.

The name Dyrham derives from '*deor ham*', a deer enclosure, and was first recorded in an early Saxon annal of AD 577. The supposition that the Romans corralled deer here is reasonable, bearing in mind that they were quite partial to venison. However, to date no villa complex has been discovered in the immediate vicinity, though the setting would seem appropriate. In 972 Dyrham was listed in the estates of Pershore Abbey, but by the Conquest was in the

Dyrham Park (E. front)

possession of the Saxon Aelfric, who in turn lost the 10 hides to the new Norman overlords.

The parish church of St Peter's, the nucleus of which dates from the mid 13th century, was rebuilt in the late 14th century by Sir Maurice Russel (depicted with his wife on a brass in the S aisle). The tower is 15th-century Perpendicular. There are several interesting monuments within the church, the most imposing being the tomb of George Wynter. Through marriage Wynter was succeeded by William Blathwayt, a man of considerable intellect whose wealth was accumulated, untypically for the Cotswolds, not through the cloth trade but by his being an indispensable court diplomat and serving remarkably under four monarchs, Charles II, James II, William III and Queen Anne. Of Cumbrian descent but groomed in London, he transformed the estate and in particular the house. The shabby Tudor pile, of which only the Great Hall now remains, was cast away when he directed Samuel Hauduroy, a little-known French Huguenot, to design a new W front. The work was completed in 1694 and became the grand baroque entrance. Within 6 years he was committing the considerable skills of William Talman to design an even grander E frontage reminiscent of Chatsworth and similarly enlivened by a cascading water garden (alas now gone). This work was concluded in 1705.

# 5. Dyrham, Tormarton and Dodington Park

The Way gently rises with Dyrham Park wall to gain an excellent view across to the impressive strip lynchet terracing beneath Hinton Hill. Unseen from this point, Dyrham or Burrill Camp annexes about 12 acres of the escarpment spur above these lynchets, the modern road passing through the original central entrance on the E side.

We are here witnesses to a historic scene, for as the *Anglo-Saxon Chronicle* relates 'in 577 Cuthwine and Ceawlin fought against the Brytwalas (Britons) they slew three kings, Coinmail, Condidan and Farinmail, at the place called Dyrham, and captured three cities, Gloucester, Cirencester and Bath'. By the mid 6th century the West Saxons had established themselves on the Wiltshire uplands and with the Battle of Dyrham they surely laid claim to the Cotswolds and possibly the lowland to the Severn shore. The western limits of Wessex thus defined, the post-Roman populace was now largely banished to the west country and Wales.

The Way now heads for Tormarton across the functional eyesore of the M4 motorway. Toll Down is skirted, as it would have been by astute travellers to avoid the early 19th-century toll house that still remains next to Dodington Park entrance rotunda (Bath Lodge). On the gentle N-facing slopes of the broad limestone ridge of West Littleton Down there is an extensive area of Celtic fields covering a 200-acre site. They are largely only visible from the air, though faint traces exist on the Wiltshire flank, and judging by the broad banks substantial stone walls originally existed. During the construction of the M4 two Romano-British settlements were revealed (and promptly destroyed!), together with a stone coffin burial.

Tormarton translates to 'farmstead upon the boundary by thorn-trees'. The boundary in question may well have been the Saxon Wessex/Mercia march, in modern terms Wiltshire/Gloucestershire, though to some extent this is blurred by the ducal Beaufortshire, the Badminton estate embracing even today over 20,000 acres in this district.

In the Domesday survey, Tormarton was held by Richard, one of King William's Commissioners charged to record the extent and worth of the Conqueror's new realm. Interesting among the persons recorded for this place was a riding man (radman or radknight), common only in the counties bordering Wales. His duties included journeying on his lord's errands, escort work, a degree of conveyancing of produce and goods, some limited agricultural service and certain obligations connected with the chase (deer hunting). The mention also of a priest must indicate the existence of a Saxon church – indeed Saxon stones have been identified in the present church tower, lending further credence to this.

St Mary Magdalene, in essence a Norman church with an imposing Perpendicular upper stage to the tower, has battlements, gargoyles and a stair-turret. An almost unique survival outside the E end of the chancel is the upper of two string-courses, a wheat-ear moulding repeated only once again in England, at Norwich Cathedral. Not surprisingly it is to the memorials that visitors' curiosity is drawn. In the nave, beneath the carpet, there is a plainly dressed brass to John Ceysill (1493), while behind the organ is a baroque tablet to Edward Topp (1699). The Gabriell Russell monument of 1663 offers praise to a trusted estate manager. Possibly the most fascinating is the 14th-century brass matrix on the chancel floor, showing the outline of Sir John de Rivere in the form of a knight holding the model of a church with a foliated cross. Sir John, who founded a chantry and college of priests here, lived in the adjacent manor, where certain medieval features have survived, including the carved arms of de Rivere beside a large chimney-stack (though most of the house has been rebuilt). A Tudor doorway remains in the churchyard wall. The Compass Inn, an old coaching hostelry, gains its name from the biblical phrase 'God encompasses us'. The route leaves Tormarton to enter Dodington Park at Seven Springs the source of the River Frome, which joins the Avon in the heart of Bristol.

St Mary Magdalene, Tormarton

# 6. Dodington, Old Sodbury and Little Sodbury

Cotswold wayfarers could proceed to Old Sodbury and be unaware that they have just passed one of the largest stately homes of the Cotswolds, so well concealed is Dodington House. The curves of the humble scarp, coupled with subtle tree plantings and the recent transformation of the parkland, through which the route wends, from grazed turf to waist-high corn, draw a mantle of secrecy over the great mansion. Dodington House is clearly the expression of great wealth, a wealth, it must be said, most disagreeably earned through the exploitation of Negro labour in the sugar plantations of the West Indies. Designed for the nabob Christopher Bethell Codrington by James Wyatt, the house would be unspectacular but for its huge portico entrance. The classical Roman inspiration evident here contrasts with Wyatt's numerous Gothic works. The transformation of the house complex took twenty years to complete. However, before the house was built, Lancelot 'Capability' Brown, that most famous of 'Romantic landscape' architects, redesigned the park. The house remained the Codrington family seat until 1983.

Dodington House

Coomb's End, recently furbished and beautified with an abundance of flowers in the garden, is a farmhouse of 1654 with gables, mullioned windows and a two-storey projecting porch, formerly the dairy wing. The Way goes

Coomb's End

uphill to enter fields by Catchpot Cottage – the name may be a corruption of Catchpoll, 'petty constable' or, earlier, 'collector of Lords dues'.

The route enters Old Sodbury along Chapel Lane, crossing the busy A432 road, mentioned in Ogilby's road-book of 1675 as running from Bristol to Burford via Tetbury and Cirencester. At the head of the scarp is the Cross Hands Hotel, which briefly gained notoriety in a blizzard in December 1981 when Her Majesty the Queen was benighted there en route for Windsor, following a visit to Gatcombe Park delivering Christmas presents.

The early medieval development and growing importance of Bristol had a magnetic influence on local trade. In 1218 William le Gros, Lord of Old Sodbury Manor, secured a royal grant for a market (and a fair in 1227) – the crucial ingredients for a healthy wealthy life for the entrepreneur squire who could extract taxes by establishing his own market town. Two fairs were established, on Holy Thursday and 24 June, for cattle and pedlary. Naturally he chose a site a comfortable distance from his residence. Thus was born Chipping Sodbury, which means quite literally 'Sodbury market'. The manorial name Sodbury derives from 'Soppa's fortified place'. Whether this refers to Sodbury Camp or some other lost site is not clear. Passing through the farmyard, notice the intriguing gable end in the small stone building depicting what appears to be a king's or noble's head, below which are two clerks and beneath them a lion.

The Way climbs a steep bank into the churchyard, where walkers will no doubt enjoy a brief rest on the Brooke memorial seat. The church lies on a prominent knoll, the likely site of a Saxon church mentioned in 783. The present church is largely a faithful rebuilding in 1858 of an early 13th-century Norman Transitional structure. Monuments include a wooden effigy of a 14th-century knight, which is barely recognizable, and a stone high-relief military figure (early 13th century), both situated in the N transept. There is a memorial to David Hartley (1813), who lived at Little Sodbury Manor and, as an envoy extraordinary and plenipotentiary to the Court of Versailles, negotiated the peace settlement with America in 1783.

Sodbury Hill Fort

The Way proceeds to Little Sodbury, passing through the largest earthwork on the entire route, Sodbury Camp multivallate fort, enclosing 11 acres. Although it has never been excavated, its rectangular form together with additional banks' traces and the discovery of eight Roman coins ranging from Gallienus to Constantius II support the view that, while its original constructors may have been Iron Age, occupation and adaptation proceeded long after into the Romano-British phase. Passing through to the farm buildings, which are in the process of renovation, notice the five-division dewpond, allowing the controlled watering of stock, the water being accumulated off the great barn roof — an ingenious device with water at a premium.

Portway Lane was the regular route between Little Sodbury and Chipping Sodbury market.

gable-end in Old Sodbury

# 7. Little Sodbury, Horton and Bath Lane

To speak of Little Sodbury is to speak of one man, William Tyndale. He represented the dawn of a new age in religious understanding and liberty and it was from this manor, while chaplain to the household of Sir John Walsh, that he began his life's work. He moved here in 1521, following receipt of his M A at Oxford. Through his scriptural scholarship and his distaste for hypocrisy and superstition Tyndale soon developed as an outspoken advocate for biblical truth. He set to work translating Erasmus's *Enchiridion Militis Christiani* into English and preached widely in the area and in St Adeline's, which at that time stood behind the manor. In 1523 he moved to London and the following year to Hamburg. By 1526 his English New Testament was printed at Worms. Only two copies of this printing exist – one in the Library of St Paul's, London, and the other in the Baptist College in Bristol.

Working in Antwerp with the assistance of Miles Coverdale, Tyndale began translating the Old Testament in 1530. The pendulum of religious thought was inevitably swinging, Martyrdom came a mere two years before Henry VIII's decree in 1538 that every church in England should hold an English Bible.

Little Sodbury Manor can be visited by prior appointment. Dating from 1486, it was extensively restored in 1919 for Baron Carlo de Tuyll. The oldest feature is the great hall, with its steeply pitched open timber roof. St Adeline's church was rebuilt in 1859 by William James, using some of the old church fabric. The dedication, unique in England, is to the patron saint of Flemish weavers. Within, the principal feature is the pulpit formed of five panels, with figures of Hooper, Latimer, Ridley, Cranmer and Tyndale, all martyred at the time of the Reformation.

Horton Camp

The route next enters Horton, which shelters on the marlstone shelf beneath the scarp. Above is a univallate Iron Age fort, called the Castles; here the crescent bank encloses about 5 acres; on the S, strip lynchets terrace the hillside, partly obliterating a hollow way. The place-name Horton appears as 'Horedene' in Domesday and suggests 'hill frequented by stags'. Widden Hill meant 'hill with willows'.

Horton Court

The oldest portion of Horton Court, the N wing (close to the church), was built with large limestone blocks in *c*. 1140, making it the oldest inhabited house in the Cotswolds. The main house was built in 1521 for the Prothonotary William Knight, Bishop of Bath and Wells. Henry VIII sent him to Rome in 1529 in an attempt to hasten the annulment of his marriage to Catherine of Aragon. It was an abortive mission surrounded with much intrigue. Knight returned from Italy enthusiastic about Roman architectural fashions, which he expressed in the Ambulatory, a kind of loggia (covered walk) built beside the house. He also added bands of Renaissance arabesques carved in oolite to the porch of his house, some of the very earliest examples of such design in England. The house and garden, administered by the National Trust, are open to the public on Wednesday and Saturday afternoons from April to the end of October.

St James's church was built in the 14th century on the site of a Norman church. The vaulted porch with unusually lively carved figures dates from 1520, when the 14th-century building was remodelled. The church interior is spacious and wholly pleasing. At the W end of the arcade, between the N aisle and the nave, there is a curious gargoyle-type figure of a man sticking out his tongue. The memorial of Ann Paston is sensitively worded, while the odd-looking tablet to Baron Carlo de Tuyll (1913) simply bristles with Art Nouveau.

The name Bodkin Hazel derives from 'hazel wood upon Beauduca's hillock'. The route sets course above the scarp, passing through a motor scramble course to join Bath Lane on an old trading route (not on the Jurassic Way).

St Mary's, Hawkesbury

# 8. Hawkesbury Upton and the Kilcott Valley

The old settlement of Hawkesbury ('Harfoc's fortified place'), like Horton and Sodbury before, lay beneath the scarp in a springline situation. It can be reached down a minor road leading by old quarries into a sequestered combe. Here shelters St Mary's church, with a rectory and some farm buildings. The church is both grand and gracious. Predominantly Perpendicular, it contains Norman, Early English and Decorated features. The interior is uncommonly spacious, though its medieval qualities were suppressed by the restoration of 1882–4, when Wood Bethell of Pitchcombe was employed to save the church fabric. He found it necessary to remove all plasterwork, leaving bare pointed stonework. None the less it is a truly delightful church to explore. The existence of a Saxon church is indicated by a Charter of 972, when King Edgar confirmed land and privileges to Pershore Abbey, including an estate of 40 hides in South Stoke (the present Hawkesbury), Hillesley, Tresham, Kilcott, Oldbury-on-the-Hill, Didmarton, Badminton and Hawkesbury Upton. The Charter states that 'these are the bounds of the seven lands belonging to South Stoke'.

Hawkesbury was evidently the centre of a large and important estate. The original foundation was an Anglo-Saxon minster church from which a small body of secular clergy provided pastoral care over this wide area. At the dissolution in 1540, both the Manor and Rectory came into the hands of the Crown and were granted to John Butler of Badminton in 1546. They passed to Arthur Crewe of Hillesley in 1609, and in 1620 the Manor to Sir Robert Jenkinson of Charlbury in Oxfordshire, a descendant of Anthony Jenkinson, companion of the maritime explorer Sebastian Cabot (the Manor was pulled down in the last century). Around the chancel are numerous monuments to the Jenkinson family. On the S wall on a mural tablet is an inscription to Charles Jenkinson, 7th Baronet (1808), who became successively Lord of the Admiralty, Lord of the Treasury in 1767 and in 1778 Secretary of War under Lord North. In 1786 he was raised to the peerage of Baron Hawkesbury and in 1796 was created Earl of Liverpool. Against the N wall is a tablet to the second Earl (1828). On the assassination of Spencer Perceval in 1812 he was appointed Prime Minister, an office he held for fifteen years.

The present incumbent is responsible for Upton, Hillesley, Tresham and Alderley as well as St Mary's Hawkesbury. With such a widely dispersed concern, communication with parishioners is always a problem, and the parson has endeavoured to minimize this by installing a vicar's letterbox by the shop.

The first reference to Hawkesbury Upton is in 972, where it is called simply Upton, meaning upper farm. It gained Hawkesbury as a prefix some six

Pool Farm

centuries later. Any settlement of the bleak wolds has the provision of an adequate water supply as a primary consideration. Hence the first settlement would probably have been upon the fuller's earth around the pond. This water factor would have inhibited its medieval growth despite its having been granted a market charter. Only when a copious supply from the Kilcott valley was established did the community expand, hence the 19th-century character of the village.

The Somerset Monument is in a prominent position and for a mere 10p you can climb the 144 steps to the 120 ft-high balcony. The monument stands at 650 ft and surveys a transitional stage in the escarpment. The regular shallow re-entrant waves of the edge now change to long valleys, or 'bottoms', reaching deeply into the dip-slope. The monument was erected in 1846 to the memory of General Lord Edward Somerset, fourth son of the 5th Duke of Beaufort, who served under Wellington in the Battle of Waterloo. His remains were interred in St Peter's, Hanover Square.

Badminton House, 3½ miles to the SE, scene of the famous annual cross-country horse trials, has been the family seat of the Dukes of Beaufort since 1608, when the Earl of Worcester abandoned Raglan Castle after Civil War destruction (the 3rd Marquis of Worcester was created 1st Duke in 1682). The present house was enlarged and rebuilt between 1680 and 1710 on the site on an old manor. It was here that the game of badminton evolved, and it is said that fox hunting also had its beginnings from the local stag hunt (the park still shelters some 400 red deer and 75 fallow deer).

At the northern end of the 3-mile ride stands Worcester Lodge, built *c.* 1746 by William Kent. This is considered by David Verey to be 'one of the most spectacular triumphs of the English genius for park buildings'.

The Way departs into the pretty Kilcott valley, a delightful woody experience. The fall of the stream has in years past been harnessed by corn and cloth mills, several of which are seen en route, notably Kilcott Mill, with its pond, sluice and associated buildings.

Kilcott Mill

# 9. Alderley, Wortley and Blackquarries Hill

The walk passes through a softened secretive landscape, the quiet proceedings of contemporary life to a large extent disguising the intense industry that once thronged these scarp valleys. For here water mills and allied trades served the considerable demands of the cloth trade in the 16th and 17th centuries.

The Industrial Revolution largely spelt death to the humble mills of these Little Avon tributaries, but at one time the Kilcott and neighbouring valleys were literally lined with cloth mills. A legacy of fine houses remain as proof of the past wealth.

The Kilcott Valley

The village of Alderley ('alder clearing') is an obvious example. Here the houses parade a sure Cotswoldian grace, in stark contrast to the workaday air of Hawkesbury Upton. The church was largely rebuilt in 1802, though it retained the Perpendicular tower of 1450. Rather oddly it is dedicated to St Kenelm, the 9th-century Mercian king who crops up again at Winchcombe. Of the church monuments perhaps the most interesting is to Matthew Hale (1609–76) who rose to become Lord Chief Justice (1671–6). In the churchyard is the pink marble headstone to Marianne North (1890), a genuine pioneer botanist who travelled throughout the world sketching, painting and recording rare flora.

Through ill-health brought on by the atrocious conditions encountered on her travels, she retired to The Mount, spending the last five years of her life creating a garden of her own and writing *Recollections of a Happy Life*. The Grange, a Jacobean house, was formerly the home of Brian Houghton Hodgson, the eminent oriental botanist who introduced the Himalayan rhododendron 'hodgsonii' to this country. (The garden is open on certain summer Sundays.)

The route proceeds down Kennerwell Lane, near the bottom of which a steady flow of water spills from a moss-clad trough – the well in question. Is the name a corruption of St Kenelm's Well, to tally with the church dedication?

The Ozleworth valley cuts the furthest trench into the Cotswold edge south of Stroudwater (in so doing forcing the Jurassic Way back from the scarp towards Chavenage Green) and harbours a group of great houses and much else of real interest to the curious visitor determined not to be straitjacketed by the Cotswold Way. High in a secluded wooded nook is Boxwell Court. Again it is a tree that has determined the place-name and over 40 acres of box wood exist here. The 15th century court on the site of a manor was a brief refuge for Charles II. Prince Rupert was also entertained here.

At the top of the bottom is Newington Bagpath (possibly 'badger path'), where there is a castle mound. On the plateau above is the Chessalls, covering 50 acres of arable ground in Kingscote parish. This is a recently excavated Romano-British villa with mosaic and hypocaust literally inches below the plough. Much more remains to be excavated within the parish. Many of the finds are in Gloucester City and Stroud Museums, while an inscribed semi-circular oolite relief, depicting Mars with worshippers, was built into the 12th-century Kingswood Abbey barn at Calcot crossroads; this is now in the Ashmolean Museum, Oxford. Lasborough Manor (open by appointment) and Lasborough Park (the latter 1794, by James Wyatt) were built for the Estcourt family, a descendant of which (Nick Estcourt) recently died climbing K2.

Lasborough church was the work of Lewis Vulliamy, who also designed Rosehill (next to Alderley church), the Somerset Monument, Westonbirt House, the White Hart Hotel in Tetbury and Chestal House at Dursley. On the N flanks of the valley stands Ozleworth Park, a fine Georgian house in close company with St Nicholas Church. The church has a very unusual hexagonal tower in the centre, which is presumed to date from the early 12th century when it may have been the nave. There is speculation that the circular churchyard points to a pre-Christian cemetery, but there is no tangible evidence for this. The name Ozleworth means 'Osla's enclosure'.

Newark Park, owned by the National Trust, is said to have been built from the stones of Kingswood Abbey following the Dissolution. James Wyatt redesigned the S front in Gothic detail. Access is only by a footpath linking Lower Lodge (S) and Lion Lodge (N).

The Cotswold Way passes close to Wortley, which translates to 'clearing used for growing plants and vegetables'. If you branch briefly L to the road

The Clump, Tor Hill

junction you will see the house on the L where Stephen Hopkins was born; he made a fortune in the cloth trade in London and sailed with the Pilgrim Fathers in the *Mayflower* (1620), establishing himself in America in a position of authority and style.

The Way climbs a hollow way up Wortley Hill, regaining the 700-ft contour for the first time since Lansdown, and enjoys grand views over Nanny Farmer's Bottom! The name Tor Hill suggests rocks but is more likely merely a reference to thorn-bushes. The Clump long barrow is passed. Ahead rises a Post Office tower built in 1965, a scaled-down version of the London landmark. Views are now into Tyley Bottom ('clearing where tiles were made').

St Nicholas, Ozleworth

111

St Mary the Virgin,
Wotton-under-Edge

# 10. Wotton-under-Edge and North Nibley

The route descends off Blackquarries Hill via Lisleway Hill, an unusual contraction of 'little way', typical of north-country dialect but rare south of Stafford. Appropriately, the approach to Wotton-under-Edge (the name being derived from the location: 'farmstead in the wood beneath the Cotswold escarpment') is alongside the mill stream, for, as John Leland remarked in the 16th century 'the town is well occupied with clothiers'. Ralph Bigland, the 18th-century historian, asserted that Flemish weavers (remember Little Sodbury Church) had come to Wotton around 1330, and by 1608 a report referred to half the community being employed in the cloth trade.

From the inauspicious Valley Road enter Coombe Road and pass, on the R, a trough with a tablet stating that it stands on Edbrook spring, the original source of the town's water supply. Indeed, as walkers approach Culverhay ('dove's enclosure') they are very much entering the unplanned Saxon town.

The parish church stands upon the site of a church which was supposedly destroyed by fire in the reign of King John, when the King's mercenaries devastated the Berkeley lands. Consecrated in 1283, it is predominantly Perpendicular. The beautiful S porch, with a fine sundial and priest's chamber, was rebuilt in 1658. Inside, notice the early Gothic Revival plaster ceilings and the organ, bought from St Martin-in-the-Fields and originally given to the London church by George I in 1726.

Monuments are plentiful, but due mention should be given to the Berkeley brass – Thomas, Lord Berkeley (1417) and his wife (1392), unfortunately lacking inscriptions but of such fine quality and early date that they deserve any visitor's attention. There is reasonable evidence to suggest that this brass was made at the same workshop as that of Lady Russel of Dyrham.

Entering Church Walk, just visible is the roof of Lisle Manor House, built in 1639. A 13th-century manor house was built here by the Berkeleys and used as a dower house. They also lived here as a second home at times when they were excluded from Berkeley Castle. Katherine, Lady Berkeley, founded the Grammar School in 1384. She was the widow of the Thomas, Lord Berkeley, accused of complicity in the murder of Edward II (the brass in the church is to his grandson).

The wool trade can be seen to have influenced much of the town, the core of activity being naturally concentrated by the stream, with Stranges and Dyehouse Mills at Coombe and Britannia and Waterloo Mills below the old town. Here also is the former Ram Inn (bearing an echo of the Cotswold sheep in its name), now a private house with bed and breakfast accommodation. Dating from 1350, it is cited as being the oldest house in the town.

stained-glass
window in the
Perry
Almshouses
Chapel

Hugh Perry's Almshouses in Church Street, built in 1638, provide a modern-day sanctuary from the busy vehicular activity in the streets. Notice the list of regulations for the residents in the gallery above the entrance passage. Within the courtyard is a truly peaceful retreat, a 17th-century chapel with a beautiful stained-glass window portraying historic images of Wotton the wool town. There are also the Dawes Almshouses and General Hospital, built in 1720 to complete the quadrangle (renovations here gained a Civic Trust Commendation in 1971).

Long Street (the shopping street) is lined with a variety of house styles. This is part of the planned medieval new town established in 1253 by the Berkeleys. In Orchard Street is a house where Isaac Pitman lived (he later moved to the Royal Crescent in Bath), and where in 1837 he formulated the shorthand writing system known as Phonography. At the corner of Market Street stands the Tolsey, dating from 1595, when the Countess of Warwick granted a market court. Originally the upper storeys were jetted. Notice the attractive Victorian Jubilee clock and the comical dragon weather-vane surmounting the cupola (a first-floor room houses the library of Wotton's Historical Society).

Market Street (off the route), where rebuilding gained a European Architectural Heritage Year Award in 1975, leads to The Chipping. Today largely a car park, this square was formerly the grass-covered market centre of the medieval town.

At the end of the briefest of High Streets, the Cotswold Way advances into Bradley Street. However, walkers may care to divert to discover the most recent tourist innovation in the town. An incredible reproduction of the famous Woodchester Roman mosaic pavement has been meticulously re-created in the former Tabernacle Church by the brothers Bob and John Woodward. Built with tiny tesserae, it depicts the story of Orpheus charming nature with his lyre. It is open throughout the summer during afternoons (except Mondays) and by appointment at other times (tel. 3380).

Merlin Haven is a rather odd corruption of Mary's Heaven. Evidently this has some religious association.

The route climbs steeply onto Wotton Hill, passing the Jubilee Plantation. Originally planted in 1815 to celebrate Waterloo, the trees fell prey to a bonfire to celebrate the end of the Crimean War, to be replanted in 1887 to celebrate the jubilee of Queen Victoria. This is Wotton's best viewpoint, though a footpath rising through the impressive strip lynchets onto Coombe Hill may well claim to be a rival. Before the Dissolution, Kingswood Abbey used these south-facing lynchet slopes as a vineyard.

The Way advances along the tree-shrouded Westridge, passing the necessarily isolated site of an illicit cockpit at the junction of paths where a meeting could easily be dispersed before detection. Of course it is a long-lost practice.

Brackenbury Ditches, formerly and more appropriately Blackenbury, was an Iron Age promontory fort annexing 4 acres of the Cotswold scarp. The route glances by the recently cleared deep outer ditch, though the main body of the encampment remains densely covered in mature woodland. The original entrance was via a hollow way up the scarp on its SE flank, suggesting the builders lived, not on Westridge, but in the vale below, and may have been the originators of the numerous strip lynchets in this locality.

The delightful sheltered interlude through the woods is succeeded by an exposed promenade along the close-cropped turf of Nibley Knoll, passing the Silver Jubilee topograph to reach S. S. Teulon's Tyndale Monument. This tapering prospect tower stands 111 ft high, with stairs leading to a gallery from where a most marvellous and expansive view is revealed across Michaelwood and the Berkeley Vale to the silver Severn and the dark ridge of the Forest of Dean. This is the good news. The bad news is that the tower is sensibly kept locked, making it necessary to descend Wood Lane to gain the key (read the notice board at the foot of the lane).

An inscription on the tower reads 'Erected AD 1866 in grateful remembrance of William Tyndale, translator of the English Bible, who first caused the New Testament to be printed in the mother tongue of his countrymen; born near this spot, he suffered martyrdom at Vilvorde in Flanders on 6th October 1536'. It

Brackenbury Ditches from the Tyndale Monument gallery

represents a genuine regard for Tyndale, and its prominent position makes it a landmark from afar. Yet the evidence does not exist to confirm either Tyndale Cottage or even the village of North Nibley as his birthplace.

Formerly, the Cotswold Way took the direct, hair-raising descent from the monument, but fortunately the landowner permitted the dedication of a new footpath to link through the old quarries to the head of Wood Lane. The old path is now discouraged, as landslipping has made it a lethal hazard and wholly unsuitable for pack-carrying walkers.

North Nibley derives its name from 'the clearing near the peak'. The 'North' distinguishes it from Nibley, on the Frome, near Yate. The nucleus of the village has several 18th-century houses and cottages and would appear charming enough but for the ill-considered design of the council houses. Nibley House is at least 17th-century, though remodelled in 1763. It was the home of John Smyth, historian of the Berkeley family, whose wife, Grace, is portrayed in a coloured kneeling effigy (1609) in St Martin's church close by.

The church, in Early English and Perpendicular styles, is worth inspecting. It has a fine 15th-century nave roof with king posts, open panelled spandrels, and carved portrait corbels of kings and queens, and a gold mosaic reredos dated 1874, an 18th-century oak pulpit, a 15th-century font and a stained glass E window of exceptional quality with plate tracery. The chancel, rebuilt in 1861, exhibits a strong French stylistic influence. Unfortunately, the chancel wall-paintings were over-painted in about 1910, thus largely destroying the impact of the fine Victorian decor.

A little N of the church is Nibley Green, where the last private feudal conflict on English soil was fought in 1470. The battle was the culmination of a long dispute between the Berkeleys and the Earls of Warwick over the rightful ownership of Berkeley Castle. It was a bloody and totally ineffective encounter: 150 men were shot and hacked to death, including the young foolhardy Lord Lisle from Wotton Manor, who had initiated the meeting with the obviously tactically better prepared William, Lord Berkeley.

Descending Lower House Lane walkers may notice (L) an old doorway dated 1607. I can shed no light on its purpose. Can any walker?

Waterley Bottom

# 11. Stinchcombe Hill, Dursley and Cam Peak

Doverle Brook, meaning 'pure water', has cut deeply into the flanks of the Stinchcombe Hill peninsula. Eventually it will break through to form yet another Cotswold outlier of this great headland.

Stancombe ('stony valley') Park, originally built in 1840, was mostly rebuilt in the same late-Georgian style after a fire in 1880. Below, in the hollow of the Park, is a romantic folly garden with a temple, laid out by the Rev. David Edwards in the late 19th century. The herbaceous borders, and new tree and shrub plantings, are opened to the public for just two midsummer afternoons.

Sir Stanley Tubbs gave Stinchcombe Hill and Woods for the benefit of the public in 1930 and a popular golf club has established itself here. Tubbs's benefaction is commemorated by a stone seat on Drakestone Point and a stone shelter above Bownace Wood (the frequent repair of lovers – so beware!)

Drakestone Point appears to recall a now unidentifiable rock that the heathen Anglo-Saxons deemed to be a guardian dragon and was therefore an object of mystique and dread.

The Tyndale Monument from Stinchcombe Hill

Stinchcombe Hill is composed of an evidently resistant Inferior Oolite which must have been least affected by the earth movements that tilted the Jurassic strata to create the scarplands, because its persistence, jutting closest to the former ice flow that created the Severn Vale, indicates minimal structural weakness.

As a viewpoint it has few equals. Indeed, the view S from the head of Hollow Combe is as near perfect a scarpland composition as is attainable anywhere along the Cotswold Way, embracing the various stages of the wooded escarpment, including both the Tyndale and Somerset Monuments, and stretching to Hanging Hill.

From the trig point there is a great western prospect into the eye of the prevailing winds that are channelled up the Severn Estuary. The M5 Motorway brings a steady drone of traffic through the air, but the spectator can readily divert his attention to more interesting objects, notably (due W) Berkeley Castle, for 800 years the almost continuous home of the Berkeley family. It is the oldest inhabited house in Gloucestershire, an imposing pile that has on several occasions figured in the history of England. The last occasion was in 1645, when it was the last Royalist stronghold in the surrender to the Roundheads during the Civil War. As a result of this action its Norman outer bailey was razed and the keep wall breached to prevent the castle being used again for military purposes.

Beyond the castle is the square block of Berkeley Nuclear Power Station, and a similar structure at Oldbury further S. Beyond this the M4 Motorway suspension bridge spans the broad tidal Severn, linking Aust with the Beachley Peninsula (where Offa's Dyke meets the sea at Sedbury Cliffs) and over the Wye to Chepstow. The Forest of Dean looms large, stretching from the bridge right up to May Hill (with its distinctive clump of trees). Overtopping the forest are the distant hills N of Pontypool, featuring Blorenge, Sugar Loaf and Skirrid Fawr. Due N beside the great sweep of the Noose is the Severn Wildfowl Trust, Slimbridge. This migratory halt for many estuarine geese, ducks and waders was developed by Sir Peter Scott, son of the famous Antarctic explorer Captain Scott. The Malvern range, whose outline will become a familiar element of views henceforward, fills the distant skyline.

Below the Tubbs shelter is the 'valley frequented by the sandpiper or dunlin', enshrined in the village name Stinchcombe. This village contains several attractive houses, notably Piers Court, which was once the home of the novelist Evelyn Waugh. The spired church has a curious dedication to St Cyr.

Dursley shelters in the shadow of Stinchcombe Hill amid an attractive landscape of little hills and beech-laden valley sides. At the Norman Conquest the Manor of Dursley was no longer in the hands of the heirs of Deersige (from which the town's name derives). It belonged to Roger Berkeley, a cousin of Edward the Confessor, who was accepted and was able to prosper within the new order. The castle is now lost, but the town that developed around it grew to become one of the principal wool and cloth centres of the Cotswolds, especially when the manufacture developed away from cottage-based industry. Though the present town has lost much of its early character, certain facets remain to indicate its former eminence. At the end of Parsonage Street (the main shopping area) stands the Market House, built in 1738. The ground floor was a sheltered arcade for a butter market. The room above, formerly a County Court, is now the Town Hall. In a niche facing the church stands a statue of Queen Anne, while the S side bears the shield of arms of the Estcourt family, Lords of the Manor, once removed from the Berkeleys. The hipped roof has dormers and a bell-turret with a cupola installed in 1747 as a fire alarm.

Across the way is St James's church, largely composed of the locally quarried tufa. There is no record of a church here before the 13th century, though Roger Berkeley is known to have founded St Leonards Priory at Leonard Stanley and his nephew, William, founded the monastery at Kingswood, so it is highly likely that a church did exist. The earliest portions of the present church are the extraordinarily stilted nave arcade arches dating from 1450. The E portion of the S aisle forms the Tanner Chapel. The W tower spire, constructed in 1480, was in urgent need of repair by the late 17th century and the necessary work was executed. However, on 7 January 1699 a celebration peal from the bells caused such vibration that the spire actually fell, ripping down the end wall of the church and killing several bystanders. The damage was reckoned at nearly 2,000 pounds, a small fortune for those days, so the town petitioned the king for money to rebuild. In due course a substantial sum was granted by Queen Anne (which explains why her statue features prominently on the Market House) and the rebuilding was completed in 1709 minus a spire (there was no wish to repeat the tragedy).

Long Street, lined with the former homes of clothiers and wool merchants whose names feature in the church memorials, is the most distinguished of Dursley's streets. The business practices and actions of certain Dursley folk in the past gave the town an unfortunate reputation. On a happier note, in Victorian times it was the custom of menfolk, while escorting their ladies home through the unlit streets, to offer their shirt tails (known as 'Dursley lanterns') to guide their wives following behind!

At the foot of Long Street is the oldest of the clothier's houses, now the offices of R. A. Lister. The broad flight of steps leads to a Tudor doorway with the inscription E.W. These were the initials of Edmund Webb, for a short time Lord of the Manor. His family were prominent clothiers in Elizabethan Dursley, and it is said they came to the Cotswolds from Holland to help develop the English cloth industry.

R. A. Lister, founded in 1867, is one of the largest industrial enterprises in the Cotswolds, with a world reputation for quality engineering. Until the present recession it steadily expanded on this site, producing agricultural equipment, engines and generators in the familiar green livery.

Chestal House (the name derives from 'ceasted' – a heap of stones) was built in 1848 by Lewis Vulliamy (see the Somerset Monument, p. 106). The Chestal Steps were cut by members of the Cotswold A O N B Voluntary Warden Service, relieving a most uncomfortable climb out of Dursley.

The name of the River Ewelme comes from the O E ae-welm, 'source of the river or spring'; it shortly changes its name to Cam, a Celtic word meaning 'crooked'. The village of Cam possesses one of the very few surviving Gloucestershire cloth mills, operated by Messrs Strachan. It manufactures superfine whites for the Pope's robes.

Cam Peak is the local name for what maps call Peaked Down. This Cotswold outlier is connected to Cam Long Down by a saddle depression. The stiff climb is rewarded by a delightful view of Dursley. In August 1974 Cam Peak was the venue for the first National Hang Gliding Championship.

Cam Peak from Cam Long Down

# 12. Cam Long Down and Coaley Peak

The route takes a sickle-shaped sweep over Cam Long Down, a Cotswold outlier capped with Inferior Oolite locally known as 'Table Land', the summit ridge of which is pitted with solifluction depressions. Oddly there is no evidence of this being used as a defended retreat, probably because of the proximity of Uleybury. There are, however, strip lynchets detectable on the warm S-facing slopes.

Uleybury is one of the finest examples of a promontory fort in Britain. Taking fullest advantage of the steep scarp slopes that fall from almost every point, its Iron Age builders further defended the spur with a rampart and ditch, creating a 38-acre sanctuary from where all the advantage lay with the defenders. It has never been excavated, but among numerous chance finds was an uninscribed gold stater of the Dobunni, preserved in Gloucester City Museum, together with more than 150 Roman coins from the 2nd to the 4th centuries. There were three entrances, on the W, E and N corners. The latter, being the most vulnerable, had additional defences. Unfortunately quarrying has damaged them. (Walkers are directed to the virtues of the promenading track orbiting the ramparts.) The camp enclosure is presently locked within the continuous cereal regime. Indeed, the prosperous days of the Cotswold sheep have, in common with so much of agricultural practice, long been swept away by an irrevocable tide of economic change and imbalance; that has meant that shepherds have been replaced by tractors and combine harvesters across the former broad sheepwalks of the wolds. Precious little sheep pasture remains unploughed except the steep scarp banks. So the face of the Cotswolds is characterized by ploughlands and waving golden corn. The recent trend towards the predominance of autumn planting of wheat and barley had adversely affected fox hunting more than walking. Traditionally ranging freely from cover to cover with little hindrance, the chase has more than ever to watch its step!

The village of Uley ('clearing among the yew trees') lies tucked under the promontory fort and presents, by the quality of its buildings, the undoubted evidence of former prosperity founded on the weaving of broadcloth.

There were fulling and fetting mills through the length of the valley and the specialist dyeing process meant that with the stream running rich in dye only one colour could be employed in each vale – hence 'Uley Blue'. Upon the church, rebuilt in 1858 by S. S. Teulon and grandly sited overlooking the village, is a monument (too high to read easily) to John Eyles of Wresden. It sports his clothmark and states that he was the first to make Spanish cloth in the parish, in the late 17th century.

Owlpen Manor is of medieval origin and is rightly considered one of the most attractive manors in the Cotswold region. Flanked by its church with a wooded scarp backdrop, it makes a superb objective on an excursion off the Cotswold Way, continuing up through the beechwoods to Nympsfield.

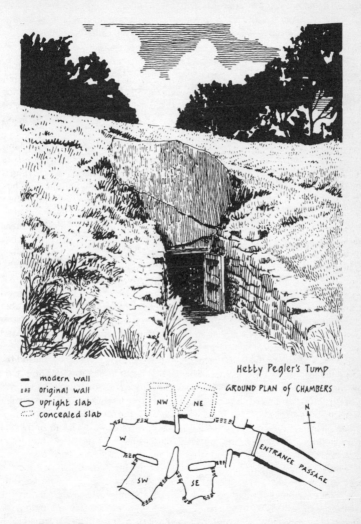

Hetty Pegler's Tump

GROUND PLAN of CHAMBERS

- modern wall
- original wall
- upright slab
- concealed slab

Hetty Pegler's Tump is the first substantial long barrow near the route (Nan Tow's Tump, sited above Kilcott, had little to offer the visitor other than its association with a witch). Up to the late 17th century, when the site was owned by Henry and Hester (Hetty) Pegler, the Tump was known as 'The Barrow'. Its position high up on the Edge was symbolic. It is described as belonging to the Severn–Cotswold group of chambered long barrows from the Neolithic period. Present evidence suggests that this cultural tradition lasted from about 3000 to 1800 BC in SW Britain. Within the group it is technically classed in the transepted gallery-grave type, which may be one of the earlier forms; it consists of a mound 10 ft high, 140 ft long and 90 ft wide. Internally a passage leads to three chambers, a further two being sealed because of their dangerous state. Like other long barrows in Britain, it was essentially a communal burial mound and the rite of interment was normally inhumation of the unburnt body, the chambered mound representing the womb of the earth-goddess. It is believed that there is a cultural link between the people who built the Severn–Cotswold barrows and the group of gallery-graves in S Brittany, which may indicate a movement by sea up the Bristol Channel. The barrow is kept locked to minimize wear and tear, but the key can be obtained from the cottage at Crawley Barns (Crawley incidentally means 'clearing frequented by crows').

The name Coaley Peak derives from 'pointed hill above the clearing with a shelter'. This was not the prominent spur upon which the AA topograph stands but rather the sub-scarp ridge over which runs the minor road from Silver Street up to the Frocester Hill turnpike. In 1725 a turnpike toll gate existed near where the Cotswold Way enters the quarry Nature Reserve but from 1780 the Frocester Hill route was used by coaching services for mail and passengers linking to Tetbury, Bath and Wotton from Gloucester. Notice the old milestone, with its misspelling, 'Nymphsfield'.

# 13. Stanley Wood, Pen Hill and Peckstreet Farm

Gatehouse to Frocester Court

Frocester ('Roman settlement near the River Frome', pronounced 'Frost-er') is a fascinating vale village. There are two Roman villa sites. Fragments of one were found beneath the church of St Peter; the other, at Frocester Court, has been extensively excavated by the farmer himself. The excavations showed that the villa consisted first of a simple strip house, to which wings and a front corridor, together with back rooms and a bath block, were later added.

Frocester Court is an interesting complex; the Hall is a fine example of 14th-century cruck construction; the picturesque timber-framed gatehouse is thought to date from the late 16th century. However, the most remarkable element is the enormous tithe barn (its finest aspect unfortunately obscured by a modern barn – poor planning control, one feels!). There is strong evidence to suggest that the entire barn dates from *c*. 1300, during the period when Abbot John de Gamages was principal of this 'magna grangia' of Gloucester Abbey. It is in a superb state of preservation and is one of the finest monastic store houses in England. The barn, comprising thirteen bays, measures 186 ft by 30 ft, including the passage-bays of two wagon-porches on the NW. Some of the associated farm buildings bear unmistakable medieval characteristics: there is a fine double dovecote and some 17th-century sheep pens.

Nympsfield Long Barrow

Nympsfield long barrow offers a simple lesson on chambered barrow construction. Having been restored from an obviously grievous state, it lacks the aura of ages possessed by Hetty Pegler's Tump. In this instance there was but one pair of transept chambers, containing at least thirteen skeletons, pottery, and a flint leaf arrowhead (now in the Stroud Museum). The upright slabs which outline the chamber have probably never been moved, but all the drystone walling is modern reconstruction. Folklore suggested it was built for lepers and consequently locals would not go near it. The village name, Nympsfield, has been translated to mean 'tract of open country belonging to a place called Nymed' from the Welsh *'nyfed'*, 'a shrine or holy place'. There is no knowing whether this was a Christian or pagan site or precisely where or what constituted the shrine, but it is certainly pre-Saxon and conceivably relates to the long barrow.

Coaley Peak picnic site car park is furnished with a small information building with display boards and a toilet block (WC on map). The County Council have prepared a useful walks guide to the picnic site and nature reserve. Buckholt Wood means 'beechwood'. (The origin of the modern word 'book' has come down to us via the Germanic '*buch*', supposedly derived from their early use of beechen boards.)

The route proceeds through and beneath the beech-capped scarp and above the old village of Leonard Stanley, one of the more interesting communities just missed by the Way. The present church of St Swithin contains good Norman carving and is grouped with farm buildings showing very early features connected with the former priory; notable are an 11th-century chapel, a barn with a medieval gable-end and a priory fishpond. Much else in the village, which surprisingly gained a market charter in 1315, is of considerable charm and age and certainly is worthy of a detour.

The name Leonard Stanley comes from the former dedication of the church 'ecclesian Sancti Leonardi de Stanleye' (1138) and the small Augustinian priory of St Leonards, founded between 1121 and 1129 by Roger Berkeley, Lord of Dursley. The latter part of the name, in common with neighbouring King's Stanley, meant 'stony clearing', the prefix 'King's' because the Manor was the ancient demesne of the crown (*regis*). The Thane Tovi held it from King Edward, then after the Conquest he held 2 hides (240 acres) from King William.

The name Pen Hill comes from the Celtic '*penno*', meaning peaked hill, as does the first rise of the Cotswold escarpment above Bath. Peck Street (17th-century farmhouse) derives from Peckestrete (1306) or Peak Street (later Pen Lane), an ancient way from a ford over the Frome up Pen Hill (followed in some part by the Cotswold Way). Middle Yard, a rather odd expansion of an apparently insignificant feature, is a dependent hamlet of King's Stanley (there are shops in both places). The pimples on Selsley Common are the remains of a long barrow known as 'The Toots', which meant 'look-out', and it is one of the best viewpoints of the Golden Valley. The plural name comes from its resemblance to two round barrows on account of a depression in the middle, though it is considered to have originally been a single-chambered cairn.

Sir Samuel Marling, who owned Ebley Mill in the 19th century, was not only a shrewd businessman, retaining a thriving company while all around floundered, but also something of a romantic, wishing to employ the Tyrolean style of the church at Marling in Austria for the new Selsley church. However, G F Bodley, that champion of Gothic Revival, clearly used French Gothic for the body of All Saints, with the saddleback tower his only real concession to Marling. If the striking exterior does not attract the visitor, certainly the stained glass should be inspected, as it was one of the earliest commissions executed by the Pre-Raphaelite Brotherhood workshop, with William Morris, Philip Webb, Ford Madox Brown, Burne-Jones, Campfield and Rossetti all contributing.

King's Stanley is a considerably older settlement than the nearby industrial conurbation of Stroud. Indeed, Domesday records that there were two mills here upon the River Frome, valued at 35 shillings, twice the value of the two recorded at Stonehouse. Its mills flourished, but the attempt to create a borough at King's Stanley failed despite the weekly market (established by 1295) and the creation of fifty burgage plots. Nevertheless, with the advent of cloth mills the village remained involved with the industry.

The grand Georgian Stanley Mill, passed where the route crosses the River Frome, is generally considered to be one of the principal monuments of the Industrial Revolution in the Stroud district. The Clutterbuck family built Stanley Mill in 1593 as a fulling mill, adding a gig mill in the mid 17th century. The gig mill raised the nap of the dyed cloth by moving locally grown teasel heads across it (sometimes called 'mosing'). A warping room, shear shop and dye-house were later additions.

Stanley Mill

With the need for specialization came a new start, taking advantage of a concept of fire-prevention first tried a few years previously in Derbyshire. A cloth mill pioneering fire-proof construction was built in 1813. The original doors were made of iron, as were all the interior columns and trusses. Built in 1802, the plant continued in use until 1954. It was originally water-powered, five wheels producing on a 16-ft fall 200 hp; in 1827 steam power added 40 hp. It specialized in worsted, a lighter material than the broadcloth made elsewhere in the Stroudwater valleys. It was unfulled, with the weave still visible in the finished cloth.

The development of steam engines put the Gloucestershire cloth industry on the rack, for the southern Pennine towns, well endowed with coal, were able to forge ahead and capitalize on the Cotswold reluctance to adopt steampowered looms. The worsted mill closed in 1954, though Messrs Marling and Evans still run the mill to meet contemporary needs. Along with Ebley Mill, Stanley Mill produces a variety of woollen materials for Marks and Spencer. Their research has led to the manufacture of highly specialized materials from man-made fibres; for instance Nomex, a fireproof material developed for racing drivers and firemen; a fine thread used in cardiac surgery; and a silvery nylon double material used as shuttering for laying concrete under water.

Preserved within Stanley Mill is a shearing machine made on the same principle as Price's original patent, from which came the inspiration for the standard lawn mower drum, invented by Edwin Budding of Dursley and first patented by Messrs Ferrabee, Millwrights, of Stroud in 1831.

Just beyond Stanley House is the parish church of St George, a Norman medieval building greatly restored by G. F. Bodley (see Selsley, above). Among the numerous copper plaques on the flat gravestones is one inscribed to Ann Collins, a barmaid (died 1804): 'Twas as she tript from cask to cask, in at a bung hole quickly fell, suffocation was her task, she had not time to say farewell'.

*striding through Pen Hill Woods*

# 14. Ryeford, Westrip and Standish Wood

The Cotswold Way crosses the River Frome at Ryeford ('Frome' deriving from a Celtic root meaning 'fair, brisk'; 'Ryeford' being the ford across which the rye-harvest was carried).

Stroudwater Canal

The Stroudwater Canal takes its name from an affluent of the River Frome. The name was also employed for various channels cut for mill purposes, like that running between the old branch railway and the canal where the Cotswold Way crosses. The canal itself was constructed between 1776 and 1779 to link the navigable Severn at Upper Framilode with Stroud. The 8-mile length proved a great success, setting Stroud ahead of all its Cotswold neighbours as the main cloth-producing town. It was the forerunner of other more ambitious schemes like the Severn/Thames link, extending from Stroud through the Sapperton Tunnel to reach Lechlade (29 miles) and the Gloucester to Sharpness Ship Canal (18 miles). The Stroudwater initially served to bring raw wool to Stroud docks and despatch the finished broadcloth. However, its trade expanded with the supply of coal as an energy source for the mills, necessitating the construction of wharves. From about 1880, when coal transportation became too expensive, the initiative for the use of steam-powered looms was readily taken by the Yorkshire mill towns in the production of their coarser worsteds.

Stroud became famous for its scarlet broadcloth (a broadcloth measured 3 ft by 24 yds). It flourished in the late eighteenth century, when fortunes were made by the gentlemen clothiers whose fine mansions adorn so many of the grand viewpoints and secluded coombes of the district. The name Golden Valley tells of the wealth this textile industry brought. The broadcloth from the Stroud and neighbouring valleys was characterized by its smooth even surface suitable for the smartest guardsmen's uniforms or hunting jacket. These Cotswold valleys had copious supplies of spring water, which also had the suitable natural salts for cleaning and dyeing. Cottage weavers were swallowed up by the advent of power mills, which in turn over-reached their capacity and succumbed to northern competition.

Wycliffe College was founded in 1883. The college emblem 'Bold and loyal' decorates the smart footbridge which links the Junior School to the main grounds (a sensible measure to keep the younger pupils and traffic apart).

There is a Bristol Omnibus fare stage at the Ryeford road junction. Stonehouse has many useful shops and a British Rail station, though Stroud has the more regular service (Gloucester to Swindon). The name Stonehouse evidently refers to the Saxon manor house. Humbler dwellings, whether in the vale or on the wolds, were invariably of timber construction, indicating the abundance of trees and woodland in medieval times. A tremendous amount of 'assarting', that is the clearing of woodland, principally for arable cropping, took place especially in the 12th century. The Domesday Book records a vineyard at Stonehouse specifying that it extended to 'two arpents' – a French measurement of unknown extent.

Doverow Hill, recorded in 1642 as Dovereys Field, continues the French connection and poses a conundrum, for the only explanation of the name has been that it is from an obscure surname taken from Ouvrouer-les-Champs in France.

The name Westrip means 'western outlying farm', corresponding with Thrupp to the S E of Stroud.

The Way wends through Fuzzies or Three Bears' Wood onto Maiden Hill (not Goldilocks, surely!).

There is an Iron Age cross-ridge dyke in Randwick Wood, known as Randwick Camp, which is rather a misnomer as it probably served only as a secondary bulwark. Curiously no gap was found when it was excavated in 1883. The lane followed by the Cotswold Way would appear not to be an ancient ridgeway. Did the dyke in fact sever the old ridge track that would naturally have materialized, possibly running up from the corresponding Peak Street ford at Ryeford?

The name Standish meant 'the stony pasture-enclosure'. The Vinegar Hill probably alludes to a vineyard that produced a weak sour wine only suitable as a pickling medium.

# 15. Haresfield Beacon, Scottsquar Hill and Washbrook Farm

The route continues through the National Trust's car park at Cripplegate. This name describes a now lost low opening in a wall to allow sheep (but not other larger animals) to pass from one field to another (literally 'creeping gate'). The cylindrical topograph will provoke curiosity with its unusual raised-relief panoramic plate.

The Way passes under the Haresfield Hill entrenchment, the Bulwarks, which appear in 1268 as Suberesburia (later changing to Eastbury), suggesting that the Saxon personal name Hersa (in the parish name) was applied to the encampment previously. Incidentally Hersa is deemed to come from an archaic stratum possibly pre-Saxon in origin, hence it is conceivable that this was 'Hersa's bury'. With the dykes, Randwick Camp, Haresfield Dyke Camp, the Bulwarks and the Ring Hill defences, we see an interesting sequence, shutting off various stages of the ridge, though without the necessary excavation it is impossible to match or date them. Ring Hill encloses the narrowest part of the promontory and but for the woodland would be a grand viewpoint. The knobbly end is known as a beacon site, though again we have no corroboratory evidence of its use. Certainly the beacon on the Malverns and possibly the Brecon Beacons could have had some correlation. Cotswold wayfarers can be forgiven for not considering Haresfield Beacon as anything special because the approach is so easy. The grandest ascent is from Arlebrook up Vinegar Hill, completing a circuit via the topograph above Standish Park, a real hill-climb, where thankfully the only opposition will be your lungs.

Ring Hill camp encloses 10 acres, with the N E and S sides defined by banks. There were five gaps in the defence, affording access via terrace-ways and a hollow way on the N side. That the camp may have been used as a Roman signal station is not beyond reason, for a Roman building has been identified near the E end. During the excavations of 1837 a pot vessel discovered inside the S entrance contained a hoard of two to three thousand bronze coins.

Students of geology may care to scramble below the N W scarp from the O S trig point to find what is considered a classic exposure, revealing the exact junction of the Upper Lias sands with the Inferior Oolite. Landslipping, fractures, cambers and a multitude of distortions obscure the true relationships of the strata everywhere in the Cotswolds except at this one location.

The significance of Cromwell House and Cromwell's Stone are more apparent than real, for there is no evidence that the Huntingdon Parliamentarian Oliver Cromwell ever passed this way. May there have been a coincidence of family names, later adapted with no wider historical significance? A more appropriate name for the stone would be 'King's Stone', as it is dated 5 September 1643, the precise day that the forces of King Charles I raised their siege on the City of Gloucester. At that stage in the Civil War the city was out of step with most of the west and north country by supporting the Roundheads.

The hastily assembled militia of the Earl of Essex advanced on Gloucester via Cheltenham (captured on the 5 September), arriving on the 8th, and after the gruelling deprivations of the long march from London were grateful to enter unopposed. Having replenished the city's food stock with corn from Tewkesbury they returned, on the 15 September, to London by way of Cirencester. Meanwhile the Royalists, recently departed, hastened with the King to Oxford. The whole strife was at this point delicately poised. Indeed it was not until 1645, when Cromwell and Fairfax brought authoritative leadership to the Parliamentary forces, that the issue came within sight of a decisive conclusion following the crucial battles at Marston Moor and Naseby Field (see Campden House, p. 188).

Beside Cliffwell Cottage stands a well-head, built in 1870, with the inscription: 'Whoer the Bucketful upwindeth, let him bless God, who water findest, Yet water here but small availeth, Go seek that well which never failest.'

The Way sweeps round a further escarpment bay. Within this wooded Stockend (farm end) is a hexagonal retreat cottage. Unseen below, near the source of Daniel's Brook, is the site of a Roman villa, robbed by the cartload for local masonry. The route quits the scarp face through Stockend Wood, crossing the quarry-scarred Scottsquar Hill. Scottsquar is an adapted place-name reflecting the extensive quarrying of recent centuries. The earliest recorded name, Sotora (1131), from O E *sceot*, 'a steep place', and O E *yfer*, 'the edge or

Scottsquar Hill

brow of a hill', whence 'brow of the steep hill', aptly describes the Stockend declivity. This is folk-etymology in action, modifying the spelling to suit the contemporary state.

Owing to the considerable dissection into the rear (dip slope) of the escarpment, the ridge between Painswick Beacon and Scottsquar is becoming a narrow isthmus. Eventually the whole promontory leading to Haresfield Beacon will be severed, forming a new outlier. The application of the name Rudge Hill to the open common beneath the ridge crest is doubtless due to a wrong analysis of such expressions as 'under edge' and association with 'ridge'.

Descending the common to the Edgemoor Inn, formerly the Gloucester House (from its situation on the Gloucester–Stroud coaching road), there are unrivalled views N E to Painswick, backed by the wooded hills of Kimsbury, Saltridge and Bulls Cross.

Washbrook Farm stands on Spoonbed Brook, an obscure valley name derived, it is conjectured, from a bed or pile of wood chippings (like Spuncombe on map 10). Washbrook Farm was built in the 17th century and was one of many cloth mills running on the Painswick and tributary streams. The name Washbrook would indicate the good wool-cleaning properties of the water. The Way passes the house upon an apparently raised ground level. Notice the initials W.A.H. and the date 1691 above a carved door lintel decorated with cherub heads. Elsewhere, on a broad label of a doorway, are the arms of the Hawkins family. In 1823 it was called Merrett's Mill and in 1830 Baylis's Mill. The change from cloth to flour (grist) mill occurred in the mid nineteenth century, continuing to the end of that century.

Outcrops beneath Haresfield Beacon

# 16. Painswick and Painswick Beacon

Climbing up the pastures the Way enters Painswick, which until 1237 was documented simply as 'Wicke', from the O E 'dairy farm'. Yet a century had passed since Pain Fitzjohn, Lord of the Manor, had died, and clearly even by the Domesday commission the settlement had long outgrown such a humble description. Walkers may choose to advance up New Street or take a more telling stroll via the churchyard.

The name New Street could be misleading. Its newness relates to the allocation of burgage plots within the Lord's demesne in 1253, along with a market charter (which explains Friday Street, Friday being market day). The manor house has long been lost, though several interesting houses remain fronting New Street. Hazelbury House has a Palladian front built before a 17th-century gabled house. This was the home of the Packer family who ran Cap Mill on Painswick stream, specializing in making caps for cloth workers. The Falcon Hotel (1711) was used by the Jerningham family, for 250 years (until 1804) Lords of the Manor, as a guest house and their family crest is depicted on the inn sign. A bowling-green was established by the Jerninghams in 1554 at the rear of the Falcon and was the regular scene of cock-fights in the 18th century, when rivalry with Stroud was fiercest. Facing the Falcon is War Memorial Ground, on the site of the Stock House, where local justice was meted out. This was pulled down in 1840 and the metal ring stocks placed across the churchyard at the top of Hale Lane.

The Fiery Beacon Gallery, with its 19th-century Gothic façade, stages regular exhibitions, notably promoting the work of natural history artists. The adjacent house, The Beacon, is mid-18th-century and has a fine Palladian frontage. There is sketchy evidence that John Wood the Younger designed it, surmised from the assumption that the owner, called Wood, was a relative. Beyond Victoria Street, New Street is hemmed in on both sides and echoes with an uncomfortable congestion of traffic. The Post Office has exposed timber-framing dating from 1428, the only example to survive in Painswick, though many houses are timber-framed internally. A little further, on the same side, is Madison House, which has a portico with Corinthian columns.

It would be a pity, having arrived at Painswick, not to allow yourself a more intimate view obtained through the pretty lych gate (1901) facing Edge Road. The timbers came from the belfry roof damaged when the spire fell in 1883. St Mary's churchyard, composed of avenues of interlocking yew colonnades 'architecturally' clipped, is truly a spectacle. The yews, largely planted in 1792, number in excess of one hundred. Tradition claims that only ninety-nine yews survive at any time. This legend arose from the difficulty of counting them. Locals admit that certainly more than ninety-nine flourish today. But impressive as these arches may be, there can be no denying the sheer quality and stunning quantity of table and tea-caddie tombs on display. They are more than just monuments of man's passing – they symbolize Painswick's golden age as a cloth town. Table or chest tombs originated from the long boxes that provided bases for recumbent effigies inside churches. The Painswick collection represent the high-water mark of their genre. (A tomb trail researched by Denzil

The old stocks

St Mary's, Painswick

Young can be purchased within the church.) The tombs were designed in the tradition of the Renaissance and display baroque style, later rococo, like the plaster-work on The Beacon. In all, seventy-three historical tombs are recorded on the excellent map in the Vicar's vestry. The principal architects were the Bryan family, active throughout the 18th century as monumental masons and carvers. Their clients were mostly the wealthy clothiers, whose elegant houses adorn this compact old town, though yeomen, mercers and woolstaplers also featured.

St Mary's church takes the centre stage, whether viewed from a distance or close to, the gracious spire rising 174 ft. Nature endowed the Painswick locality with much beauty and the materials for man to express his gratitude. The silver-grey stone gleams from the ashlared walls of the church, which was created with the loving care and sophisticated skills of the Cotswold master mason. While Domesday mentions that a priest served the community, neither the likely Saxon nor later Norman church, when a possession of Lanthony Priory from the 12th century to the Dissolution, have survived the rebuilding begun *c*. 1378; only the fabric of St Peter's Chapel and N aisle and arcade date from this time. The total effect of the interior is most harmonious. The nave of *c*. 1480 is exceptionally wide, while the aisles appear narrow, a composition of scale. Decoration too shows a rare sensitivity, particularly the chancel and sanctuary roofs. The tower dates from 1430, and the spire was added in 1632, at the height of the cloth trade prosperity. The tower contains a peal of twelve bells, a number which only thirty other English churches can match. In 1815 Stroud increased its peal from six to ten, whereupon Painswick raised its peal from ten to twelve in 1821 – an example of the rivalry which existed between 'strutting Stroud' and 'Painswick proud'.

To the S of the churchyard stands the Court House, a traditional gabled Cotswold house built in 1604 for the clothier Thomas Gardner. To the S of this is another large house, Castle Hale (*c*. 1653), which is presumed to occupy the site of the medieval manor. Near the junction of Victoria Street with St Mary's Street is the vicarage, formerly Loveday's House, a delightful example of a small early 18th-century classical town house. The steeply descending Tibbiwell Street, like the narrower Hale Lane, leads down to Painswick Stream. The stream is lined with mills which are now largely private residences of charm and distinction.

Much of the noise and hard labour of the boom years of the cloth trade in the 17th and 18th centuries were concentrated deep in the valleys, hence the mill owners and allied well-to-do could reside aloof on the ridge with the blessing of a S-facing aspect. Tibbiwell has several typical and picturesque 17th-century houses. Entering Friday Street from the Cross a particularly pleasant group of gabled houses holds the L corner. A bomb struck this street in 1941, and the subsequent rebuilding removed some of the charm. Bisley Street, along with the subsequent Gloucester Street, was the original main street of the village of Wicke (the lane proceeding down the valley towards Stroud on the opposite side to the modern A46 highway is still known as Wick Street). To the R is the Institute, built in 1906 by William Curtis Green, architect of the Dorchester Hotel in London. Each August the varied skills of the Guild of Gloucestershire Craftsmen are exhibited here. Facing Friday Street is Byfield House, Tudor with an 18th-century front. At the back is a 17th-century wool barn, now a dining-room. Further up the hill are some of the oldest houses in the town, dating from the 14th century. The Chur, once a coffee tavern, has an arched doorway with a studded oak door, a packhorse entrance through which the burden of wool was carried. Little Fleece (the National Trust bookshop) is part of what was an inn. The name harks back to the early years of Painswick's woollen glory. Wickstone has a packhorse entrance too, though blocked in. On the opposite corner is New Hall, first mentioned in 1429 as a cloth hall (warehouse).

Leaving the old town up Gloucester Street, the Way passes Pound House, which stands by the lost gathering enclosure where sheep were held before and after common grazing upon Painswick Hill. Painswick House dates from 1730 and was curiously first called Buenos Ayres. The route passes through The Plantation, planted by W. H. Hyett of Painswick House and presented to the people of Painswick in 1946. Among the numerous benefactions bequeathed to the town probably the two most significant were from the brothers Frederick and Edwin Gyde. Frederick died in 1872 placing £10,000 in the hands of trustees. Uppermost in his hopes was that it should help develop a railway link from Stroud to Painswick, but this was not realized. However, of far greater importance, the fund was used in 1906 to initiate a radical improvement in the town's water supply and drainage.

In 1872 Edwin gave the clock on the church tower in memory of his brother. On his death in 1894, Edwin left the bulk of a large fortune for the establishment of charitable institutions in Painswick; the Almshouses were first to be completed, designed in 1913 by Sidney Barnsley of the Arts and Crafts Movement, followed in 1919 by the completion of the Orphanage, which is now affiliated to the National Children's Home.

The route climbs onto Painswick Hill, passing Catsbrain Quarry. This peculiar name is derived from 'cattes-brazen', a medieval phrase applied to mottling, rough clay mixed with stones. At this point the Way rises over Paradise, a fanciful name for an exquisite hamlet setting. Walkers may like to ascend to Painswick Beacon, so far the highest point on the Cotswold escarpment. Although much pitted with minor quarrying, Kimsbury, sometimes known as Castle Godwyn, is a fine example of late Iron Age hill fort construction, being multivallate except on the N, where it is univallate. It encloses an 8-acre ridge site with a pronounced inturned entrance near the S E corner. Kimsbury, which means 'Cynemaer's fortification' (a Saxon personal name that occurs again in Gloucestershire at Kempsford), was the temporary and bleak camp of the Royalist forces after they lifted their siege on Gloucester on the night of 5 September 1643, while King Charles rested comfortably in the Court House!

The Welsh-looking river name Twyver derives from '*wefer*', 'winding stream', the initial 'T' slipping in from the expression 'at Wyver'.

# 17. Prinknash Corner, Cooper's Hill and Witcombe Woods

Idel Barrow, like idle thoughts, derives its name from the fact that the cairn had been emptied, doubtless for treasure, in Saxon times. There is no trace of a mound, which is only located as the junction of three parishes, Upton, Cranham and Painswick.

The Retreat, Prinknash Abbey

Prinknash (pronounced 'prinage') derives from 'Princa's ash-tree' (from O E *'princ'*, 'blinking of an eye').

In 1928 a Benedictine community moved from Caldey Island in Carmarthen Bay to Prinknash, where they took over the Retreat, a small mansion built as a grange and hunting lodge for the abbots of Gloucester. It was an idyllic setting but cramped for their needs, and plans were made to build a suitable monastery. The Second World War interrupted progress and the original Gothic design had become impossibly expensive, so a radically modified scheme was begun. The plans of F. G. Broadbent eventually gained acceptance, though its plain lines yielded nothing to the Gothic ideal. The five-storey monastery and church, built with the gorgeous yellow Coscombe stone – contrasting with the pale grey traditional-style Retreat – was opened in 1972. Prinknash flourishes, attracting many visitors with a highly successful pottery, a farm shop and tearooms.

High Brotheridge is a name that on the face of it smacks of monastic land, but in 1838 it was recorded as 'Broadridge', describing accurately the plateau leading to the escarpment edge; there are traces of an incomplete Iron Age dyke bounding a 200-acre settlement site. A downfaulted mass of Great Oolite resting upon fuller's earth clay is the main reason why the Cooper's Hill spur protrudes so massively, creating a high-level springline which might explain the Iron Age settlement on High Brotheridge.

Cooper's Hill is famous for the cheese-rolling event, a hair-raising custom of unknown antiquity staged each spring bank holiday. If you stand at the brink, next to the maypole, you will surely admire the courage of contestants who undertake the fearful plunge, racing to be the first to reach the foot of the slope after the release of a wooden drum representing a cheese. The winner takes many bruises and a 7-lb Double Gloucester cheese as his reward. The race, which appears in similar guises elsewhere, was formerly held on Midsummer day. It is suggested that the drum symbolizes the sun. Thus the act of chasing it may have been an attempt to arrest the shortening day and ensure its longevity – a pagan desire possibly linked with the inhabitants of the great High Brotheridge settlement.

Be sure to use the Haven Tea Garden (and sign the visitor's book) before tracking through Witcombe Woods. The names of Buckholt and Buckle Wood show them to be mature beechwoods. Cranham is derived from 'meadow haunted by herons'.

Like so many sheltering combes, Witcombe ('wide valley') has attracted springline settlement since at least Roman times. Witcombe Roman villa (sometimes opened to the public by Mr Hicks-Beach), discovered in 1818, dates from the 1st century. Excavations have suggested that it stood up on an earlier Iron Age enclosure. The unstable nature of the site seems to have caused the Roman occupiers to resort to thick walling to compensate, yet they remained here throughout the Romano-British phase, the presence of Cooper's Hill Farm being a perfect illustration of at least 2,000 years of settlement at this spot.

# 18. The Peak and Crickley Hill

Place-names can be either descriptive and revealing or just plain vague. Birdlip appears to answer to the former model, yet while we can be reasonably happy about 'lip' as 'edge' the first element teases us in its earliest spellings, which suggest 'bride', and the significance of some incident or folk-tale may be completely lost. The village stands very much on the lip of the escarpment upon the Roman Ermin Street, linking Glevum and Corinium (Gloucester and Cirencester). 'Ermin' derives from the Anglo-Saxon folk (clan) Earningas. The Way, which formerly entered Birdlip, complies with a terrace-way track of easier gradient than that of the modern road ascending Birdlip Hill; it is likely that this was also the course of Ermin Street (note also the clear ramp, marked by the footpath dots on map, in the pasture below where the Way regains height up to the road).

The name Peak aptly describes a short spur of the scarp. The earthworks of a dubious promontory fort are hidden within the Peak Plantation. The Peak, where once the Cotswold Way descended the sharp nose, offers superb views, much to be preferred to the Barrow Wake lay-by viewpoint, if only on grounds of relative solitude.

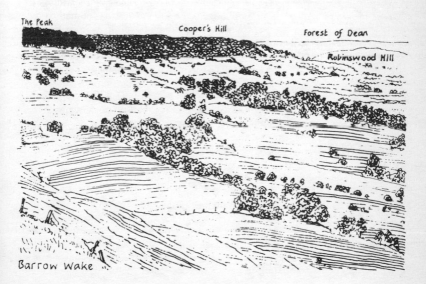

During quarrying to the east of the Barrow Wake highway, an Iron Age inhumation cemetery came to light in 1879. There were burials apparently found together in cists lined and covered with limestone flags, presumably a cairn burial. The group consisted of a female with an ornamental bronze mirror (only two have ever been found in Britain from this period, this one being referred to as the 'Birdlip mirror'), two bronze bowls, an iron knife-handle with a bronze bulls-head terminal, a silver-gilt fibula datable to within the early 1st century, a bracelet, rings, tweezers and other bronze objects, together with beads from a necklace of amber, marble and shale. With her were two 'unaccompanied' skeletons, thought to be male. A fourth skeleton, found nearby in a shallow grave, was accompanied by the remains of a bronze-mounted wooden bucket and an iron dagger, with a 13-ins. blade (all these 'grave-goods' are in Gloucester City Museum). Could the principal female inhumation be the 'bride' of Birdlip? We shall never know.

Two notable topographs have been erected for the steady stream of visitors who enjoy one of the finest Cotswold panoramas literally a few paces from the comfort of their cars. In 1970, near mile 63, a rectangular platform was recognized as the site of a Roman building. The Way passes the Air Balloon public house, established on the old turnpike, later the coaching road between Gloucester and Oxford, before following the steepening edge out to Crickley Hill promontory fort. Local tradition relates that the name Air Balloon recalls the late eighteenth century, when Crickley Hill was the venue for hot-air balloon ascents. (There is a potted history on the bar wall.)

The place-name Crickley embodies reference to these earthworks, the 'clearing near crik-hill' coming from Celtic *'cronco'* meaning 'mound', as in Churchdown Hill. The excavation of the site, begun in 1969, has proved to be one of the most successful and enlightening undertaken in this country. It reveals that the site was occupied over some 3 acres at the tip of the spur during Neolithic times. Behind this sweeps the principal rampart and ditch enclosing some $9\frac{1}{2}$ acres: this dates from two phases of Iron Age settlement.

The Neolithic occupation, within a causewayed enclosure had two lines of ditches breached by two entrances: the re-cutting and back-filling that occurred imply the intermittent use of the site. The final settlement phase is indicated by the strengthening of the earthwork defences, with dry walling topped with a palisade. The discovery of flint arrowheads against burnt fencing, in one of the passageways, implies a sudden end of Neolithic occupation some 5,000 years ago.

Between the Neolithic and Iron Age use of the Crickley Hill site, it appears that times were more peaceful, hence the supposition that there was occupation over broad areas of the wolds and vale. Traces of such lower-lying sites have long been obliterated.

The Iron Age phase of occupation has been dated at 700 BC. Although a few fragments of Early Bronze Age (Beaker) pottery were discovered, with contemporary flint arrowheads dated *c.* 2000 BC the Late Bronze/Early Iron Age really becomes evident only with the hill fort of around 700 BC.

This phase consisted of a rampart overtopped by dry walling and a palisade walkway, with a quite straightforward central entrance. Behind this ran a roadway between lines of rectangular-plan barn-like houses. Groups of small square huts, possibly crop storage sheds (as there was no trace of hearths), stood in attendance. Only about a third of the ground area has been excavated. The evidence suggests that the occupation lasted for, at the most, two generations, and suffered a cruel termination.

A piecemeal rebuilding seems to have taken place with the entrance restructured on a massive and complex scale around the early 5th century BC. The settlement is defended by a pair of stone bastions, the approach being checked by a second gate in a large outwork. The settlement took on a different form from its predecessor. A great roundhouse, nearly 50 ft in diameter, stood directly beyond the inner gate, with smaller roundhouses in an irregular ring; other structures, presumably used as granaries and store houses, lay in the general vicinity.

This second group of settlers appears to have arrived from points east, for pottery and house styles are similar to those discovered in the mid and upper Thames valley. Again their existence here was unlikely to have been more than say thirty years before the fort was attacked and laid waste.

Crickley Hill itself remained deserted until the foundation in the 2nd century of a small Roman farm whose ranch boundaries have been traced within The Scrubbs.

The County Council own the old quarry and hill fort site and pay a full-time warden to serve the public. There is a Crickley Hill Trust which seeks sponsors to support and advance excavation and preservation of the hill fort site. (The current Hon. Secretary is Mr R. E. Burke, Ermine House, Hucclecote, Gloucester GL3 3TH.)

Beneath the hill fort is a prominent line of cliffs, exhibiting the largest exposure of the Pea Grit formation in Britain, reaching 40 ft; they are very fossiliferous, teeming with fragments of sea urchins, polyzoa and various brachiopods.

The
Birdlip
Mirror

# 19. Shurdington Hill, Leckhampton Hill and Seven Springs

On the prominent Shurdington Hill headland rests a long barrow (no access) contemporary with the first, Neolithic, inhabitants of Crickley Hill.

Crippets (from the M E surname Cropet found in the district during the period 1230–1330) was the home of Edward Wilson, the eminent zoologist, who died along with Captain Robert F. Scott, Captain Lawrence, E. G. (Titus) Oates, Lieut. Henry (Birdie) Bowers and Edgar (Taff) Evans, on that ill-fated Antarctic expedition of 1911–12. Wilson's dramatic paintings of the ethereal effects in the Antarctic skies, executed before the fateful trek, survive as witness to a sensitive observer and brave companion.

The Greenway Lane came into existence as a sheep drove-road linking the manor of Badgeworth with Upper Coberley, when Eafe, Abbess of St Peter's, Gloucester, acquired Pinswell and Upper Coberley, some time between 734 and 767, expressly as a sheepwalk.

The route runs above a further deep combe; geologists consider that these great scoop-shaped hollows were formed by the action of nivation during the glacial period, each combe being a place where a snowfield collected, progressively frosting and down-shifting material. The action of water alone would only create a regular V-shaped valley tending towards convex valley slopes, whereas Cotswold escarpment combes tend towards the concave.

Ullenwood ('owls' wood') is the home of both the National Star Centre, a further education college for the physically handicapped, and the Cotswold Hills Golf Club, which moved here in the mid-1970s from the bleaker course on Cleeve Common.

Salterley means 'salt-dealers' clearing', indicating that a salt-way passed this way, presumably from Droitwich. Whether it strictly implies the residence of salt tradesmen is not clear.

Leckhampton Hill, together with Charlton Kings Common, provides the best high-level promenade on the Cotswold Way. The air is bracing and the prospect impressive and revealing, particularly over Cheltenham, though it must be stated the Eagle Star Insurance skyscraper is a vertical incongruity amid the intrinsic proportional eloquence of the spa's Regency town planning. Leckhampton Hill was famous for its quarries through the late 18th century and 19th century, which grew with the laying of tramways and railway links. Indeed it was the making of the upper incline that, in due course, gave rise to the Devil's Chimney. This curious landmark came into being when the upper incline was necessarily cut into the quarried cliffs; a slender silhouette arose upon the Cheltenham skyline. Georgian writers hastened to proffer an explanation

The Devil's Chimney

that was far removed from industry, for their readers were the fashionable society of the rising spa who sought an aura of mythology. Attributing the ragged outcrop to the works of the devil proved an irresistible publicity hoax and the quarrymen entered into the spirit of the tale, progressively trimming it back until by the 1830s the distinctive column we know today stood in bold relief, its makers revelling in the fantasy and hiding the simple truth. The collapse of the chimney is a matter of real concern, hence climbing on it is now forbidden.

Dead Man's Quarry, the source of much of the stone used in the building of Regency Cheltenham (in 1810 blocks of dressed stone cost only one old penny per ton delivered), offers geologists the greatest exposure of Inferior Oolite in the Cotswolds. The face consists of (from the bottom up): resting on Upper Lias Clay, 32 ft of Pea Grit (pisolitic limestone), then the massive

145

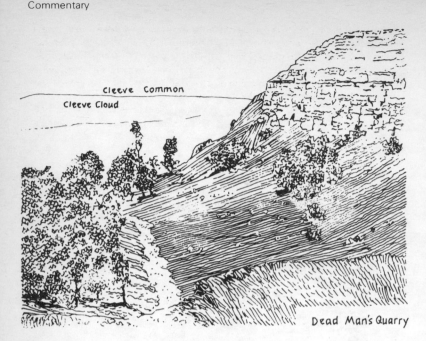

Cleeve Common

Cleeve Cloud

Dead Man's Quarry

75 ft of Lower Freestone, topped by 10 ft of Oolitic Marl, 30 ft of Upper Freestone and a 20- to 30-ft crust of ragstone. The name 'freestone' was possibly coined because neatly rectangular slabs could be removed 'freely' from the quarry face. Oolitic Marl is a white chalky rock which weathers into rubbly masses because it is not strongly jointed. Brown Stone Quarry was exclusively for ragstone extraction, the upper layers being useful only for dry walling and roadstone. Ragstones are bedded hard limestones which break up irregularly, and were popular in the late 19th century for neo-Gothic architecture, its ragged texture being reminiscent of medieval material.

Above the unprotected edge of Dead Man's Quarry is an Iron Age univallate hill fort enclosing 7 acres. The E and S side are defined by a rampart with an outer ditch. Near its N end the rampart crosses a gully, subsequently utilized by a quarry tramway; the entrance is in the E side a few yards S of the tramway cutting. A possible Iron Age square ditched barrow was excavated without material result in 1925; this lies 30 yds S E of the fort entrance (marked tumulus on the map).

Seven Springs occur at the base of the Pea Grit and draw upon the great reservoir beneath Hartley Hill. They are the source of the River Churn, which is the longest tributary of the River Thames. Understandably, locals have long claimed them to be the true source of Old Father Thames – indeed their claims were even discussed in the House of Commons in 1937, when the then recent-edition OS maps had confirmed Thames Head near Kemble as the true source. The debate, of course, effected no change; in fact Lord Apsley introduced a further complication by suggesting that the real Thames was a stream known as the Willbrook, which rises in Wiltshire!

The tiny circular thatched building was a parcel house erected for the mail coach service by William Hall, who built Seven Springs House and Ullenwood Manor for his daughter.

St Giles', Coberley

# 20. Seven Springs, Wistley Hill and Lineover Wood

The river-name Churn derives from Corinium, the Roman sub-capital of Britain. Slang speech produced the variants Churn, Cern and Ciren, the latter represented today in North and South Cerney (near where the Churn joins the Thames), and Cirencester.

Walkers would not be disappointed if, having enjoyed the view over Cheltenham, they chose to branch off Hartley Hill to reach Coberley. The name Coberley (pronounced Cubberley) comes from 'Cuthbert's glade'. In 1540 Leland erroneously thought that local speech was obliterating the Norman Lordship when he wrote 'Cow Berkeley', unaware of its clearly earlier Saxon association.

It is a most pleasant stroll down to the church, the discovery of which has an element of surprise, as the outbuildings of Coberley Court and a private garden shield its approach. The oldest parts of St Giles are the W tower, S porch and S chantry chapel. The nave and chancel were rebuilt in 1869–72. Until the 18th century Coberley Hall stood in what is now a horse paddock, next to the church. A branch of the Berkeley family (of Dursley) settled here, building the hall some time after c.1200, hunting their estate for deer upon Chatcombe and Hartley Chase and flourishing in an idyllic setting.

Evidence of the Berkeleys exists in the church in effigy monuments and in the carved coat of arms on the diagonal buttress of the Perpendicular tower. In the Sanctuary there is a rare heart-burial, unique in the Cotswolds. The heart belonged to Sir Giles Berkeley, the remainder of his body being interred at Little Malvern in 1295; the body of his horse was, unusually, laid to rest in Coberley churchyard. Sir Giles's son, Sir Thomas Berkeley, fought at the Battle of Crécy and is the principal effigy in his own chapel, beside a Lady and girl effigies. Sir Thomas's second wife, Joan, being widowed in 1352, later moved to Pauntley, marrying Sir William Whittington. Their son, Sir Richard (Dick) Whittington, spent much of his childhood at Coberley Hall. It is claimed that he rose to become both successful in commerce and three times Lord Mayor of London – a great benefactor to the City. The effigy of a young man on the S wall is also 14th-century.

Upper Coberley is a shrunken medieval village, its inhabitants having been forced to retreat by the inadequacy of the springs. An interesting string of Saxon names may be readily traced within the ensuing stretch of the route. Needlehole, from OE *'naet holh'* meaning 'wet hollow', is aptly named, as walkers traversing the field by the pond will confirm! The English landscape takes many body-blows gracefully – nature has many means of healing man's impositions – but the electricity transmission lines in this vicinity are starkly profuse. How many pylons can you spot? (The author noted at least twenty-eight!) The name Chatcombe is derived from an OE personal name giving 'Ceatta's valley', and in the same way Ravensgate Hill is from 'Hraefn's gate'. Wistley, which from its setting might appear to be 'the clearing where the wind whistles', in fact comes from OE *'wisse'* 'clearing near a swampy meadow'.

Wistley Hill is a majestic viewpoint and may fairly claim to be, ahead of Broadway Tower, the highest point en route along the Severn/Thames water-shed. California may be contemporary with the opening-up of the 'West' in America. Lineover appears in a reference *c.* 800, to *'lind ofres heafdan'*, which describes a boundary along the scarp edge above the lime-tree bank. Rossley is the glade where rafters or beams were got (from OE *'hrost'*, as in hen-roost).

The route descends to cross the old railway, completed in 1889, linking Banbury with Cheltenham (along which the author remembers frequently travelling in his youth). The line offered a shortened route from London to Cheltenham and proved valuable in the conveyance of ironstone to South Wales. The nearby station at Andoversford developed a fatstock market which thrives to this day, long after the Beeching axe fell in 1963.

Lineover Wood

Hereford cows & bull

# 21. Dowdeswell Reservoir and Piccadilly

The A40 London to Fishguard highway developed as a mail coach route. From Andoversford the descent into the Chelt valley was fraught with difficulties of gradient and a poor road surface. The earliest coach route left the turnpike at Cold Comfort Inn above Kilkenny. This route fell from favour about 1796, coaches preferring the steep sinuous course through Dowdeswell village. Then, in 1825, a new route was developed, coming down the head of the valley from Andoversford direct. This well-surfaced road better served the demands of the mushrooming spa of Cheltenham.

In 1718 a saline spring was first recognized on the site of Cheltenham Ladies College (W of the Promenade) and was progressively developed for its medicinal properties. In 1738 Henry Skillicorne erected the first Pump Room, then in 1776 his son William built an Assembly Room by the original well. A steady stream of patrons were attracted and in 1784 a larger Assembly Room and theatre were built in the Old High Street.

In 1781 Simon Moreau, the 'Beau Nash' of Cheltenham, forsook Bath to orchestrate the programme of social events during the summer season. The spa had begun, but its shortcomings – poor access and flow of water, and lack of hot springs – were sufficient to restrict its growth until 1788, when royalty was lured to 'take the waters'. Following the five-week holiday of King George III's household, the spa immediately became, like Bath after Queen Anne's visit, the fashionable place to be seen – in fact superseding Bath. Cheltenham had arrived and had become 'the merriest sick resort on earth'.

Under the patronage of Earl Fitzhardinge, the theatre, balls, musical promenades and gambling (in all its fashionable guises, such as cards and horse-racing) flourished. This second stage in the new golden age of spas (initiated by Bath) resulted in a spectacular growth in the town's population, making it possible to plan and build on a grand scale never before known in England (towns had previously grown up piecemeal). So, in oolite and brick, Regency Cheltenham arose in tree-lined avenues, duly followed by Leamington Spa. The Victorian age stifled the flamboyance, converting Cheltenham into a rather staid and snobbish residential town, an image it tries hard to shake off today.

Many wells were sunk to satisfy the needs of the growing town, but towards the end of the 19th century it became necessary to create a greater reserve – hence Dowdeswell Reservoir, which acts as a compensation reservoir.

The river-name Chelt has a very definite shroud of mystery about it. A. H. Smith, in his place-name survey of Gloucestershire, tentatively offers 'Celta's water-meadow', but he is far from convinced, for the element 'chelt' may parallel 'chilt' in the Chilterns, though whether it is topographical or personal in origin is not known.

Charlton Kings is quite a smart quarter of suburban Cheltenham, lying agreeably upon a thick band of sand. Yet this was not always so. As the place-name tells us 'Charlton' comes from the Saxon for peasant's farmstead ('Kings' because it was an ancient demesne of the Crown and to distinguish it from Charlton Abbots, which belonged to Winchcombe Abbey).

Place-name scholarship is an exclusive discipline in the main barely emerged from a dark age of understanding. Archaeologists are inclined to dismiss the whole subject as too coarse-grained to be capable of revealing solid new evidence. Yet sound new strata are emerging and surely will continue to come to light, particularly with the application of computer technology. One such discovery was made in 1967 by Dr Margaret Gelling and is represented at Syreford near Whittington. This is a field-name, Wycomb, where a Roman settlement, covering at least 20 acres and classified as a 'small town', has recently been excavated. *'Wic'* is a loan word from the Roman (Latin) *'vicus'*, first entering the O E vocabulary to describe actual Romano-British settlements or administrative units, later developing a variety of allied meanings such as 'salt-working centre' (Droitwich) and the more common 'dairy farm' (Painswick).

The walk up beside Dowdeswell Wood is inclined to be uncomfortably slippery. The wood is private, with no access – a good thing too, as it is said that the ghost of a local man, the last to be hanged for sheep-stealing in this neighbourhood, haunts its innermost glades!

Colgate is not 'cold gap', though it seems appropriate, but M E *'colle gate'*, to match the portal of Ravensgate across the valley.

Before 1800 the minor road ascending past the Hewletts, crossing the ridge into the Puckham Valley bound for Whittington, Syreford, Shipton Oliffe and Northleach, was the only way out of Cheltenham to the E. This was the route by which the Earl of Essex, advancing to relieve Gloucester, entered the town in 1643. The 15,000 march-weary militia camped upon the ridge for two rain-sodden nights somewhere in the vicinity of the Cotswold Way.

Piccadilly derives its name from fashionable dress collars no doubt paraded at the spa.

# 22. Happy Valley and Cleeve Common

The Way from the Happy Valley to Padcombe, traversing Cleeve Common, provides the best open country walking en route, reminiscent in parts of wild mountain terrain, a real treat.

Happy Valley

The curious dry valley feature known as the Happy Valley was created by a lateral dip and fault structure. It has parallels elsewhere in the northern scarp, on Cleeve above Postlip Warren, on Shenberrow Hill and at Broadway Tower.

Another interesting and commercially beneficial fault system occurs in the nearby Puckham valley, where, through block down-faulting, a large mass of base bed Great Oolite from the Stonesfield Slate series has been preserved from erosion. The valley provided a valuable source of roofing tiles, extracted both as 'presents' (by open quarrying) and as 'pendles' (by mining).

The Way enters the Common by a large notice board and proceeds along the edge through the ramparts of Cleeve Cloud Iron Age hill fort, which encloses 3 acres of gently W-sloping ground. The earthwork is bivallate, with an intermediate berm. Unfortunately quarrying over a long period has removed a considerable length of this rampart, including the entrance portal, which would seem to have been on the N side judging by the extent of quarrying.

The name Cleeve Cloud embodies OE *'clif'* and *'clud'*, meaning 'edge of the rocky outcrop'. The breezy, invigorating advance along this rocky edge is one of the highlights of the Cotswold Way, best enjoyed towards evening, with the setting sun highlighting the western horizon and picking out, beyond May Hill and the Malverns, the Black Mountains and the Herefordshire uplands.

Below the edge is Huddlestone's Table, named from the family of Sir John Hudleston, who were granted common rights in 1548. Nutterswood refers to nut-gatherers, while Queen's Wood commemorates Queen Elizabeth (wife of Edward IV), who held Southam Manor in 1550.

Castle Rock

At the end of the outcrop is Castle Rock. Composed of Lower Freestone upon Pea Grit, this is the biggest and soundest exposure of rock in the Cotswolds. It is the regular venue for local rock-climbers, particularly on the warmer evenings when they can develop their skills at leisure in advance of weekend adventures in Snowdonia; the hardest routes are on the N end.

The Way now climbs to the trig point and accompanying Rotary topograph. Some idea of the development of escarpment outliers can be gauged from this coign of vantage. The ridge continuation N runs by an isthmus to Nottingham Hill. On this spur is a large Iron Age promontory fort covering 120 acres. Its Saxon name was Cocca Burh (Cockbury). To the NE is Langley Hill, a severed outlier. The two hills embrace the Isbourne Vale, within which shelters

Winchcombe. Beyond, separated more fully by low land from the escarpment, Bredon and Dumbleton Hills can be seen. From this popular Cheltonian viewpoint it is only a short descent to Cleeve Hill Youth Hostel.

The Way descends to pass several mysterious Iron Age earthworks: the first, the Ring, encloses $\frac{1}{2}$ acre and contains a possible hut-platform; adjacent is a platformed ringwork, its flat interior 30 ft across, also containing a hut-platform. Proceeding along a contouring track, the Way passes above an area of ancient (undated) enclosures above old quarried slopes, marked by 4-ft-high banks.

Tewkesbury Borough Council own the Cleeve Hill Municipal Golf Course, which is 6,152 ft long (par 70). From the vicinity of the club house the route runs parallel to the first and second fairways (Winchcombe Way, 582 ft, and Hare's Run, 299 ft) before plummeting into the Postlip Valley. Domesday records that Godric held Postlip prior to the Conquest but subsequently it had been transferred to Ansfrid de Cormeilles and among its possessions were two mills. Indeed, the mills (c.1700) have remained; John Durham converted the corn mill below Corndean (*cweorn denu* – 'valley with a mill') into a paper mill. The hardness, purity and constant flow of the Postlip stream ensured the mill's continuity. In 1824 it passed through the Lloyd's to the Evans family and developed a reputation for quality coloured papers and board. Under Evans Adlard Ltd the mill has prospered, producing highly specialized filter paper for industry.

The Washpool

The name Postlip comes from either 'Pott's chasm' or 'declivity near a deep hollow'. Sheltering in the trees is Postlip Hall, a gabled Elizabethan mansion on the site of Robert de Solers' Manor (he had married the granddaughter of Walter de Cormeilles). The fine 14th–15th-century tithe barn has a W gable finial effigy said to be Sir William, Robert de Solers' son. He is said to have built the Roman Catholic chapel to St James. It was desecrated after the Reformation and used as a sheep-cot until 1891, when it was reconsecrated for Catholic worship (one service a year). Postlip Hall is now a commune. The route slips into the deep Washpool valley. The spring occurs at the base of the Lower Freestone upon Upper Lias clay: the porous oolitic rock and Liassic sand act like a giant sponge, steadily releasing water from its vast reservoir to flow into the Washpool. Notice the keyhole-shaped sheep dip below the dam. (The most copious spring, because of the peculiar synclinal tilt structure of Cleeve Hill, exists at Syreford: see Wycomb (p. 151), which explains why the Romans favoured that location.)

The Way climbs onto the wild expansive shoulder of Cleeve Common, the last vestige of unenclosed waste in the Cotswold region. Padcombe ('Pata's valley') is the source of the River Isbourne ('Esa's stream'). Here we are at the zenith of the walk, approximately 1,060 ft up; the highest point on the common, 1,083 ft, on West Down, is also the highest point in lowland England E of the Severn. Cleeve Hill persists to such an extent because of its considerable thickness of Middle Inferior Oolite, laid down 180 million years ago beneath a clear, shallow, Mediterranean-type sea with a coastline somewhere in the Welsh borderland (Offa's Dyke is not a relic shoreline!).

effigy of
William de Postlip

# 23. Wontley Farm, Belas Knap and Sudeley Castle

Wontley Farm is not a 'clearing' type place-name, for an Anglo-Saxon boundary reference of 769–85 mentions, *'to Antan hlawe'*, meaning Anta's mound. This cairn feature, now unidentifiable, was apparently located close by. The buildings conform to a traditional Cotswold grouping of barn, hovel and yard probably dating from the time of the first Enclosure Acts, when these wolds above Charlton Abbots were still but sheep pastures. The stone building to the L, short of the main group, looks like a sheep-shearing house and wool store. The ubiquitous barley acres that dominate the present-day uplands have arisen only since the Second World War with the advance of mechanization.

False entrance portal of Belas Knap long barrow

Belas Knap means 'beacon hill', though it is unlikely that the beacon had any connection with the long barrow, which dates essentially from *c*. 3000 BC. Archaeologists have recognized a relative chronology defining three categories of Neolithic chambered long barrows: the initial phase, the true-entrance or transept gallery type (such as Hetty Pegler's Tump), where the burials were placed either side of a central passageway approached from the front portal; then, possibly in answer to grave-robbing, the 'false portal' type with side chambers (Belas Knap falls into this category); later still the regularity of the side transepts was abolished and chambers were apparently sited randomly.

Belas Knap is a remarkable monument to the Stone Age agriculturalists, who must have been the first to impose some semblance of order on the primeval landscape. Some 5,000 years after it was built we can still appreciate its impressive dimensions and fine construction. It presently measures 178 ft long, 60 ft at maximum breadth, and 13 ft 6 ins high, though originally it would have been about 200 × 80 ft. Judging by the meagre finds, it must be assumed that despite its design the mound was entered over succeeding centuries and major grave goods removed. Indeed Romano-British potsherds, revealed in the mound near the false entrance, suggest that this part of the barrow may have been opened during the Roman period (Wadfield Roman villa is situated immediately below Humblebee How).

The mound was explored rather crudely in 1863–5, bringing to light, in the blocking of the false portal, the skull of a round-headed young male adult and the remains of five children (possibly inserted during the later Bronze Age). Within the NW chamber were the remains of fourteen individuals; in the NE chamber there were twelve, all but one being long-headed; the SE chamber had two males and two females, together with animal bones, pottery and a few flint flakes. The S chamber was probably only an enclosed cist (without the approach passage of its restoration); within were parts of a human skull. A 7 ft diameter circle of stones between the NW and NE chambers was destroyed during these excavations. This was possibly a degenerate survival of the rotunda found within earlier barrows, like Notgrove. All chamber passages were sealed.

The chambers were constructed with large slabs of Inferior Oolite placed upright and as over-capping (though the last restoration unfortunately used concrete). The false portal, of which only the lower layers remain undisturbed, was constructed with tilestones from the Puckham valley. It is often asserted that this dry-walling is the antecedent of all the enclosure walls of the present day, but palpably this is not true, for the Neolithic builders obviously preferred the regular wafer quality of the Stonesfield Slate (this material barely, if ever, occurs in subsequent walling). This hard tiling, moulded to form the flush curves that characterize the false portal, give it a unique mystique of distant millennia.

The enchantingly named plantation Humblebee How does not derive its name from an association with the bumblebee, as a reference of 1771 gave it as Hamelihou, from *'hamol hoh'*, meaning 'scarred (scree) hillside'.

The tiny village of Charlton Abbots at the head of the Beesmoor valley was blighted from any growth because the Abbots of Winchcombe Abbey kept it as a hospital for lepers; however, the present Manor House is a most beautiful Elizabethan and Jacobean building in an exquisite spot.

Wadfield Roman villa (for access ask at Humblebee Cottage) was discovered during ploughing in 1863 and was excavated in 1894–5. It lies just below the junction of Cotteswold Sands and Upper Lias, near springs on an E-facing slope. Subsequently a wall (incorporating re-used stones) was constructed around a large portion of the site. The villa was built, somewhat piecemeal, around a courtyard, and contained at least two heated rooms and two with mosaic tesserae. The tesselation in Room 1 was partially reconstructed after having been removed to Sudeley Castle in 1863 (a shed now protects this floor). Among small finds were coins from the reigns of Domitian, Hadrian and Arcadius. In 1969 a further Romano-British building was discovered 53 yds S during trenching for a major natural gas pipeline. At the same time a contemporary burial was found just W of the minor road immediately above the villa. Another larger courtyard-type Roman villa exists exposed in Spoonley Wood towards the head of Beesmoor Brook.

Wadfield

The word Wadfield comes from 'woad field', a plant used to create the blue dyes for the woollen industry. The centrepiece of this 18th-century farm is an elegant ashlar-faced mansion.

The Way approaches Sudeley crossing ridge and furrow which is a new sensation, as this is, remarkably, the first time the route has negotiated such pastoral corrugations.

Sudeley Castle often catches the eye in its parkland setting during the descent from Cleeve Common, its golden masonry radiating a sun-drenched warmth. The route passes the Almsbury Lodge entrance, a rusticated castellated archway lodge with tower and Gothic windows, built in 1893 for Emma Dent.

Sudeley, which unflatteringly means 'clearing with a shed', from the O E *scydd* ('shed'), was recorded in Domesday as belonging to Harold, son of Earl Ralph and great-grandson of King Ethelred the Unready.

The Beesmoor and Isbourne valleys had always been welcome harbour for selective settlement, but it was not until the early 12th century that the first actual castle was built, apparently illegally, during the turbulent years of King Stephen's reign. In 1367 Joan de Sudeley married William Lord Boteler of Wemme, whose family henceforward held the estate. Ralph Boteler, who succeeded in 1398, became Lord Chamberlain and was made Baron of Sudeley. In 1440–50 he rebuilt the castle; the earliest remaining features of the present castle date from this time and include the inner and outer courts (the S side of the inner court is missing). The most considerable remains are the chapel to the E, which featured in the Palliser plays on BBC TV, and the ruins of the great barn to the W. Ralph was both a fighting man and local benefactor, but because of his allegiance to Lancastrian ideals during the Wars of the Roses King Edward IV confiscated his property, granting it to the Duke of Gloucester (Richard III) in 1469, who rebuilt the E side of the inner court as a splendid state apartment. It then passed to Henry VII, who granted it to the Duke of Bedford for his lifetime.

Henry VIII retained it as a royal seat, appointing Sir John Brydges as Constable. Although Henry visited it with Queen Anne Boleyn, it was Katherine Parr who is principally connected with the Castle. After Henry's death she married Lord Seymour, who had been granted Sudeley by Edward VI in 1547. Katherine lived there, gave birth to Mary in 1548 and died a few days later. Her daughter's life after early childhood remains a mystery. Katherine was embalmed and buried in a lead coffin. There are numerous accounts of the fate of her remains, telling of the opening of the coffin in 1782, the removal over a period of years of most of her hair for keepsakes, etc. The effigy over the remains of Katherine Parr was carved in 1859. It gives possibly an over-gentle impression of a lady of immense vitality and drive.

Katherine Parr was a convinced Protestant, which explains the appointment of Miles Coverdale to the post of almoner. He was in attendance at Sudeley at the time of Mary's birth and subsequently conducted Katherine Parr's funeral in English, a radical move for those times. Miles Coverdale continued William Tyndale's work of translating the Bible into English (see Little Sodbury, p. 102). Lord Seymour was beheaded in the Tower of London within a year of Katherine's untimely death.

The castle came next to the first Lord Chandos, who largely rebuilt the outer courtyard with wide mullioned windows typical of Tudor work. The 6th Lord Chandos held the castle for King Charles I in the Civil War, and, although he later changed sides, his house was 'slighted' (like Berkeley Castle) and most of the inner courtyard demolished. For almost 200 years it was allowed to decay, until the estate and castle were purchased in 1863–7 by the Dent brothers, prosperous glove makers. They commissioned Sir Gilbert Scott to restore the beautiful little chapel, and he and J. D. Wyatt restored part of the house to contain their collection of art objects. That there is anything left to see, let alone glory at, is totally to the credit of the Dent family; over the succeeding years they cherished the estate and castle with genuine regard for its future.

The castle is open to the public from March to October daily from 12 to 5.30; the grounds are open from 11.00. The rooms open to the public occupy one side of the outer courtyard. The interior decoration is largely 19th-century; there is a collection of lace in the first-floor corridor, a rare Sheldon tapestry of the late 16th-century and paintings by Rubens, Van Dyck, Constable and Turner. The probable site of the great hall, dividing the two courtyards, is now by a Victorian corridor in which Emma Dent's collection of autographs of eminent men is displayed. The great dungeon tower in the inner courtyard is used for exhibitions (for example, in 1978, of Anna Karenina's costumes from the BBC TV production which was filmed at Sudeley). It also contains the largest private collection of toys and dolls on view in Europe. Peripheral attractions are the 19th-century gardens, ruins of the Great Banqueting Hall and an adventure playground to relieve your children of any remaining energy not sapped by the crossing of Cleeve Hill!

Sudeley Castle

# 24. Winchcombe and Hailes Abbey

The small town of Winchcombe, or Winchcomb (O E *'wincel'* 'bend', making 'valley with a bend in it') developed in the shadow of both the castle and the earlier abbey. King Offa, famed most for his attempts to emulate Charlemagne as a unifier and protector of Mercian England (Offa's Dyke), established a nunnery here *c.* 790. Offa was succeeded briefly by his son Egrid in 796, then by Kenulf, who founded an abbey, dedicated in 811 by the Archbishop of Canterbury; both Kenulf and his son Kenelm were buried here. A legend connected with the death of young Kenelm expanded into saintly proportions – hence St Kenelm's Well, on Sudeley Hill, from where in 1887 Emma Dent's benefaction of a town water-supply was laid in commemoration of Queen Victoria's Jubilee (see also Alderley, p. 109).

During the period of Mercian ascendancy, Winchcombe was a royal seat: it is thought that Offa may have lived here and at nearby Cropthorne from time to time (Cropthorne is linked to Winchcombe by the Wychavon Way). The decline of Mercia brought a decline in the abbey and it was not until *c.* 970, with the accession of King Edgar and establishment of Benedictine orders by St Dunstan, that the abbey saw a revival. On the turn of the first millennium AD the Mercian districts, administered from royal manors such as Winchcombe, were reorganized as shires on the Wessex model: hence Winchcombeshire, which lasted a mere twenty years before the amalgamation with the greater shire unit based on the city of Gloucester. Incidentally, following the Norman Conquest, it is stated in the *Anglo-Saxon Chronicle* that in 1085 '... at midwinter the King was at Gloucester with his counsellors ... and held very deep speech with his wise men about the land, how it was held, and with what men'. The outcome was the Domesday Book survey, the single most treasured document on the historic landscapes of England.

Winchcombe Abbey rose to great wealth through shrewd land purchase, and many Cotswold manors were transformed (some may say degraded) into vast sheepwalks, ousting the mixed economy: evidence of this can be seen at Enstone, in Oxfordshire, where a great tithe barn belonging to the abbey remains. Yet while the town grew alongside, benefiting from pilgrims visiting either St Kenelm's Well or the 'Holy Phial' at Hailes, it did not develop its own industrial base, maintaining its strongest links with agricultural interests and not blossoming as a 'wool town' like so many others.

By the end of the 15th century the monastery was said to be 'equal to a little university'. In 1539 the abbey was confiscated by Henry VIII's commissioners. Within a few years its entire fabric had been removed, much finding its way into various town houses, only Abbey Terrace, facing the market place, perpetuating its location in the heart of the old town.

The loss of the abbey was a near mortal blow to the town. There were lean pickings for the inhabitants. The petition for additional markets and fairs to generate local trade was granted by Elizabeth I in 1574. A return of 1608 records that there were four mercers dealing in cloth fabrics; one of these, Chris Merrett, had a son, educated at Worcester College Oxford, who became an accomplished natural scientist and whose published works included the first printed list of British wild birds.

Among the town's short economic adventures was the growing of tobacco. From about 1619, when the Farmcote landowner John Stratford purchased land and began its cultivation, the crop proved very successful, giving much needed employment. However, the government of the time was more intent on developing the recently settled Virginian colony than on encouraging home-based economies. It took nearly seventy years before tobacco growing was completely extinguished.

Winchcombe fails to convey any distinct cohesion or architectural unity, owing in no small part to its lack of any sustained latter-day prosperity. The Way enters Vineyard Street, the former Duck Street, where a duckboard stool was employed in the Isbourne as wet punishment. At Abbey Terrace visitors are directed off route along Gloucester Street, a name it must have held long before Cheltenham expanded to dominate the vale below Cleeve Hill. Soon the visitor will see St Peter's church, crowned with its gilded weathercock. This is one of the prime Perpendicular wool churches of the Cotswold region, though it is simpler than most and has no chancel arch. It was completed in 1465, the combined product of the Abbot, William Winchcombe (the chancel), and the parish, largely in the person of Sir Ralph Boteler. While genuine church explorers will enjoy the decoration and general fabric, and perhaps query the architects' wisdom in putting so much strain upon the clerestory mullions, the more casual visitor will gain sure delight from the comical array of gargoyles that ensured the devil and his own were banished without, while the church remained a sanctuary of peace and salvation.

Opposite the church is Jacobean House, one of many houses restored by the Dent family and a fine example of a 17th-century merchant's house (formerly the King's Grammar School). Immediately behind, in the alley off Queen Square, are the Chandos Almshouses, with the coat of arms of Chandos of Sudeley dated 1573. Built at right angles to the Abbey Terrace (Market Square) to the S are the Sudeley Almshouses; built by Sir Gilbert Scott in 1865, they have a crisp Victorian style.

In the High Street the John Wesley Café is a 16th-century timber-framed gem. On the opposite side stands the Town Hall, built in 1853 in Tudor style, housing a small local folk museum. Outside reside the town stocks, used in the last century to sober the unruly. A regularly up-dated list of local accommodation is posted on the wall outside the museum: a valuable local service for 'through' walkers.

*The Stocks at Winchcombe*

The pre-Reformation George Inn, almost opposite, was evidently built by the abbey for pilgrims to stay in, for the doorway carries the initials of the penultimate Abbot, Richard Kydderminster (RK). He resigned in 1525, having previously earned great favour and respect from Henry VIII and Thomas Cromwell. His death in 1531 saved him the horror of witnessing the confiscation and demise of his life's devotion at the hands of supposed friends.

Hailes Street, apart from the delights of the Pilgrim's Way Café, has several appealing Tudor houses with timber-framing and over-hanging first floors. Notice the house, midway down to the L, called 'Hwicci'; the name in this connection may be new, but its significance is genuine enough, for the Hwicce were a major Saxon people forming a principality covering Worcestershire, part of Warwickshire, Gloucestershire and the Oxfordshire Cotswolds, effectively South Mercia. Winchcombe was one of their power bases, which is probably why Offa in his endeavour to develop stability throughout his kingdom put such emphasis on the town. Indeed even today the impression of the town from Sudeley Hill, Cleeve Common or Langley Hill is of a complete and secure settlement wedded to the landscape much as King Offa would have envisaged.

The Way sets off for Hailes precisely as many thousands of medieval pilgrims will have done, along Puck Pit Lane, from O E *'puca pytt'*, meaning 'goblin-haunted hollows'; whether the pilgrims coined the name, their suspicions roused along the boggy track, aware that mischievous spirits might dissuade them from their mission, is not known.

Despite its spartan proportions Hailes is an ancient community. The place-name holds links with the largely lost Celtic language. It is thought to mean either 'folk dwelling on the stream called Salia' or, with the salt-way connection in mind, 'salt folk'. In the Domesday Book it was stated that Osgot the Thane held it before 1066 and the estate extended to 11 hides (1,320 acres). The moat of an early Norman defended castle/house might help to explain the location of such an old Norman church here (*c.* 1130).

Though the church plays second fiddle to the Cistercian abbey, its rather plain exterior hides a truly special interior, worthy of more than a passing glance. The principal treasures are the wall paintings of *c.*1300 in the chancel, with shields of arms and heraldic devices including the eagle of the Earl of Cornwall and castles of Eleanor of Castile, together with fantastic animals and monsters. In the nave further wall paintings depict a huge St Christopher on the N and a sporting scene with three lurcher dogs hunting a hare on the S. In the splays of the windows are two female saints; the one on the N is an exceptionally pretty girl.

Hailes Abbey

The manicured order and crisply defined foundations and masonry that characterize the Hailes Abbey ruins today conspire to deny the visitor the quality he may most desire – 'romance'. Shaggy ivy-clad ruins embowered to give just a hint of mystery are the ingredients so starkly missing, yet these are the very worst conditions if any monument is to survive and be genuinely cared for.

The Abbey was founded in 1246 by Richard Earl of Cornwall, younger brother of Henry III, in fulfilment of a vow made on return from a Crusade in the Holy Land, when his ship was all but wrecked off the Scilly Isles. Hailes Abbey was one of the last Cistercian houses to be founded in England, some 180 years after the Order first established itself at Waverley in Surrey.

In 1245, three years after the Scilly episode, Henry III granted his brother the Manor of Hailes, and within a year the nucleus of a monastic community had assembled from Beaulieu Abbey in Hampshire. Five and a half years later the Abbey was sufficiently developed for it to be dedicated on 5 November 1251; the company included the King, Queen Eleanor, Earl Richard and several nobles, and no less than thirteen bishops.

The community struggled through its early years until 1270, when Earl Richard's second son Edmund presented a phial of the Holy Blood, which he had purchased from the Count of Flanders in 1267. This bore the guarantee of the Patriarch of Jerusalem, later to be Pope Urban IV, that it was the authentic Blood of Christ! On 14 September, amid due ceremony, the Holy Blood was placed in a specially built shrine. So distinguished a relic demanded a worthy setting, and accordingly the whole E end of the church was rebuilt into a coronet of chapels radiating from an ambulatory around an apse (known as a chevet and directly inspired by the E end of Westminster Abbey). Henceforward, Hailes prospered in leaps and bounds, becoming one of the great pilgrimage centres of England. Chaucer mentions it in the *Pardoner's Tale*: 'By the blode of Crist that is in Hayles'. Just prior to the Dissolution and surrender by the Abbot in 1539, the relic was discredited in analysis and found to be nothing more than 'honey, clarified and coloured with saffron'.

What remains gives little more than a suggestion of a once great abbey. Only three cloister arcades and walling on the NW and E sides stand to any height. Visitors are recommended on arrival to take a careful look at the displays within the museum and gauge for themselves the beauty in stone so lovingly fashioned by the medieval master masons: witness the six bosses from the Chapter House vault. The abbey, owned by the National Trust, is open throughout the year at specific times; the entrance fee is nominal.

# 25. Beckbury, Wood Stanway and Stanway

The Way ascends the old lane towards Farmcote ('cottage amongst the ferns'), passing the intensive orchards of Hayles Fruit Farm, where the first crop of tobacco in the district may well have grown back in the early 17th century. Within Hailes Wood is an area of confused ridges and gullies, known as Hailes Camp; this site has been discredited. Similarly, upon the exposed hill beyond Beckbury, a series of ovals clearly defined in aerial photographs has been attributed to a natural geological quirk.

Farmcote was a grange of Hailes Abbey: the barn and farm buildings show all the hallmarks of their medieval ties. Within the charming little chapel-of-ease, St Faith's, are some attractive furnishings. Only the nave of the Norman church remains. It contains a stone effigy of William Stratford and his wife Ann Walwyn, recumbent in civilian dress, of 1590.

Beckbury Camp, enclosing 5½ acres at the edge of the plateau, is a univallate Iron Age hill fort. The entrance appears to have been the 40-ft gap in the SW between the bank and the scarp edge. No excavation has been carried out here, so any genuinely useful knowledge is locked within the turf. Regrettably nothing is known either about the stone monument at the NW corner – there is no inscription other than graffiti, though the tall niche would appear to have held a figure and some association with Hailes Abbey and the Blessed Virgin Mary is hard to avoid.

At Quarry Plantation the Way rejoins the Jurassic Way for the first time since Dyrham Wood, 78 miles back! The small group of barns seems an unlikely location for a sheepwash on the dry plateau, yet the dew pond, into which four walls converge, must have served as such. A corrugated shed shows the purpose of staddle-stones, a common garden ornamentation in the Cotswold region, their 'mushroom' lids preventing rodents entering a grain store.

At Stumps Cross, there is indeed the stated stump, just by a sheep pen. Of more visual interest, however, is the nearby Coscombe (Guiting) Quarry, still extracting the beautiful rich honey-coloured freestone employed to such wonderful effect locally. Toddington Manor is frequently in view from high points along the Way (3 miles as the crow flies NW of Stumps Cross); it is probably the most impressive local building constructed from this stone. The Dissolution Acts brought a property bonanza to wealthy Tudor families like the Tracys. They lived initially in the Abbot's lodgings at Hailes until they built Toddington Old Manor (of which only the gatehouse survives today). When this was abandoned in the early 19th century Charles Hanbury-Tracy designed and built for himself the stupendous mansion between 1820 and

1835, an aristocratic piece of Gothic style, much influenced by the Oxford colleges. Hanbury-Tracy's architectural wisdom was confirmed by his appointment as chairman of the Commission (in 1835) to select a new design for the Palace of Westminster, and it was largely due to his persistence that Charles Barry's plan was adopted.

Bredon Hill from Coscombe

The blind corner at the top of Stanway Hill, through which walkers are obliged to slip, is succeeded by a truly gorgeous prospect down Coscombe towards Bredon Hill. Lower Coscombe is no rustic arcadia, being efficiently managed for equestrian interests. It stands upon the site of the summer residence of the Abbot of Hailes, who obviously knew a good view when he saw one! The name Coscombe derives from 'Costa's valley', where *'cost'* is OE for 'excellent', so this name might in fact refer to the quality of the land and climate. The ensuing steep pastures exhibit some of the best ridge and furrows on the entire route, sweeping at various angles to the path and pointing to a time when many teams of oxen and horses will have been working to satisfy the needs of a large rural populace.

Wood Stanway, a hamlet of Church Stanway, has several large 17th-century and 18th-century farm houses and cottages. The name Glebe indicates that this farm at one time belonged to the church: Tewkesbury Abbey owned the manor for 800 years. The OE *'fyrhde'* (modern 'thrift'), confirms the age of the wood above the hamlet.

The Domesday Book has an interesting entry for Stanway, mentioning that it had a monastery; no trace of it remains. However, an engraving by Kip of 1713 shows the Abbot of Tewkesbury's 'fair stone house' sited right where the present mansion rests. It seems probable that the monastery preceded the present church. It is interesting to note that the estate owned a salt-house in Droitwich. The old 'stone way' (from which Stanway derives its name) was a salt-trading route: the route either ascended the scarp here via Old Hill or at Hailes, going up Salters Lane.

Stanway is a typical estate village, with the great house and church as its centre-piece and the homes of estate workers dotted around in the vicinity (it could be likened to the Iron Age community on Crickley Hill, with a little stretching of the imagination!).

Below the Lidcombe Woods is Papermill Valley, where a paper mill was

War Memorial at Stanway

established before that at Postlip. At the crossroads beyond the charming Old Bakehouse is quite the most impressive war memorial in the Cotswolds. Sir Philip Stott (see Stanton) provided the plinth, upon which was mounted a simply gorgeous bronze, 'St George and the Dragon', by Alexander Fisher; the immaculate lettering was the work of Eric Gill. It deserves a wider fame for its all-round excellence.

The Tracy family acquired this estate too and built Stanway House in Elizabethan and Stuart times. It has descended from the Tracys to the Earls of Wemyss, who care for it today (living in the gatehouse). The principal rooms are in the long S-facing range, with service and domestic rooms at right angles, a departure from the traditional Tudor hall. The house is particularly notable for its windows.

The Gatehouse of Stanway House

The gatehouse defies flippant description. While the designer remains a mystery, it has been linked with Timothy Strong, from Little Barrington in Oxfordshire, who clearly understood the Renaissance forms being introduced by Inigo Jones from Italy. The scallop-shell motif derives from the Tracy coat of arms, which features above the doorway. Next, the church of St Peter. Much of the masonry of the nave and chancel belong to a 12th-century rebuilding. The interior suffered an over-enthusiastic restoration in 1896. The churchyard, which offers a fine prospect of the great W window of Stanway House, contains in its bounding wall various bits of carved masonry and coffins of the

12th and 13th centuries, indicating the extent of the 1896 restoration! Here lies buried Dr Thomas Dover, who introduced mercury into medicine and who it is said captained the ship that rescued Alexander Selkirk (the original Robinson Crusoe) from the island of Juan Fernandez in 1708. Within the grounds of Stanway House, behind the church, is an enormous 14th-century tithe barn, confirming Tewkesbury Abbey's pre-Reformation link with Stanway. Used today for social gatherings, it is constructed with cruck frames supporting an immensely heavy stone tile roof. Notice the unusual curved finials. The gabled porch on the N has a small stone 13th-century doorway, inserted, it is thought, from another of the Abbot's buildings. Across the road is a cricket pitch with the pavilion mounted upon staddle stones to protect the valuable equipment from the eager teeth of rodents (mice in particular)! This is credited to Sir James Barrie.

Manorway, Stanton

# 26. Stanton, Shenberrow Hill and Burhill

The Way crosses old ridge and furrow to enter Stanton by Chestnut Farm into Manorway, where there are some tidy modern additions to the compact village housing stock.

If you have sped from Stanway, then dawdle here, for Stanton is just the place you should remember long after your journey ends. There is an element of formality about the place derived, no doubt, from a desire to respect such bountiful beauty. The village is largely a 16th-century grouping of farmhouses and cottages growing very naturally in the mode of the time, yet somehow it has all worked out so well that the modern visitor cannot but admire the simple perfection of the place.

But it is well to remember that when Sir Philip Stott arrived at the Court in 1906, his architectural instincts were filled with compassion for so run down a place. Until his death, in 1937, he spent much of his time and money restoring and revitalizing the battered fabric of the community, bringing so basic a commodity as water (hence the tap niches up the street) down from a reservoir and creating a discreet, and at that time incredibly novel, innovation, a swimming pool for the parish. He even brought in timber-framed barns (like that opposite the village shop in Manorway), now agreeably converted into a residence, Dove Cottage.

We cannot but applaud his efforts, and those of his successors, for respecting Stanton's rare architectural cohesion. Who can look at such houses as Warren House (the original manor, which was extended in 1577 by Thomas Warren) or Warren Farmhouse (up the main street to the R beyond the Cross) and not commend them as major elements in the rich treasury of Cotswold domestic architecture. Each house in turn bears its own distinct character without regimentation. The village is akin to the composition of a master painter who knows that if his work is to endure it must draw the spectator's eye on with mounting curiosity.

The oolite, hewn upon the scarp, is seen in mellow perfection, the textures in soothing tones of apricot and ochre; was ever a stone a better complement to its setting? Thankfully, the virtues of Stanton have not been downgraded by commercialism – compare Broadway and Bourton-on-the-Water. As it lies well away from the main A46 Stanton, to all intents, is a cul-de-sac; one is as likely to encounter a horse-rider as a car.

Stanton was held by Winchcombe Abbey until the Dissolution and has always had its roots in herding and tillage. The name means 'farmstead within a stony enclosure'. This early Saxon site presumably lay sheltered upon the

St Michael's, Stanton

upper scarp and will have been wholly timber-framed. Until the 15th and 16th centuries all but exceptional structures took advantage of the abundance of hardwood that clothed the vale and scarp alike – after all it was easy to haul and fashion this wood into practical dwellings, barns and hovels.

Stanton

Although the majority of buildings line the streets in an obvious picturesque manner, there are several notable exceptions. Firstly, Stanton Court, built it is said by the Izods, Lords of the Manor during the reign of James I, a major landowning dynasty that came to the Cotswolds in c.1450 from Chapel Izod in County Kilkenny. The family have never lost their farming appetite – indeed a main branch of the family exists to this day as a large farming enterprise and as good neighbours of the author (see Westington, p. 188). The Court is shrouded by fine trees at the foot of the hill opposite the cricket field. A tall, dignified, well-balanced hall with steep-pitched roofs and projecting gable-wings, its E elevation, clearly seen from the churchyard, has survived subsequent alteration, notably at the hands of the Wynniatts and latterly by Sir Philip Stott.

The medieval market cross is surmounted by a 17th-century sundial and globe. Just here a lane leads off to the parish church of St Michael. Could a more fitting church be conceived, scaled and fashioned for this one setting? The neat spire is proportioned like hands in prayer, and the porch treated as one with the S aisle. The tiny room above the porch now houses a quaint collection of artifacts; previously it may have been a parish treasury.

The predominant features of the church are Perpendicular, though the earliest parts are 12th-century Norman. The interior has the undeniable woody feel of a medieval meeting-place – the clever work of Sir Ninian Comper in the first quarter of the present century; as Verey says, he 'cast this subtly mystical spell'. Notice the E window, incorporating 15th-century stained glass from Hailes Abbey; the organ loft; pews; rood screen; wall paintings; and the pulpits where John Wesley preached while staying at nearby Buckland Rectory on vacation from Oxford. Among the monuments are painted stone tablets with coats of arms to Henry Izod (1650) and John Warren (1728).

Advancing up the street, the Way branches R to pass Sheppey Corner, so named because this is where flocks of Cotswold sheep will have entered and left the village bound for the broad sheepwalks upon and above the escarpment. Leave not in haste, for Stanton holds two further surprises.

By taking the L fork the thirsty, travel-weary wayfarer will, if his or her timing is right, be rewarded with welcome refreshment in convivial surroundings at the Mount Inn (no accommodation), and enjoy an excellent viewpoint to boot. The lane continues up the bank to Stanton Guildhouse, the product of Mary Osborne's dream. Built over the period 1963–71 by a totally voluntary labour force, its concept was, and remains, to provide a centre to rekindle and nurture country crafts and skills together with the many forms of artistic expression from painting to musical appreciation. Long may this bold venture flourish: it is analogous to the Cotswold Farm Park at nearby Temple Guiting, where rare breeds of domestic farm animals are bred to ensure their survival.

The Way climbs the narrowing combe, beyond two hydraulic rams pumping water up to Shenberrow Buildings, to reach Shenberrow Camp, a bivallate Iron Age hill fort enclosing $2\frac{1}{2}$ acres. The name derives possibly from O E *'scene'*, meaning 'bright, beautiful fortified hill'. The allusion is not obvious, though there is no denying the grand prospect through the trees. The site was excavated in 1935, producing finger-marked pottery, two bone needles, a spindle-whorl of Lias limestone, a bronze bracelet, and a tanged iron knife (finds in Gloucester City Museum), together with evidence of the original defences' substantial size.

Stretching back from the Edge at this point is the high sweeping wold associated with that Saxon chieftain 'Cod', whose name has also endured in the village name Cutsdean. 'Cod's Wold', or, as it later became, 'Cotswold', has over the years expanded its meaning to embrace the entire stone belt from Bath through Cirencester to Chipping Campden.

The Way tracks N through No Man's Land, which is claimed by Stanton's parish boundary. There appears to be a dyke feature (unrecorded) running parallel with the N wall from the gate. Could this be an ancient estate boundary abutting the disputed patch? Incidentally, this field-name occurs again locally, close to (S E of) the Fish Inn; named 'nanesmonnes land' in 972, it is a remarkable case of long survival.

Just after No Man's Land look E towards the village of Snowshill on the far hillside, just beneath the scarp edge. Old quarries flank the track as the Way passes Laverton Hill Barn and gently declines with a hollow way; this must be quite an old way, for it exhibits sunken characteristics despite the underlying rock. The stone used to build Laverton and Buckland probably came by this route. Laverton, a dependent hamlet of Buckland, has a most charming derivation, 'farmstead frequented by larks' – or was it that the farmers rose early 'with the larks'?

The Way proceeds past the new Manor Farm buildings created by the present owner of the Buckland estate, who has transformed the old buildings in the upper village into superbly appointed holiday cottages. The name Buckland bears no relation to the 'beech tree', but signifies 'land held by grant of a charter', in this instance granted to St Peter's, Gloucester, by Coenred (Kynred), King of Mercia. The village shelters beneath Burhill: in 1960 a univallate hill fort was discovered on this marlstone spur. A 972 land charter of Pershore Abbey refers to Burhill as *'wadbeorh'* (woadhill). This was later to become Burrell, and finally assumed its present name.

Buckland, though of tiny proportions, contains two buildings of considerable character and history. The church of St Michael preserves an almost un-broken architectural history spanning the 13th to 17th centuries, though perhaps the strongest influence is pre-Reformation Perpendicular. In the churchyard is a table-tomb of Colonel Granville, who died in 1725, a relative of Sir Bevil (see Lansdown Monument, p. 91). Close by stands the Manor. The existing 16th-century buildings were much altered in late Victorian times. The prime attraction, with the church, is Buckland Rectory, quite the oldest parsonage in Gloucestershire still used for its original purpose. The stone-faced exterior looks like a rambling farmhouse, except for the mullioned windows of the great hall in the centre. It was built between 1466 and 1483 as an addition to an existing small house. There are 17th- and 19th-century additions, but the main features include the open hammer-beam roof in the hall, the medieval window-glass and the stone stairs. The Rectory is opened to the public on weekdays during the summer, the Rector being the well-informed and amusing guide.

Shenberrow Camp

175

# 27. Broadway, Broadway Tower and the Fish Inn

At the edge of the map the Way enters Worcestershire, which in the local government re-organization of 1974 came into unnatural union with Herefordshire. The route slips through Broadway Coppice, descending to the West End Lane. West End Farm contains elements of Baldwyn Sheldon's Manor House of 1540. The Sheldon dynasty was not only wealthy, but also talented: one member of the family who had been Warden of All Souls College, Oxford, rose to the exalted position of Archbishop of Canterbury in 1663. In that same year his friend, Sir Christopher Wren, completed the Sheldonian Theatre in Oxford (with £12,200 given by Sheldon). This was Wren's first work of architecture and provided the centre stage for university ceremonies.

Badsey Brook, which has cut back deeply into the scarp along a fault weakness, drains through the Vale of Evesham, which must have been settled and tilled for thousands of years.

The route ascends the pasture known as the Wilderness, so named from the overgrown ruins (now long removed) of Sir Francis Winnington's Manor, burnt down in 1815. In Church Street opposite, Austin House is an attractive Georgian house of *c.*1700, former home of Lord Lifford, in whose fond memory the village hall was built. To the L stands the 'new' parish church of St Michael's, built in 1839 to save parishioners the long trudge beyond the Very End (Bury End). Within is the sumptuous Elizabethan pulpit (removed from the old church) and an interesting organ.

At the end of Church Street (the Snowshill road), beyond the old Court gatehouse, is St Eadburgh's, named from one of the patron saints of Pershore Abbey. Fortunately this fine 12th-century church was saved from destruction, the common fate of many churches superseded by Victorian edifices. St Eadburgh's is worthy of a visit.

Before 1875 the ancient 'broad way' to Snowshill commenced up Coneygree (rabbit-warren) Lane, proceeding by Middle Hill on a sinuous and somewhat devious course.

Snowshill, sheltering on the breast of the scarp, was presumably so named because the snow lay longer here than elsewhere in the locality. The village formerly had closer ties with Stanton, as both places belonged to Winchcombe Abbey. Snowshill Manor, a National Trust property, is a real crowd puller, for this attractive Cotswold mansion contains the most diverse 'magpie' collection, exhibiting Charles Paget Wade's passionate nostalgia for the Victorian empire.

Turning into Broadway proper, the Way passes the Crown and Trumpet

St Eadburgh's

and several charming houses to reach the Green. On the L, shielded by a yew hedge, is the Abbot's Grange (c.1320). This was the summer residence of the Abbots of Pershore and is the oldest domestic building in Worcestershire.

It is a hard but necessary task for the visitor to gaze up the 'broad way' from the Green. Imagine the scene bereft of tarmac and traffic, with a slightly sunken track, flanked Mesopotamian fashion by tiny streams: set back, the homes of a community still largely orientated to farming and allied trades. This is the village which, having lost its former importance on an arterial coaching route to London with the coming of the railways, attracted the admiration of a body of Victorian artists, writers and seekers after the archetypal English village such as William Morris, Sir Alfred Parsons, Frank Millet, Sir John Sargent, Henry James and Mary Anderson de Navarro.

The qualities they found have, to all intents, been submerged in a sober urbanized conformity, overlaid by a strong current of commercial commitment to please the eye and catch the pocket of the modern itinerant. Brodi, as the locals would pronounce it, derives its name from the 'broad road', but there is considerable doubt as to which of the two old ways the name refers. The older road passing St Eadburgh's, where the original settlement lay, must be the 'Bradsetena' of c. 860.

When manorial expedience shifted, the nucleus moved E of the Green (N of the church demesne) and the name, very properly, was transferred with it.

Broadway had been granted to the Benedictine monastery of Pershore in 972 by King Edgar; during the 550 years to the Dissolution, Broadway had developed to provide one quarter of the Abbey's total income. This carefully nurtured agrarian prosperity, supplemented in the stage-coaching era (of the 17th and 18th centuries) by the provision of accommodation and fresh horses ahead of the severe haul up Fish Hill, goes a long way to explain the stature of the modern village.

The Green has been the focal point of the village from the earliest days, and the scene of the Tuesday market and Whitsun Fair through medieval times. The small Almshouses are of c. 1600, and Broadway Hotel, dated 1575 on an inside door, has been both a blacksmiths and bakehouse. The High Street stretches ahead towards the escarpment. This is an exceptionally long street, longer than that of many similar small towns; remember Wotton-under-Edge. Nevertheless, the arrangement and form of the houses is sufficiently unpredictable, standing forward and back with pretty flower gardens, with thatch and tiled roofs, alternating in levels to retain an underlying village character.

There is a full range of shops, tearooms and hotels, of which certainly the most impressive is the Lygon Arms (pronounced Liggon). Originally a large private residence (owner unknown), it became the White Hart Inn in the 16th century. Following the purchase of the Springhill Estate (above Snowshill) by General Lygon (who fought in the Battle of Waterloo), the inn was acquired by his steward, who promptly capitalized on the rising coaching custom to develop the hotel, shrewdly using his squire's coat of arms. The front of the Lygon Arms has a recessed centre with projecting gable wings, the door being added in 1620; to the R a dining-room/ballroom was built sympathetically in 1910. The real transformation came when Sydney Russell bought it in 1904, with extensions to the rear and a massive interior facelift. The hotel has risen to pre-eminence as one of the best-run and smartest country hotels in Britain. Russell's second son, Gordon, was detailed to repair the hotel furniture, from which small beginning sprang the world-famous Gordon Russell Ltd, making high-quality furnishings. There is a factory and showroom behind the Lygon in Back Lane.

Further up the street, notice the surprising Broad Close field, owned by the North Cotswold Hunt. Its survival from building development is quite amazing. Today it is protected by an open space preservation order.

At the corner of the Willersey Road stands Prior's Manse, which is contemporary with the Abbot's Grange. Here the Abbot's steward lived. Until 1877 a large barn adjoined the E end.

Where the street starts to curve, notice the old turnpike milestone against the Milestone Hotel wall. The stone was removed in 1939, when all forms of directional aids were banished (to confuse the enemy if they occupied the country), and reinstated in 1953, Coronation year.

Flea Bank, High Street, Broadway

The Cotswold Way now leaves the High Street to begin its ascent to Broadway Tower. However, it is worthwhile taking a short stroll up the remainder of the street. To the L is the much-photographed group of 16th-century cottages on Flea Bank, known as Shakespeare Cottages; these were condemned in 1930, though fortunately restored during the last war. Beyond the cottages is a series of distinguished former farmhouses.

Clump Farm, of 1722, has a beautiful barn to its rear. Orchard Farm, with its long frontage to the road, was the home of the late Sir Gerald Nabarro, the renowned politician. Previously, at the turn of the century, Lady Maud Bowes-Lyon and her mother the Countess of Strathmore had bought the farmhouse and converted it into this grand house. The Queen Mother, when a girl, is said to have stayed here with her aunt.

Top Farm, now called East Lodge, was bought by a Mr Wells, who turned it into a splendid model farm. From humble stock at Alveston near Stratford-upon-Avon he set forth to America to make his fortune – achieved by the invention of Quaker Oats! He returned to his homeland, living here until his death in 1910. The Bell Farmhouse was enlarged and renamed Court Farm. The original house was of 14th-century cruck-framed structure. Beyond is Turn Pike Cottage (a toll gate spanned the road here until about 1865), from where rises the serpentine Fish Hill.

Broadway Tower Country Park provides nature walks, countryside exhibitions and facilities for family picnics. It is entered, as it were, by the 'back door', so if you wish to climb the tower or otherwise partake you are obliged to pay.

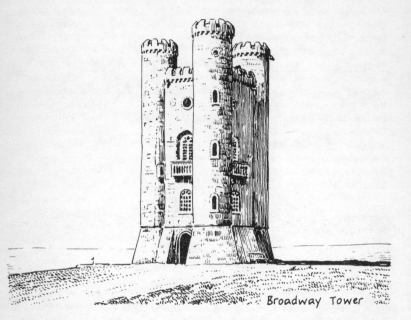

Broadway Tower

Broadway Tower was built on a beacon site at 1,024 ft at the whim of the Countess of Coventry, wife of the 6th Earl, in 1798. The Earls of Coventry owned the connecting estate at Springhill, before General Lygon, and commissioned James Wyatt to design the prospect tower (see Dodington House, p. 99, and Newark Park, p. 109). The tower, a landmark of distinction and some grace, is composed of three round turrets with canted sides, looking for all the world like a miniature Norman castle keep. The Coventry's family seat, at Croome Court (4 miles W of Pershore), is littered with a profusion of folly structures, including a Panorama Tower designed by Robert Adam in 1766. Bredon Hill completely obscures Croome Court from Broadway Hill, and the only visual connection with their land was with Springhill. The view from the foot of this 55-ft tower is only marginally less than from the battlemented top, embracing the fertile plain to the distant heights of the western Midlands; the clearest visibility is needed to see the Wrekin (NNW), or the

Black Mountains (W); Bredon Hill figures large above the Isbourne valley and Evesham (pronounced ev-esham) on the Avon is easily seen (NW); beyond are the Malvern Hills, and the Clee and Clent Hills.

From the tower the Way enters a smaller version of Cleeve Hill's Happy Valley. At the edge of the old quarry, a pagan Anglo-Saxon cemetery was found in 1954 when a mechanical digger threw up human bones. Eight burials were found, simply set into the rock (no coffins) with some grave-goods. The bones were well preserved but had been badly broken by the weight of quarry machinery. The suggestion is that they related to a very early Anglo-Saxon settlement somewhere in the vicinity of the Fish Inn. The Fish Inn was built for Sir John Cotterell of Farncombe House as a summer house. Lord Torrington called it 'the most extraordinary gaze-about in the world'.

Over the busy A44 stands a beautiful topograph which lacks but one thing – a view! The old coaching road descended through the quarried area below the topograph and still can be followed peaceably on foot today, briefly recalling the feel of the old turnpike days. Beyond the picnic site the Way re-enters Gloucestershire, crossing Buckle Street, named from an Anglo-Saxon lady called Burghild, who is known to have owned land down in the vale where the Buggildway (earlier name) coincides with the Roman Ryknild Street. Ryknild is Ickneild Way, gaining the 'R' by corruption of ME 'at there Ikenild Strete' to 'at the Rikenild Strete'.

Izod Fingerpost.
Cross Hands

181

# 28. The Mile Drive, Dover's Hill and Chipping Campden

The Mile Drive complies with the parish boundary of Weston Subedge and Campden, and as such formed a skyline landscape feature from Campden House. Originally it may have formed some ridgeway link; more recently it served as a sheltered ride for the Earls of Gainsborough, possibly even a private racecourse; it has recently been partially absorbed into an arable field.

Campden House can be seen down in the Combe valley to the R. From 1153 the land belonged to Bordesley Abbey: a muster roll of 1608 confirmed it to be the home of two yeomen, a husbandman and a shepherd and not the residence of a gentleman. By 1628 Sir Baptist Hicks had bought the estate, though there is no evidence of the Hicks family here until 1846. The descendants of Sir Baptist, the Noels, were created Earls of Gainsborough by Charles II. However, the family seat was Exton Hall, in Rutland, so they were absentees until they returned to enlarge Campden House (this Victorian extension was demolished in 1928).

The Kifts Gate Stone, standing shyly in the undergrowth of Weston Park Wood, is a remarkable survival. It may not be in situ, having possibly been removed from an original setting on Spelsbury ('speech hill'), adjacent to Kiftsgate Court above Mickleton. At this stone, on that moot-hill, the Anglo-Saxon Hundred Court would have assembled to hold their routine inquisitions and make proclamations regarding important local and national issues. The 'gate' would imply that it lay on a main thoroughfare serving the district comprising the hundred, most likely the White Way.

With the Dover's Hill scarp 'amphitheatre' the Cotswold Way bids farewell to the Cotswold Edge. The view, as confirmed by the topograph, is extensive, though slightly blinkered when compared with Broadway Hill. To the NE is Meon Hill, at 635 ft the final vestige of the scarp. Beyond is Stratford-upon-Avon and Warwick.

Dover's Hill, formerly Campden Hill, is named after Robert Dover who, according to Samuel Rudder in his *A New History of Gloucestershire* of 1779, '... instituted certain diversions on the Coteswald, called after his name, which were annually exhibited about Willersey and Campden ... every Thursday in Whitsun-week at a place called Dover's Hill'. Dover, grandfather of Dr 'Quicksilver' Dover of Stanway, started these 'Olympick Games', as they became known, in 1612. He probably modified existing Whitsuntide festivities in such a manner as to gain support from Sir Baptist Hicks and other members of the gentry.

An anthology of poems in praise of the Games, called *Annalia Dubrensia*

(1636), possesses, on its cover, a woodcut of Robert Dover, dressed in a fine suit and feathered hat, riding proud on a white horse (see the National Trust collection box in the car park). This dress was presented to Dover by Endymion Porter of Aston Subedge, having been given to Porter by Prince Charles while he was groom to the Prince's bedchamber.

Dover, thereafter, opened the event upon his steed, supported by a flourish of cannon fire from a mock castle sited near the present topograph. Competitions were many and varied and not a little brutal! Included were singlestick fighting, the aim being to clout the opponent's head; shin-kicking, to floor the opponent; wrestling; throwing a hammer; racing on foot and horseback; hare-coursing; cock-fighting; and for the more genteel bowls, chess and cards, the last two competitions being held in tents.

Dover's Hill

The Games ceased when Puritanical influences banished such wild frivolities, but in 1725 they were revived. Dover's Hill Games became progressively more lively occasions, culminating during the period 1846–53, when Irish and Black Country navvies, engaged in the construction of the Campden Tunnel for the Oxford, Worcester and Wolverhampton railway, indulged in riotous behaviour in the neighbourhood. Locals were reviled, and through the persistence of Canon Bourne an Act of Parliament was granted enabling the open common behind the edge, known as Kingcomb Plain, to be enclosed. As a result it became possible to abolish this annual unruly debauch. This brought new emphasis on the Scuttlebrook Wake fair, held in Leysbourne (where until 1831 flowed the Scuttle Brook).

In 1920 philistine proposals were afoot to develop Dover's Hill as a hotel site. Mercifully it was saved from desecration by the selfless act of the artist Frederick Griggs, possibly Campden's most influential resident this century. He bid against the speculators at auction and bought the hill for £4,000. Over the next two years richer friends, among them the historian G. M. Trevelyan, were able to pay him back in full and then hand it over to the safe custody of the National Trust in 1929.

The Way makes its final descent away from the escarpment down the aptly named Hoo Lane (from O E *'hoh'*, 'ridge-end'). It is to the good fortune of the Cotswold Way that the finest jewel of the Cotsallers art, enshrined in Campden town's motto 'History in Stone', should form the natural culmination of this superb adventure.

The Way enters Chipping Campden's distinctive curving High Street with its sloping greens and island buildings within the market place. Sheep Street enters from the R. On this corner are Robert Welch's showrooms and, behind, the Silk Mill where the Hart family continue their silversmith trade, being one of the very few to stay on after the demise of Ashbee's bold venture in Arts and Crafts. When de Gondeville laid out his new borough in 1180, Sheep Street was created to draw custom off the White Way. The name tells of its principal trade, though in the main only the fleece will have been conveyed this way.

The modern shop and hotel frontages parade their wares with an unpretentious and discreet honesty. The flower of Cotswold vernacular architecture blooms fair throughout the diverse styles, amid a living, caring community.

Beyond the 16th-century Island House stands the Town Hall, which has some 14th-century fabric, suggesting that it began as a wool exchange, or court house for the burgesses in the heart of the market thoroughfare, or even developed out of the lost chapel to St Catherine. The War Memorial was designed by Frederick Griggs. The last building in the market-place is the Market Hall (National Trust), built by Sir Baptist Hicks in 1627.

Probably the oldest house in the street is Grevel's House, a late-14th-century town house. It has a two-storey Perpendicular bay window giving daylight into a full-height hall. The moulded arch doorway will have been for packhorses laden with their staple of wool. The Grevel family flourished beyond the wool trade. Through judicious marriages their line advanced to Warwick Castle in 1605. They rebuilt the castle, subsequently becoming Earls of Warwick.

Woolstapler's Hall, across the way, probably built by Robert Calf, was contemporary with Grevel House. It was here that merchants met to assess and purchase the staple on offer. Renovated in 1902 for his own use by C. R. Ashbee, it exists today as an interesting local museum and tourist information centre.

Entering Church Street notice the Eight Bells Inn (named after the church tower ring of eight bells), probably the oldest hostelry in the town. The road (a one-way system with on-coming traffic, so beware!) swings L, with the Sir Baptist Hicks' Almshouses forming a beautiful approach to the church steps.

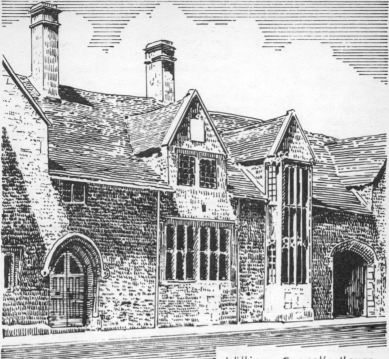

William Grevel's House

Down to the R, notice the old cart wash where wagons were drawn to soak their wooden wheels to prevent them shrinking and falling apart during a dry spell of weather.

That completes the Cotswold Way, but Chipping Campden has one more 'treat' in store: the Ernest Wilson Memorial Garden, established in 1983, to commemorate the work of an extraordinary horticulturalist. Born into a long-established Campden family (the Wilsons appear in the church records as far back as Baptist Hicks' time) Ernest left the town in 1876, soon taking up a post at the Birmingham Botanic Gardens. During his career he travelled widely, most notably through the Far East and China, from where he introduced into this country a multitude of plants; many are now common garden species.

As one might expect the $\frac{1}{4}$-acre retreat contains many of the plants he brought back. It is situated in Leysbourne, just off the High Street, and entered through a wrought-iron gate. Weary walkers will undoubtedly take pleasure from a short, soothing period of relaxation within this peaceful sanctuary – a fitting finale for any journey through the garden of England.

# Campden Town

This fine old town merits a historical postscript. Locals have long dropped the 'Chipping' in speech (to contrast with Chipping Norton, which is colloquially 'Chippy'). It is a well-loved country town leading a dual Cotswold/Evesham Vale existence today.

It resides in an area formerly known as Henmarsh, implying marshy pockets frequented by moorhens (the name survives in Moreton-in-Marsh). There is evidence that the locality has long been populated – indeed, it may be that a Romano-British estate formed the basis of the place-name, which embodies the Latin *'campus'* and Germanic *'denu'*, giving 'Valley with enclosures'. By Domesday the Anglo-Saxon manor of 'Capedene' extended to 15 hides (1,800 acres) with twenty-one ploughs tilling the fertile sheltered vale: obviously a valuable estate, owned by the Crown and handed by William the Conqueror to his nephew Hugh, Earl of Chester. Being invested with many estates throughout the kingdom, he was largely an absentee lord of the manor. A century later, because of disloyalty the 5th Earl of Chester had to forfeit the estate to Henry II. Campden then passed to Hugh de Gondeville, a courtier knight who had been involved in the plotting which led to the murder of St Thomas à Becket.

De Gondeville was the effective founder of the Campden we know today. On his initiative a new borough was laid out, sweeping down from Coombe to Leysbourne, with narrow burgage plots running to the Cam and Back Ends. The famous curve was in response not merely to the lie of the land but was also a prudent attempt to reduce the funnelling effect of the bitter Cotswold wind. The plan also accommodated a market place giving a swollen midriff effect. The ancient White Way that branched from the Jurassic Way above Springhill was obliterated by this new arrangement; it was important to the burgesses that all potential custom should pass through their emerging trading centre. For several centuries the dwellings of these craftsmen and market traders were humble timber-framed structures.

The town was granted its first market Charter in 1180. This was confirmed in 1237 by Henry III. In 1247 the burgesses had obtained a three-day fair about St James's Day in July, and in 1360 a further three-day fair was instituted about St George's day in April.

Campden was able to draw on trade from a wide area and the population grew in accord. By the mid 13th century the prefix 'Chipping' (from O E meaning 'market-place') had been given – proof, if any were needed, of the sub-regional importance of this trading centre.

The drier turf of the Cotswold uplands had, as long as man had farmed, been the special range of sheep. The landed Flemish knights, rewarded for their service in the Conquest, soon realized the opportunities of opening up an export trade back to Flanders; a popular saying of the 12th century ran:

> In Europe the best wool is English,
> In England the best wool is the Cotswold.

(Though Herefordshire wool commanded the higher price, Cotswold wool was more plentiful.)

By 1273 the Lord of Campden Manor possessed the right to graze 1,000 sheep on the wold about the town, and his tenants and freeholders would have kept many more. Domesday records twenty-seven ploughs tilling the environs of Berrington; yet, 200 years after, the emphasis had shifted to pasture and a new age of prosperity was dawning, based solely on sheep. A further hundred years on and we see even fewer cultivated strips, though this was not only the result of the spread of sheep-rearing – the Black Death had taken a colossal toll, reducing the population of England by half.

Chipping Campden was blessed by its position. The ancient trade route running from Cirencester, still known in parts to this day as Campden Lane, drew in the wool from the vast high wold estates. Furthermore, it became the emporium for large quantities of wool produced in Wales and the Marches, so it was no wonder that merchants should rise here to great wealth, trading to the Low Countries, Spain and Italy. Among the 102 burgesses at the Inquisition held in 1273 were the names Grevel and Calf, families who feature prominently as merchants rising on the crest of the wool trade.

After the death of Roger de Somery, Campden Manor was divided between his four daughters; during the following three centuries it was further partitioned. However, Thomas Smythe, friend of Henry VIII, managed to reunite the estate; his marriage to Elizabeth Fitzherbert brought half the manor (she purchased it for him) and the rest of the estate was added through astute purchases, completed when Anthony Smith, Thomas's son, obtained Broad Campden from Thomas Russell (a friend of William Shakespeare).

History does not paint a handsome image of the Smiths, and during their time the wool trade began its painful decline; between 1350 and 1400 the export of raw wool had already dropped from 32,000 to 19,000 sacks (each holding $3\frac{1}{4}$ cwt). So, while the Lord Chancellor may have continued to sit fair and square upon his 'woolsack', changes were afoot. The ever-increasing tax on wool exports, imposed by a greedy monarchy, made it more expensive. The pendulum had now swung in favour of the central southern scarp valleys, where the clear swift streams could be harnessed to power fulling mills to serve the cottage weaving industry where fine cloths were being produced, again with Flemish expertise a prime factor. The staple of wool was now but half of the commodity, and dye-houses sprang up even at Campden (Dyer's Lane) to make the complete product for the cloth trade, which was now oriented to the export of bales of finished cloth.

In 1606, a new figure, of friendlier disposition towards the town, appeared, to purchase the Smith estate. He was Sir Baptist Hicks, a London merchant, whose wealth may be judged from the fact that at various times he lent James I sums amounting to £150,000, and bestowed £100,000 on each of his three daughters. Yet it was his civic gifts that have endured: the Market Hall, built 1627, providing shelter for the sale of perishable commodities like butter and cheese, and the Almshouses, built 1612, planned in a capital 'I' in respect for James I. In 1613 Sir Baptist Hicks built Campden House, an opulent Jacobean manor. The house lasted only thirty years.

With the Civil War, Sir Baptist's family allegiance was clearly Royalist: Charles I had ennobled him as Viscount Campden and Baron Hicks of Ilmington in 1628. So Campden House was garrisoned by Royalist troops, ostensibly to guard their line of communication from Oxford to Worcester, along which the king might receive reinforcements from Wales and Ireland. They remained there until 1645 and were, in every dimension, a pox on the neighbourhood. Under Sir Henry Bard's command they pillaged ruthlessly, as far afield as Winchcombe, for sustenance. When summoned to march to the decisive battle at Naseby Field, their final act of barbarity was deliberately to set fire to their billet. Hence all that remains to indicate the style and extent of Hick's Campden House are the gatehouses and banquet pavilions.

From this time it would appear that Campden was in a moribund state, reverting to a greater diversification in agricultural practice; the urban town turned back to country town, but not completely. Roads had by now changed, communications had a different emphasis. Campden Lane, for instance, was falling from favour and a route from Gloucester via Winchcombe had gained preference.

Westington Manor, which came into being some time after de Somery's four-part partition in 1273 (the dovecote bing the oldest element), was the home of the Izods, formerly of Stanton. It was Nathaniel Izod who erected the famous Cross Hands fingerpost in 1699. It still decorates the ancient crossroads, pointing, in antiquated fashion, to Gloucester, Warwick, Oxford and Worcester.

The earliest 14th-century stone houses of William Grevel and Robert Calf were supplemented during the 'Great Rebuilding' in the late 16th century, keeping rigidly to de Gondeville's frontage, to give Campden a rich heritage of solid, elegant town houses. The Enclosure Act of 1799 gave new wealth to some landowners, and their houses, together with those of other gentry and middle-classes, adorn the High Street in all their Georgian and Regency ashlared glory. The 19th century was basically a 'hollow barrel' economically for Campden, and Victorian Gothic architecture is fortuitously absent.

By the end of Victoria's reign the town was sorely in need of a new purpose. It came in an unexpected way when C. R. Ashbee, founder of the Guild of Handicrafts in 1888, persuaded a body of forty craftsmen to leave their Whitechapel workshops in London and join him in the rural backwater that was the

Campden of 1902. In 1904 the Campden School of Arts and Crafts was opened: it seemed that there would be ample opportunities to develop and practise skilled trades – the products of which could renovate and adorn the many fine cottages, houses and churches in the district.

The experiment faltered in 1909 and many craftsmen left the community; but the beacon they lit flared across the world in their time, and lives on in many distinguished guises today. The Arts and Craft movement influenced many, including Sir Gordon Russell, who attended Campden Grammar School and lived for fifty years in Kingcombe House, built for him in 1925. He wrote of the vitality and enthusiasm the craftsmen inspired in him and his contemporaries through the 'surging activity of skilled handwork grafted on to the fine Cotswold tradition'.

The story of the town does not level there, for in 1904 F. L. Griggs; who as we have seen saved Dover's Hill and designed the War memorial, settled in Campden (he was involved in the line illustrations for the still popular Highways and Byways guides, drawings of exceptional quality). His influence in the first quarter of the present century proved crucial in developing the town's awareness of its rich architectural heritage. Griggs was instrumental in the formation of both the Campden Society in 1924 and the Campden Trust in 1929. Campden owes a great debt to the sensitivity and foresight of Griggs in suppressing the vulgar face of commercialism.

The wool trade spawned an abundance of superb vernacular houses in the Cotswold region, but of greater importance were the pious benefactions of rich wool merchants, employing the finest master masons with the finest building stone in England, the oolitic freestone.

As you approach Campden from the Fish Hill topograph there is but one focus for your attention, enhanced by sunlight: the tall elegance of the parish church tower. In the traditional Cotswold context the pinnacles of architectural excellence are expressed by the three 'wool' churches of Cirencester, Chipping Campden and Northleach. Much as Bath Abbey held the centre stage, so too does Campden church, as a monument to Perpendicular virtuosity.

From the steps before the church an avenue of twelve limes, planted in 1770 in reverence for the twelve apostles, lead to the porch. Both Cirencester and Northleach excel in their porches. Here the emphasis lies elsewhere, notably in the tower and in the simplistic harmony and unity of the whole building, largely the product of the final stages of Perpendicular development in the late 15th century.

As to its predecessors we have scant record, though it is likely that the large Saxon community had some church. The Earl of Chester gave the tithes to St Werburgh's Abbey at Chester in 1093; the Abbot still held the advowson at the Reformation. If there was a church (timber-framed), then it is reasonable to suggest it stood in the vicinity of the present one, beside Berrington ('borough farmstead') – the original Saxon settlement. Apart from the muzzled

St James' from the Cart Wash in Church Street

bear corbel in the muniment room and the remnants of the font beside the pulpit, there are no traces of a Norman church. Hugh de Gondeville bequeathed 3 hides at Westington to found a chapel dedicated to St Catherine, though the precise location of this building is not known. He also granted, c.1184, the four mills of the manor to the 'Mother Church'.

The early medieval growth of the town as a wool emporium had direct expression in the development of the church. The earliest fabric contained in the present building is the S aisle, dating from 1260; followed by the N chapel; the buttressing of the S aisle; the addition of N aisle and S porch; finally the rebuilding of the chancel: all completed by 1400.

The munificence of the town's merchants was clear, though there is no record of their identity until the death of William Grevel in 1401, in whose will £66 was set aside for 'the new work to be carried on' in the church. This sum will have been used in the N aisle and N chapel where he was buried. His brass in the chancel (not in situ) is the largest in Gloucestershire, and shows him with his first wife, Marion, in civilian dress. Around it is inscribed '... The flower of the wool merchants of all England' – he obviously had a full measure of vanity! However, there were other merchants in the second half of the 15th century who made bequests to the church, for example William Welley, who died in 1450 (Will unknown), and William Bradway, who died in 1488, leaving to 'the Bylding of the nave and body of the church one hundred marks' (£66). Others there must have been, for this was the major period when the church one sees today emerged in all its calculated Perpendicular grace. The tower came at the end of this rebuilding phase, with thin flat pilasters soaring up to culminate in ogee arches; above are battlements and pinnacles, immensely eye-catching (within is a peal of eight bells installed in the 17th century). Tradition has it that a couplet on a tomb in the churchyard reads:

> Here lies the body of John Bower
> Built Gloucester Cathedral and Campden tower!

Throughout the church the master masons chose an uncluttered form and ornamentation producing a lofty spaciousness.

Sir Baptist Hicks contributed the brass falcon lectern (possibly of Flemish origin) and the oak pulpit; amongst his other pious offerings he leaded the chancel roof and walled the churchyard.

Through succeeding centuries the church has been kept in beautiful order and is a joy to behold. Of its treasures a brief note should be made. The muniment room contains an exhibition of old church records. Beneath the tower two notable vestments are preserved in glass cases: firstly, a crimson velvet cape of c.1380 with the figures of four saints embroidered on each side of the orphrey; secondly, an embroidered representation of the Assumption of the Blessed Virgin, the centrepiece of altar hangings bequeathed by William Bradway in 1488.

Brasses include the merchants Grevel (1401), Gibbys (1484) and Lethenard (1467).

Commentary

The monuments are significant and include (the disliked) Thomas Smythe (1593) as a recumbent effigy in armour with his family; notice the Renaissance canopy. The Earl of Gainsborough's family mortuary chapel has the grotesque black and white marble edifice (costing £1,500) to Sir Baptist Hicks, Lord Campden (1629), with associated Noel monuments in attendance.

lime-tree approach to St James'

# Index of Place-Names

# FOR THE BEST IN PAPERBACKS, LOOK FOR THE 🐧

In every corner of the world, on every subject under the sun, Penguins represent quality and variety – the very best in publishing today.

For complete information about books available from Penguin and how to order them, write to us at the appropriate address below. Please note that for copyright reasons the selection of books varies from country to country.

**In the United Kingdom:** For a complete list of books available from Penguin in the U.K., please write to *Dept EP, Penguin Books Ltd, Harmondsworth, Middlesex, UB7 0DA*

**In the United States:** For a complete list of books available from Penguin in the U.S., please write to *Dept BA, Viking Penguin, 299 Murray Hill Parkway, East Rutherford, New Jersey 07073*

**In Canada:** For a complete list of books available from Penguin in Canada, please write to *Penguin Books Canada Limited, 2801 John Street, Markham, Ontario L3R 1B4*

**In Australia:** For a complete list of books available from Penguin in Australia, please write to the *Marketing Department, Penguin Books Australia Ltd, P.O. Box 257, Ringwood, Victoria 3134*

**In New Zealand:** For a complete list of books available from Penguin in New Zealand, please write to the *Marketing Department, Penguin Books (N.Z.) Ltd, Private Bag, Takapuna, Auckland 9*

**In India:** For a complete list of books available from Penguin in India, please write to *Penguin Overseas Ltd, 706 Eros Apartments, 56 Nehru Place, New Delhi 110019*

# FOR THE BEST IN PAPERBACKS, LOOK FOR THE 🐧

## PENGUIN BESTSELLERS

### Dreams of Other Days  Elaine Crowley

'A magnificent and unforgettable story of love, rebellion and death. 'You will never forget Katy and the people of her place . . . a haunting story' – Maeve Binchy, author of *Light a Penny Candle*

### Trade Wind  M. M. Kaye

The year is 1859 and Hero Hollis, beautiful and headstrong niece of the American consul, arrives in Zanzibar. It is an earthly paradise fragrant with spices and frangipani; it is also the last and greatest outpost of the Slave Trade . . .

### The Far Pavilions  M. M. Kaye

The famous story of love and war in nineteenth-century India – now a sumptuous screen production. 'A *Gone With the Wind* of the North-West Frontier' – *The Times*. 'A grand, romantic adventure story' – Paul Scott

### The Mission  Robert Bolt

History, adventure and romance combine in the most exciting way imaginable in this compulsive new novel – now a major motion picture.

### Riches and Honour  Tom Hyman

The explosive saga of a dynasty founded on a terrible secret. A thriller of the first order, *Riches and Honour* captures the imagination with its brutally chilling and tantalizing plot.

### The World, the Flesh and the Devil  Reay Tannahill

'A bewitching blend of history and passion. A MUST' – *Daily Mail*. A superb novel in a great tradition. 'Excellent' – *The Times*

# FOR THE BEST IN PAPERBACKS, LOOK FOR THE

## PENGUIN BESTSELLERS

**Lace**  Shirley Conran

'Riches, bitches, sex and jetsetters' locations – they're all there' – *Sunday Express*. 'One of the most richly entertaining reads of the year' – *Options* magazine

**Lace 2**  Shirley Conran

The gilt-edged obsessions and unforgettable characters of *Lace* are back in this incredible novel of passion and betrayal set in the glittering, sensation-hungry world of the super-rich.

**Out of Africa**  Karen Blixen (Isak Dinesen)

Passion and compassion, intelligence and an acute understanding of an alien culture. Now the subject of a major motion picture.

**The King's Garden**  Fanny Deschamps

In a story which ranges from the opulent corruption of Louis XV's court to the storms and dangers of life on the high seas, Jeanne pursues her happiness and the goal of true love with all the determination and high spirits of one who is born to succeed . . .

**Paradise Postponed**  John Mortimer

'Hats off to John Mortimer. He's done it again' – *Spectator*. A rumbustious, hilarious new novel from the creator of Rumpole, *Paradise Postponed* is now a major Thames Television series.

**The Garish Day**  Rachel Billington

A sweeping, panoramic novel of spiritual and sexual crisis. 'Rachel Billington's marvellously readable novel . . . is a real treat. Telling insight and poker faced humour' – *Daily Mail*

# FOR THE BEST IN PAPERBACKS, LOOK FOR THE

## PENGUIN OMNIBUSES

### Author's Choice: Four Novels by Graham Greene

Four magnificent novels by an author whose haunting and distinctive 'entertainments' and fiction have captured the moral and spiritual dilemmas of our time: *The Power and the Glory*, *The Quiet American*, *Travels with My Aunt* and *The Honorary Consul*.

### The Collected Stories of Colette
Edited with and Introduction by Robert Phelps

'Poetry and passion' – *Daily Telegraph*. A sensuous feast of one hundred short stories, shot through with the colours and flavours of the Parisian world and fertile French countryside, they reverberate with the wit and acuity that made Colette unique.

### The Penguin Complete Novels of George Orwell

The six novels of one of England's most original and significant writers. Collected in this volume are the novels which brought George Orwell world fame: *Animal Farm*, *Burmese Days*, *A Clergyman's Daughter*, *Coming Up for Air*, *Keep the Aspidistra Flying* and *Nineteen Eighty-Four*.

### The Great Novels of D. H. Lawrence

The collection of the masterworks of one of the greatest writers in the English language of any time – *Women in Love*, *Sons and Lovers* and *The Rainbow*.

### Frank Tuohy: The Collected Stories

'The time has come for him to be honoured for what he is: a great short-story writer, an absolute master of the form' – Paul Bailey in the *Standard*. From Poland to Brazil, from England to Japan, Tuohy maps the intricate contours of personal and racial misunderstanding, shock and embarrassment. 'Exhilarating fiction' – *Sunday Times*

### The Nancy Mitford Omnibus

Nancy Mitford's immortal, unforgettable world in one scintillating volume: *The Pursuit of Love*, *Love in a Cold Climate*, *The Blessing* and *Don't Tell Alfred*.